The Weight-Pile Murder

Thank you for all of your support. May God richly bless you. Peace & Love

E. B.

Phil. 4:13

The Weight-Pile Murder

A Tiger Price Mystery

Erick G. Benson

Writers Club Press
San Jose New York Lincoln Shanghai

The Weight-Pile Murder
A Tiger Price Mystery

All Rights Reserved © 2001 by Erick G. Benson

No part of this book may be reproduced or transmitted in any form or by any means, graphic, electronic, or mechanical, including photocopying, recording, taping, or by any information storage retrieval system, without the permission in writing from the publisher.

Writers Club Press
an imprint of iUniverse.com, Inc.

For information address:
iUniverse.com, Inc.
5220 S 16th, Ste. 200
Lincoln, NE 68512
www.iuniverse.com

ISBN: 0-595-13367-3

Printed in the United States of America

Preface

A man can work an entire career and his net worth can still boil down to one moment in time.

Acknowledgements

DeJoiré Benson, thank you for being a great first draft editor and a supportive wife.

Norris and Edie Benson (mom & dad), thank you for teaching me to strive to be the best at everything I do.

Thank you to my brothers, Norris and Gary and to my sisters, Elaine and Angela.

Thank you Ericka and Déja (daughters) for sharing me with my writing.

Pastor Chuck Singleton, keep on preaching and teaching those inspirational words of our Lord and Savior, Jesus Christ.

Tony Williams, Chief Deputy Warden at the California Institution for Men, your technical assistance is appreciated.

Thank you Greg Johnson, for your words of inspiration and for being my midnight prayer partner.

Additional thanks to Carla Baugh, Gina Copeland, Henry Harris, Anthony Herron, Marc & Keema Houston, Kathleen Marusak, Maxine Tago and Steve Wilson.

One

Lunchtime couldn't have come at a better moment, as I drove the faded blue, state-issued vehicle into the parking lot of Lou's Fish Hut. I always looked forward to that rare moment when I could relax and gaze out at the busy world through the dirt-ringed windows of my vehicle. For a moment, I envisioned the former state-issued vehicle I drove when I worked in the field as a parole agent. That vehicle was definitely a piece of work. I kid you not; the interior of that vehicle was home to paper goods from literally every fast food chain in the Pomona Valley. Pomona is a fairly large city about 30 miles east of Los Angeles. I love to eat, and the car just seems to be my ideal haven.

"May I take your order please," a fuzzy voice announced from the outside speaker. The car briefly stalled as I positioned it closer to the drive-thru speaker box. "Let me have ahhhhh, a catfish lunch. Hold the cold slaw, and I'll have just French fries and bread with the fish." I reached into my pocket hoping to find my last ten-dollar bill. Being a once-a-month paid employee definitely has its downfalls, and today could possibly be one of those moments.

"Thank God," I said aloud as I pulled the crinkled ten-dollar bill from my pocket.

"Anything to drink with that order today, sir?" "No thank you, but I will take a cup of ice water." The gentleman reached his hand through the small, sliding glass window and took my money.

My mouth watered as I anticipated munching on the fresh-fried catfish. Viewing the interior of the restaurant, I could see flames bouncing off the grill as smoke filled the back portion of the small restaurant. People really love this joint. It's definitely not a pretty spot, as the outside brick is covered with gang graffiti. The interior walls have a beige undercoat, which clearly shows through the base layer of dark green paint.

Fortunately for many others and me, the food is delicious. So quite frankly, the small stuff didn't matter, like the wall paint. "Here's your order, sir." I reached out my car window and grabbed the bag. "Thank you, and please come again."

The parking lot was practically empty, so I decided to maneuver my vehicle into one of the parking spaces that faced Mission Boulevard, a rather busy gateway that leads through the heart of the city.

What a relaxing way to spend lunch. The homeless, businessmen, prostitutes, and children were my view as I gazed out of my window. What an interesting, but crazy world I thought as I gathered the remains of my fast food lunch.

Oh, what I would give to be able to take a short nap. That would make my day. As I adjusted the position of my car seat, I was prompted to shut my eyes with no pre-determination of falling asleep. Closing my eyes without falling asleep is one of my specialties.

Sometimes I wish that I had never gotten out of Paroles. Many people in the Corrections business believe that parole agents have a plush job. It was fun while it lasted. I remember the first week in Paroles; I was part cop, social worker, attorney, psychologist, pastor, father, baby-sitter, and occasional friend. Boy, did that job carry a wallop of responsibilities.

The paperwork was enormous, not to mention the inordinate hours that were required.

Quite frankly, I was infuriated with tasks such as having to collect urine from parolees as I watched them release their waste into a two-inch plastic bottle. After fifteen years as a urine collector, I felt I deserved a break. One of the worst obligations concerning the job other than the multitude of paperwork was the unpleasant experience of making home calls. Not only did danger exist within every neighborhood, it was a challenge just to think of the filth that I had to endure on a daily basis. It was appalling. Trash on the floor, used diapers containing feces sprawled across the room, beer cans, wine bottles, and used condoms, etc. Not to mention the exposed needles and syringes that I had to dodge on numerous occasions. Thank God, many parolees were placed into custody because of creating such horrid environments.

I opened my eyes and squinted briefly, hoping that my immediate surroundings were still safe and secure. Once again, I closed my eyes and continued to reminisce over some of the reasons I left Paroles.

That darn office phone drove me crazy. How can such a small object possess so much control? It was the only object in the office that I literally hated. Amid the yellow paper post-its plastered on my walls, the desk that was covered with piles of manila caseload files, and an old, out-dated computer that presented information at a snail's pace, still existed my archenemy, the phone.

The volume of phone calls were enormous. Parolees took advantage of the open invitation in the bargain of placing unlimited collect calls to the office. The collect call policy was especially convenient when they were incarcerated. I remember one call that I received prior to going home on a Friday evening.

"Agent Price, may I help you." I took in a short breath of air and I twisted my mouth in disgust. "This is me, Mr. Price, I got picked up this morning," the voice on the other end said. I twisted my mouth towards my other cheek. "I didn't even do anything. I was just walkin' down the street and the cops rolled up on me." "Who is this?" I demanded, as I pounded my fist onto my cluttered desk. "This is Johnny Garza, prison number K697…" "Your name is sufficient. Don't you ever call up here at ten minutes to five as I'm about to go home just to tell me you got arrested for your own stupidity." Within moments, I heard Garza gasping for air. He sounded desperate yet he failed to utter one word for a full minute.

"Garza, Garza, what are you doing?" His breathing became more rapid as he attempted to utter my name. "Calm down, Garza, and take a deep breath." There was silence for a short moment. I attempted to communicate with him, but my efforts were useless. There were two loud bangs and static immediately assaulted my eardrums.

The next morning the local jail authorities told me that Garza had suffered a heart attack. He survived and thank God, neither the Parole Division nor myself was sued.

Most of the time, I was the one on the receiving end of the treacherous calls made by testy individuals.

Social Services workers called on a daily basis with the intentions of verifying the need factors of our clients. Police officers would phone our offices and our homes literally 24 hours a day when they were investigating a parolee or if they had one in their custody. The District Attorney was constantly jockeying between us for information to possibly increase the punishment level in reference to parolees who were being housed in county facilities for recent crimes committed.

The remainder of the phone time was spent explaining to a family member why their father, mother, sister, brother, cousin, son or daughter was in jail. These people were demanding and wanted action taken immediately, totally selfish, with no respect for one's time or job responsibilities.

I yawned, sucked my belly in and stretched my arms away from my body as I peeked out of my vehicle, hoping the coast was still clear.

I'm not a worrywart, but whom can you trust these days? I presume it boils down to the savvy of law enforcement. Being aware and in control of one's surroundings becomes monumental.

What the heck, I pondered, thinking that a few more moments of shut-eye couldn't hurt anything.

Speaking of hurt, my stay in the Parole Division was the only period in my career that my life was threatened.

I remember the dreaded phone startled me as I reached past my computer to answer it. "Price speaking, may I help you?" With raised eyebrows, I tilted back in my large, black, neck-level office chair asking the caller to repeat his last statement. "But why would he want to hurt me, I didn't even place him in custody."

I listened patiently for over ten minutes as a prison psychiatrist reiterated the possible fate that awaited me.

The parolee had been arrested and placed in custody for drug sales. Ironically, a parole agent who didn't even supervise his case arrested him. I was told that the parolee immediately blamed me for his incarceration.

The situation was clearly not a joking matter as the prison psychiatrist had spent several hours attempting to reach me by phone. "Please take this matter seriously," stated the psychiatrist in a stern voice. A subtle feeling of gloom overwhelmed me as I sat silently anticipating my next maneuver. I praised God inwardly, recalling the multitude of outward blessings that He had already fulfilled in my life.

For the first time in my life, since I was a kid, I was actually scared. This dirt bag had threatened to kill me by tearing me limb to limb. He also pledged to slaughter anyone else who happened to be in my presence.

A gentle peace crept over as I assured the psychiatrist that I would be careful and I would also notify the necessary management personnel concerning this serious incident.

Thank heaven there was never a phone call of that caliber ever again in my career as a parole agent. A few years later, I left the Parole Division and become an Investigative Lieutenant.

I must admit, stopping here in this restaurant parking lot definitely reminded me of the days back in parole. I'm eager to leave the prison gates when there's an investigation that leads me into the community.

"Put your hands where I can see them, now!" My eyes bucked open immediately as I heard the muffled voice coming from a bullhorn. With my eyes blurred, I focused in on what appeared to be several human figures dressed in black.

"It would be to your advantage to comply with our demands or suffer the consequences." I twisted my head slowly from side to side as I raised my hands cautiously to the steering wheel. For some unknown reason, the police surrounded me. My heart pounded rapidly as a multitude of thoughts raced rapidly through my head. I wanted to speak, but knew that a slip of the tongue could result in a slip of the finger. Black and chrome-plated nine-millimeter pistols were pointed directly in my direction and I was void of expression.

"Step out of the car with your hands in plain view." Maybe I could flash my badge once I got out of the car and this nonsense would be over. I reached over to the door with my left hand and pushed the door out as wide as it could go. My legs were shaking immensely, but I managed to step outside of the car. Lord knows I hadn't done anything, but I was still daunted by the circumstances.

"My name is..." in unison, the sound of chambered magazine cartridges could be heard throughout the airways.

Anger had now overcome my fear and I decided to proceed with the scenario before me, presented by the officers. What right did these officers have to physically threaten me without an explanation? A medium build, blond-haired fella walked slowly in my direction. I was blinded by the glare as the sun glistened from his silver chest badge.

"Slowly drop to your knees and keep your hands where I can see them." Still angered, I reluctantly replied, "I need to say something." The remainder of the police mob moved in closer with the look of subduing me at the proper moment.

"Shut-up mister, 'cause you won't be doing any talkin' until you're handcuffed and the situation is secure."

Like a pack of hyenas charging their prey, the group of officers subdued me.

After my upper body was searched, while I was still on the ground, I was quickly jolted to an upright position. The search continued as my pants were twisted and pulled. The insides of my front pockets were visibly inside out as they hung to my sides. My back pockets were searched and an officer proceeded to remove my wallet from my left rear pocket.

"Lower your guns men, we may have some brass here." The officers lowered their weapons and holstered them to their sides.

"Do you have any other identification to prove that you're who you say you are?" I bit my bottom lip, just short of penetrating my skin as I contained my anger. "First of all, I've never had the chance to speak. Second of all, you know just as well as I do that there are certain questions you can ask me to prove the validity of my peace officer status."

The officer removed a small, four-inch by two-inch cellular phone from his top shirt pocket and handed it to me. "Here, why don't you get your lieutenant on the phone and we'll possibly let you be on your way." I raised an eyebrow, "I am the lieutenant."

A gray-haired, middle-aged officer bearing stripes on both shoulders took the initiative to intervene.

"Lieutenant, please accept our apologies. This restaurant was just robbed within the last fifteen minutes. My men were merely following up on the description concerning the assailant."

Prior to leaving the location, I walked into the restaurant, flashed my badge, and asked to speak to the manager. Within moments, the manager appeared before a grease-covered counter top. His face portrayed a multitude of worry and his food-stained apron illustrated a hard-working man with integrity. "My name is Lieutenant Price and I was hoping that you could answer one question for me." I placed my badge and identification back into my rear pocket as I anticipated his response. "Sure, no problem, everyone has questioned me, I guess one more person won't hurt." "What is the description of the person who robbed this restaurant?" He gave a stifling sigh prior to speaking. "He was a short guy about 5' 7" with huge muscles. His head was completely shaved off. He had a mustache and kind of a paper bag skin tone." "Do you remember what he was wearing?" "Hey that's two questions," he stated jokingly. I smiled momentarily while awaiting his answer. "He wore a white T-shirt with UCLA written in blue across the front."

I thanked him graciously for his input and I proceeded to my car. A few on-lookers were still present on the sidewalk in front of the restaurant. Yellow police tape draped the entryways heading into the restaurant.

Unbelievable, I thought to myself, I'm six-foot two and clean-shaven with a head full of hair. I've been told I have the body of a thirty-year-old and to top it off, I'm chocolate brown. How in the world could I be mistaken for the description of the robber? These are the types of situations that anger me to the core. God created me just as equal as anyone else and I have the right to be treated with respect. Twenty-nine years on the job and three weeks away from retirement, and I must admit that not much has changed in the world in terms of the treatment of people. I wondered within myself why did I ever get involved in law enforcement. Did I believe I could actually change anything?

All my life I've struggled to be the best I could be at any task I encountered. But, it's a shame that even today as I operate my private vehicle I often cringe whenever a police vehicle is spotted in my rearview mirror. I imagine it's a built-in fear of black and whites and what they represent in my mind, imbedded from the past. At least now I can enter a department store and not feel that I'm the center of attention. That just goes to show the misnomer that a badge grants a free ride. At least I can clearly say that wouldn't be an issue for me.

Two

The evening traffic rarely avoids its curtain call, as my vehicle weaved back and forth throughout the maze of automobiles. My day had already been considerably rough and the busy drive sure wasn't helping matters.

I flicked on the radio and pressed the pre-programmed buttons hoping to find an informative talk show. Wouldn't you know it, a couple of talk show hosts named Josh and Ben were still discussing the O.J. Simpson murder case. The multiple trials had been over for years. These people really needed to get a life.

Traffic appeared to be moving quite well since I had managed to clear the crossing of three major freeway interchanges.

The aroma of cow manure became increasingly stronger as I neared the prison. Slowly rolling up my window, I quizzed myself on the issue of whose idea was it to mix cows and humans together on a permanent basis.

A pasture of well-manicured green grass was fast approaching as the prison could be seen far in front of me. There were inmates operating farm machinery, while others worked near the edge of the roadway. They were all conforming to a dress code of navy blue jeans and light blue denim shirts. One by one, the inmates would gaze expressionless as I passed slowly in front of them.

Within moments, I reached the security station, which was located outside of the prison walls. California Men's Prison South is the sister facility to the old Chino prison located just about five miles southwest. Or as some would label it, "The down wind plaza." No other facility in the prison valley area could capture the "stinks title" away from the old Chino facility.

"Good afternoon Lieutenant Price", projected the petite female officer who was fashioned neatly in her green, formal dress uniform. "How are you today?" "I'm fine, now that it's almost time to go home." She signaled to the officer present in the large cement tower, which was before us. "Take care," I said as I pulled the car to the entrance that was made of circular barbed wire and a four-inch solid steel barrier, which retracted electronically.

A whole different world opened before my eyes. Anything goes and the meaning of "fair" is non-existent. Behind these walls, every man is for himself. Prison represents many things to those who are privy to its atmosphere. A place where black is black and white is white. Racism is very real, an absolute way of life. Lies are common language and stealing is an expected occurrence. Drug use is considered recreational. Rape and homosexuality are viewed as an inward human need. Sporting events act in the capacity of a tranquilizer that often diverts strong emotions and feelings, which could result in a cell fight, uprising, or a vicious murder. Manipulation is boundless and pity is an emotion found only in the midst of the prison visiting room.

Prison is hell on earth and I was in the core of its venom. After parking my car in the usual location, I walked towards the administration building. This two-story, brick-layered building is considered the main command post for decision-making within the prison. The Warden, Chief Deputy Warden, and the four Associate Wardens are housed within this building. Also, the Captain who is the highest-ranking uniformed officer is housed in this building as well. Other key employees housed in this building include personnel clerks, records specialists and the prison's training and security coordinators.

"Good afternoon Lieutenant," pronounced Betty Wilkins, in an extremely high-pitched voice. It was always a pleasure to hear Betty's voice. Betty's a small, middle-aged, white female with fiery red hair. Her peppy mannerisms were a rare commodity in this straight-laced, collar-tight environment. "Hey Lieutenant, you look kind of worn-out," she said as she inspected my appearance from head to toe. "Yeah, you're right," I said as I took the opportunity to rest my elbow against the counter that separated us.

"I really wish you would stop working so hard for these folks. You're going to be retiring in three weeks and dying of exhaustion wouldn't look good on your tombstone," said Betty. "Work is all I know, and retiring won't change that." "Let me tell you something T.P., you can work your fingers to the bone around here and it won't make a bit of a difference." "It's time to let go and live your dreams. And you shouldn't have any regrets about anything left behind around here. I'll tell you what you need to do, you need to let somebody cook you a pot of greens, some corn bread, candy yams, black-eyed peas, macaroni and cheese, and some finger lickin' fried chicken and I'm just gettin' started." "Betty, would you stop tryin' to get me married." I smiled slightly and proceeded to change the subject. "Tell me the latest gossip Betty, you know I'm dying to know." "Meet me in the cafeteria in about five minutes and I'll spill all the beans." We both laughed as I continued walking down the long, waxed corridor floor, nestled between the vanilla-colored walls. These walls featured photographs of VIP personnel, information documents, job and vacation schedules, and also a number of signs instructing inmates where they could and could not go. I walked right through the north corridor and passed the offices of several administrators. The smell of baked chicken floated throughout the building like a delicious mist. My thoughts immediately switched gears to food. But, my destination was nearing as the Captain's door became more vivid with each step I took.

Captain Davenport's nameplate was crafted in rich pine wood. I knocked gently on the door, being ever so careful not to damage the cherished nameplate. Captain Davenport, a tall, slender, gray-haired older gentleman, wore a uniform like no other officer. His shirt and pants were creased to perfection. His lower sleeves were adorned by twelve mini-hash stripes, each representing three years of service. His shoes were buffed to a glassy pearl reflection and his double gold bars on his collar reflected a brilliance of beauty. He knew the functions of a prison inside and out.

"Come-on T.P.," stated the Captain in a cheerful manner. T.P. is a nickname given to me by the uniformed personnel and the inmates. Rumor had it that my investigation skills were fierce, relentless, energetic, and full of courage, as likened to a tiger. "How was your day?" "If I told you Captain, you probably wouldn't believe me. Thank goodness I did manage to close out the Peters case with the Pomona DA." "Great, now maybe you can tie up some loose ends around this camp while preparing for your retirement." Captain Davenport sat down on his old, black leather recliner and placed his feet upon his spotless oak desk. "Have a seat and rest yourself." As I sat in the scarred wooden chair, I marveled at the array of plaques, ribbons, medals and photographs which covered the interior of his 15' X 10' office. This man truly loved his job; retirement for him was just an afterthought.

"Three weeks is the magic number Captain, then I'm out of here. It was fun while it lasted, an adventure too, but now a man has to do what a man has to do." I raised an eyebrow, waiting patiently for his response. Not many employees knew my future plans upon shifting into retirement, but Captain Davenport had earned the right to share in my future undertaking. "Never lose that 'Tiger' instinct Price, it'll keep a warrior like yourself in business. I do believe that Los Angeles is in for a treat." "I'll do my best sir, I promise you that." I re-positioned myself in my seat as I nervously awaited his uninvited blessing concerning my future endeavor. He was the white father that I never had, though I love my natural black father immensely. It all boils down to the fact that this man was in my corner and he wasn't black. That presented an enormous degree of sacrifice in a society that embraces injustice under the guise of genuine equal opportunity. My time had come to venture out on my own and I was going to do it. Owning my own private investigation company was soon to become a reality. I'm fifty years old and soon to be fifty-one. The department had utilized my skills and pulled my strings since I was a young, twenty-one year-old man. My plans have been a long time comin', but it's definitely been worth the wait.

Captain Davenport raised his head up and his eyes began to slightly water. "Call me if you need me, but I have a feeling that you won't." Caught up in emotion, he swirled his chair around, leaving the back of his head and chair in my sights. "Now get out of here," the Captain said through tight lips. I walked out of his office and gently closed his door.

Captain Davenport disclosed a part of himself that I had never experienced in the twelve years that I've known him.

Venturing back down the shiny corridor floor, I made a pit stop at the prison cafeteria. The food failed to capture my attention at this point, but the fresh smell of brewed coffee teased me. The cafeteria reminded me of my high school cafeteria as several food special signs were displayed with various color markers. There was no clear theme or format, just faded, white walls plastered with prices and featured entrees.

"Medium decaffeinated coffee, T.P.?" asked Manny Parra, a small-framed man with curly black hair and a lip-lined mustache. "You know it Manny, that's the only way I'll make it through the remainder of the day." Manny is the kind of guy that would give you his last nickel. Many employees would agree that Manny is definitely a person who enjoys his position. A genuine people person who seems bothered to even charge for his services. If anyone is ever broke, never fear, Manny's food tab is here.

"Busy day today?" "Tell me about it Manny, I had a very rough day too. My feet hurt, my body aches, and my mind is operating on overload." I sipped my coffee, "Another great cup of coffee." Manny handed me a couple of napkins and I went on my way.

Lord knows I would give anything to feel the fit and comfort of my tennis shoes around my throbbing feet. Things could be worse. The department could have forced me to wear a necktie to go along with my navy-blue blazer, light-blue cotton shirt, gray slacks, and these narrow-ass Italian shoes.

After exiting the administration building, I prepared myself for the long stroll to the lock-down portion of the prison. This was an everyday occurrence as my office was situated on the farthest yard in the prison.

A sixty-yard, narrow path of cement led me away from the administration building to the first steel-wired fence, which was controlled by the Tower II officer. Once visual contact was made through a motion camera, an invisible laser-beam reflected a signal from my identification badge, which was hanging in plain view from my left upper coat pocket. The gate opened and I was allowed to pass through. If for some reason an unauthorized individual passes through these sets of gates, the security checkpoints have only just begun. The tower officer gestured with a hand signal as I walked through to the next checkpoint. He activated the electronic steal-wired gate and it opened up to an area known as a sallyport. A sallyport is an area or inner-location that is between two electronically operated gates. Only one of these gates is allowed to be opened at one time, unless under emergency procedures. The sally port is commonly filled with in-or outgoing employees through one gate, prior to opening the second gate for them to proceed to the next incoming or outgoing checkpoint. It is also a gateway for narcotics and contraband to enter the prison. It's quite an adventure with the employees during the three shift changes in a 24-hour period. As I proceeded to the next checkpoint, I passed through a circular module where a force radiated my body down to the skeletal structure. This procedure prevented weapons and other illegal materials from being smuggled into the facility. The final checkpoint was the molecular hand probe. This small device was located in the security checkpoint room and is securely positioned on a smooth, wood countertop. Besides a few security documents posted in an orderly manner, the room was virtually void of any other equipment.

The lone officer seated behind the counter greeted me as I approached the molecular hand probe. "Good afternoon, Lieutenant Price", he stated in a boyish tone. Most new officers addressed me by my name preceded by my position. They tended to remain totally professional, until they'd paid their dues. Once my hand was placed into this device, information was fed into a computer, which automatically revealed my identity. The security room officer then allowed me to pass through a large, brown door that led into the prison plaza.

The plaza was the main floodgate that led into the various channels of the prison. There were literally four separate prisons within the main prison. Each prison yard operated independently of the other yards. There were five separate housing facilities on each yard that facilitated a maximum of two hundred men. Supervising these men were two floor officers who mingled amongst the inmates along with one control officer. The control officer managed all the cell doors electronically and he maintained the weapon stock. His job was to monitor the behavior of the inmates while protecting his fellow officers from harm. The yard office housed a lieutenant, sergeant, S&E officers (security and escort), and the correctional counselor staff. There was an inmate kitchen and cafeteria on each yard along with a small medical facility and inmate canteen where they could purchase toiletries, specialty foods, and other items. A large tower soared over the inmate kitchen and allowed an officer to see all the housing facilities, the yard offices, the basketball court, the handball court, and the baseball field, across a large, grassy area that interlined the entire facility.

Yard "A" contained one housing unit strictly for immigration inmates. Yard "B" was utilized as a reception center where new inmates were processed and classified. Yard "C" was slightly larger due to the fact that prison industries were present there. Inmates worked in the various industries, such as optical technologies and rubber industrials. Inmates who took their positions seriously usually could find a job in that particular trade once they paroled. Yard "D" was the yard I worked on. Everyone was aware that this facility housed the place called the "Hole". In the administration jargon, it was commonly known as Administrative Segregation (Ad-Seg).

Inmates who assaulted staff, assaulted other inmates, and were caught with weapons or drugs were kept in an isolated area. Inmates were placed in protective custody as a result of being a crucial witness, or because someone or a group of individuals had a contract out on their lives.

I proceeded through the plaza area and observed my assistant, Sergeant Little, approximately twenty yards in front of me.

"Little!" I blurted out with no regard or care for who was in earshot. He turned around abruptly and waited for me to reach his location. Sergeant Little was far from being a small man. He possessed a portly belly, centered between a large body-frame. His thick, bristled mustache lay neatly below his nose, eyes, and a vivid receding hairline.

"For a man who's retiring soon, it doesn't seem like you've slowed down a bit to me." I reared back with a puzzled expression. "What do you mean?" "You left here just before noon headed to the L.A. and Pomona District Attorneys' offices and you're back already?" We both continued to stroll through the plaza. "No need to delay my work," I stated, "my stuff will be tight before I leave this joint in your hands." "What have you heard?" he stated in a hurried fashion, "you know something I don't know?" "If I told you, I'd have to place handcuffs on you and throw you into one of these prison cells." We both laughed and continued on our way.

An inmate was being escorted into the prison hospital as we passed in front of it. The hospital was located midway through the plaza. This off-white building had no windows, but did have a large, double-door entrance. There was a small grass area in the forefront of the hospital and inmate workers were busy planting summer flowers.

A loud buzzing sound could be heard in the direction of the security checkpoint room. Sergeant little and I turned the opposite direction and began running. This loud buzzing sound was a security device, which was activated to alert all department personnel that someone's safety may be in jeopardy. All officers in the area were required to respond to the location in question immediately.

While running, we observed a flashing blue light illuminated on top of the building that was located approximately fifty yards in front of us. "T.P., it looks like the prison visiting room alarm."

The assessment was mutual, but to conserve energy and my precious breath I kept my head straight and continued running without uttering a word.

Once we reached the entrance to the prison visiting room, we walked in and noticed the calm and realized it was a false alarm. Several uniformed officers began exiting. One of the officers assigned to the visiting room approached us, appearing disturbed. "Sorry for the false alarm, I accidentally pushed the button," Conners stated softly. "These darn things are so sensitive." She pointed at the small device, which resembled a garage door opener. "Accidents happen to the best of us, Conners." Her thin, dimpled face was red from embarrassment, though she managed to muster a smile. She flipped her chest-length ponytail behind her back and walked towards her desk.

"That was a great job of chewing her out T.P.," stated Sergeant Little as he folded his arms in disgust. "Just our presence here was scolding enough, don't you think Sergeant?" Puffing up his chest, "Oh yeah, yeah, a lieutenant and a sergeant in the same room together."

The man had been a sergeant over five years. Was he just realizing he had a little clout, I thought to myself.

The situation appeared stable and the inmates and their family members resumed their visiting.

Located across from the hospital was Central Control. All movement and coordination on each facility was spearheaded through this technological forum. Present in this large room were several computers that produced continuous data in reference to various prison operations. There were charts and electronic maps that displayed strategic security checkpoints throughout the entire prison. All the security and safety equipment were housed in this room as well.

I walked up to the equipment window waiting for an officer to assist me. The officers appeared to be busy as they answered the phones while completing various documents. Sergeant Little walked up from behind. I'm sure he was wondering what was taking so long.

"By the time we make it to the yard, our shift will be over." I glanced behind my shoulder, "Maybe, maybe not, I'm not in the mood to flex my wings today."

If he only knew what I'd been through today. Officers surrounded me, I had guns pointed at my head, and I was suspected of robbing my former favorite grease joint. Not to mention the fact that the man I honor and respect was emotional concerning my departure from the prison. Sergeant Little was not about to get on my bad side. I remained calm, reminding myself that patience is a virtue.

"T.P., sorry it took so long, we had a problem in the immigration building." I handed him two brass coin chits that had my last name engraved on them. These chits were utilized when equipment was being checked out.

"Sergeant Little was just saying how hard you officers work in Central Control," I stated. "Isn't that right, Sergeant?" He reached up and grabbed his shirt collar while twisting his neck. "Oh sure, this prison couldn't function without the expertise of the Central Control staff." I sensed a growl in the sergeant's voice. That'd teach him a lesson for messing with me while I was in a less than pleasant mood.

"A radio and a set of handcuffs," I said plainly. "Coming right up," said Officer Scott. Officer Scott, a blonde-haired, blue-eyed, medium-built youngster was quite impressive concerning his work ethic. Good things were said about this kid amongst the upper ranking officers. Too bad I wouldn't be around to observe how fast he moved up the ranks.

"One radio equipped with a functional battery, and one set of cuffs," announced Scott. Sergeant Little and I gestured to the officer as we walked away from the window.

As we walked past Central Control, Sergeant Little asked if I would wait for him while he went into Receiving and Release, commonly known as R&R. He stepped into the love-hate arena while I waited out front. The love inmates had for R&R was when packages of food or clothing arrived addressed to their attention. Also, when it came time for an inmate to parole back into the community, R&R was the place. The hate inmates had for R&R was when they were received into the prison. In this room, they received underwear, outer clothing, and shoes. They were given a small cardboard box full of limited toiletries and given verbal instructions concerning the rules that govern the institution. I often stayed clear of R&R to avoid the zoo-like atmosphere of boxes, packages, clothing, and naked bodies. R&R is a necessary function within the prison, a job that someone must do. But, just not me, I thought to myself while waiting for Sergeant Little's departure from R&R. For a moment, I heard a voice telling me, "Sergeant Little is probably munching on someone's lunch." Another voice told me he wouldn't dare have his supervising officer stand by in the midst of the plaza, in the hot sun, waiting for him. I'd just count to five and if he wasn't out there by then, I was on my way. I began to whisper, "One, two, three, one-thousand four, one-thousand..." dashing out of the R&R door came Sergeant Little.

"You were about to be left behind." "Forgive me, T.P.," sounding apologetic. "I didn't think I took that long." Sergeant Little scurried along slightly ahead of me. "What is that on your chin," I said. Sergeant Little appeared startled as I pointed at his chin. He swiped two or three times at his chin, while attempting to conceal any signs of eating food at the expense of my time. I chuckled under my breath. The joke was on him, literally.

Thank God we had finally arrived at the "D" yard entrance gate. The "D" yard plaza gate officer exited the small, wooded guard shack, removed a large key from his wrist area and walked briskly to the gate. A large, steel-wired fence, crowned by barbed wire, encased this small, wired gate. Officer Garcia placed the key into the key slot and opened the gate that led into the "D" yard. Garcia, a thirty-something year old man of sizable muscle, was an officer of few words, a dependable officer who never missed one day of work.

"Hello T.P. and Sergeant Little", said Garcia. He propped the gate back and allowed us to pass through. I gestured with an effortless salute. Sergeant Little took the initiative to speak for both of us. "Smooth yard today?" "No complaints from me, Sergeant." Garcia shut the gate, locked it, and returned to his post.

With an unclouded view of the yard, several inmates of various races were gathered within the weight-pile. This location was the oasis of pleasure and the plantation of relinquishment of enslaved emotions. A gathering point to exemplify manhood through muscle and sweat.

The summer sun was gleaming bright at the pivotal hour of two o'clock.

We commenced to walk across the yard in the direction of the building in which my office was located. I anticipated the assemblage of inmates in our pathway as we made our journey through the sea of men. I'd made this crossing several hundred times, but each trip across this courtyard of criminals caused my spine to tingle with fear. The feeling was genuine, but somehow seemed to dissipate within a matter of moments. I have never relied on the false sense of security represented by a lone gunman situated in a tower, high above the yard. My sole protection is far higher than some tower and with this in mind I'm able to function.

"Looks like all one-thousand inmates are on the yard today," stated Sergeant Little in a low tone. "Thank God we'll be going home in a couple of hours." I raised an eyebrow and continued walking. "How does that make you feel?" I said. Sergeant Little displayed an uneasy look. "What do you mean? I assume you're speaking of these inmates." "Yes, Sergeant, I'm speaking about the inmates." I paused while taking a deep breath. "Sometimes I wonder how many of these guys are actually guilty of committing the crime they're convicted of." Sergeant Little shrugged his shoulders. "Come-on Lieutenant, practically all these guys are guilty as mud-colored sin." His eyes maneuvered a horizontal pan of the yard. "Believe me, I'd say the percentage falls in the ninety-nine percent range for being guilty." His words captured my attention and caused me to halt my steps. "Look around and tell me what you see?" Sergeant Little narrowed his eyes and unconsciously glanced at the yard once more. "Notice all the blacks and the Mexicans, Sergeant. Imagine every prison in America with the same percentage of races coast-to-coast. That would mean that ninety-eight percent of all criminals in America are Black and Hispanic. Something is terribly wrong with the system and one day I plan to do something about it." A positive thrust of energy pulsated through my veins. It really felt good to get that off my chest, I thought. "Boy T.P., how long you been holding that in?" I motioned with my left index finger. "Let's go."

Approximately twenty feet in front of us, we were about to encounter our first set of inmates. "What's up T.P.," shouted an inmate standing amongst his yard dogs (friends). "Now you know my job is never done as long as you're around," I said. "That's a cold shot T.P., you know we got your back." Small talk is never really small talk on the grounds of a prison. When a person says, "I've got your back," he more than likely will have your back. I'll admit it only to my self-conscience that I liked knowing that in a case of a major prison riot, these inmates would probably spare my life.

"We're still waitin' on that steak dinner," shouted another inmate as we passed the softball field. "Keep writing those letters to Sacramento, something is bound to happen," I said.

Sergeant Little was practically an invisible person when he was present on the yard with a Lieutenant. Inmates tended to dispense all of their attention and loyalty to the highest-ranking officer who happened to be in their presence. They realized that action took place at the top.

"Don't you ever get sick of their meaningless comments?" growled Sergeant Little. "Can't they just ever allow us to walk to our unit in peace?" "Did you have a rough night Sergeant? This place is the same yesterday, today, and tomorrow. Some of these guys have seen my face and yours as well, for the past twelve years. I applaud anyone who has a sense of humor after having their freedom taken away." Sergeant Little is really pissing me off, I thought to myself. But, of course everyone wasn't as logical as I was when it came to prison life. I regained my composure and continued to speak. "Whether an inmate is guilty or innocent, he is still a human being. Sometimes I'm sure that's hard to conceptualize in this atmosphere, but we owe them the dignity of respect if nothing else." I know for a fact that showing respect can be a good thing at times.

"Lighten up T.P., don't have a heart-attack before you retire. These inmates aren't worth it. I don't understand you sometimes. You don't owe these fools a damn thing." He just pushed the wrong button. My inner emotions were boiling and invisible fumes were probably seeping from my ears. This guy was really starting to get to me and I didn't understand why. His comments never bothered me in the past. I imagine reality was kicking in that I was going to be gone soon from this depressing, dreadful place. I restrained myself once again and decided not to use Sergeant Little as a springboard to air my concerns. "Remind me that I need to complete your yearly evaluation before the end of the week," I said. I cut my eyes at Sergeant Little, but still managed to smile. "Don't worry, I'll tell the truth."

We walked directly in front of the weight-pile and received a host of hellos and body gestures from black, white, and Hispanic inmates, some whom we've known for years. Sergeant Little was cordial and took the honors to speak on our behalf.

Prior to reaching my unit, Sergeant Little remembered that he needed to complete some unfinished duties in the culinary facility. We departed company and I eventually arrived at my office.

My office door was open as usual and no one was inside the faded, beige-colored, 10' X 15', scarcely furnished office. I don't believe in decorating an office with material not associated with the job and since the things that are associated with the job are somewhat tasteless, I chose to cover the walls with only a calendar, employee work assignments, and my sports clock that my late wife gave to me. As time passes on, I continue to think about her every day.

My desk was made of dark, oak wood and was seldom cluttered with files or paperwork. I kept a 5" X 7" photo of my two daughters Carmen and Cathy, right smack in the center of my desk. Cathy, my beautiful, full-figured, twenty-one year old is a senior in college and is soon headed off to law school. Lord, help her. My baby Carmen, whom I must say looks as though she just walked out of the pages of Vogue magazine, is doing great as ever. Quite the model type, she is. Her freshman year in college has been tough but she's doing her best and that's all that any caring parent desires. I love my girls so much. They're all I've got now and I'll continue to make sure that they have the best.

In the bottom right drawer of my desk I kept my stash of red licorice candy. There's nothing like the delicious taste of red licorice. I reached down and grabbed a hand full and immediately placed a couple in my mouth. I placed my black leather office chair in a tilt position and twisted my chair in the direction of the window. On occasions when I wasn't busy preparing lengthy reports, I'd stare out of this window for several minutes at a time. The view from my window allows me to see practically the entire yard. Sometimes I'll isolate a particular inmate on the yard and attempt to incorporate a story to match his lifestyle and background. The scenario would include a cast of characters and situations that may have influenced his life in a negative fashion. After completing my field adventure, I would find out the inmate's name, explore his central file, and eventually discover the essence behind his actual incarceration. In the past few years, amazingly I was able to guess correctly on four separate individuals.

Were my actions legal? Who knows, but it was fun.

"Sorry to disturb you T.P., but I just needed to know if you had any special yard tasks that needed to be completed before the end of the day." There was no mistaking the southern dialect of Officer Mulberry. Mulberry is a six-foot, red-haired, freckled-faced, S&E (Security and Escort) officer assigned to the "D" facility. He has discovered more contraband (illegal items) than all the other S&E officers within the prison combined. Gopher would probably be a more suitable name for Mulberry due to his unmatched detective skills.

I declined to disrupt my window view of the prison yard by turning my chair toward Mulberry. Instead, I retained my position with an eagerness to answer.

"The yard seems pretty quiet today. I guess it must be the sun," I said in a relaxed fashion. "That's why I'm here T.P., things are kind of boring out there. I'm sure the inmates are just making the best of their time after being locked down last week." I nodded my head in agreement. "Maybe you're right." I ruffled through a small vanilla-colored tablet on my desk, hoping to find a special job assignment for Mulberry. "Everything seems to be taken care of for the moment. I suggest you and your men just continue to walk the perimeter of the yard," I said. I removed a small portable radio from my bottom drawer, placed it on the desk, and flicked it on while attempting to find any station that would provide reception.

"That will be all, Mulberry." He provided a hand salute as he exited the office.

Three

Peering out of my window, I observed a small crowd gathering around the basketball court. As I stood up for a better view of the situation, I could clearly see two black inmates involved in a pushing match. As I continued to visually examine the ongoing incident, the inmates escalated the confrontation by exhibiting punches. Officer Mulberry is the officer in charge of the yard operations, but he was still inside the building. There was an old pair of army-style binoculars that I kept on top of the file cabinet in the corner. I grabbed the binoculars and quickly scanned the perimeter of the yard. The tower officer who is positioned high above the prison yard appears to be aware of the circumstances. He was holding a microphone in his left hand and an assault rifle in his right hand.

"Everyone lay on the ground. I repeat, everyone lay on the ground now!" The commands of the tower officer could be heard clearly over the P.A. system.

Some inmates laid down on their stomachs, while others continued to taunt the inmates to proceed with their affray.

"All available staff, please report immediately to the basketball court. Black inmates are involved in a heated brawl," I announced over my hand-held radio. The tower officer blurted out another command and the remainder of the inmates were all chest down on the ground. By this time, Officer Mulberry and several other officers had the two inmates who were fighting in handcuffs. The two inmates were immediately escorted off the yard and placed in administrative segregation, which is located in my yard.

Anticipating the commands from the tower officer, the remaining inmates on the yard looked anxiously up at the officer awaiting his permission to rise to their feet.

"Everyone is ordered to report to their housing units immediately," stressed the tower officer. The yard is routinely shut down after serious altercations to allow time to determine if an investigation is in order. The basketball court area was clear and the baseball diamond and the handball court were clearing fast of inmates. The inmates present on the weight-pile are always the most sluggish individuals to clear the yard.

"I'm ordering you to stand to your feet and leave the weight-pile, now!" shouted the tower officer over the P.A. system.

The yard was totally clear except for one inmate who was still lying in the weight-pile. The tower officer appeared fidgety from my vantage point as he leaned out of the tower, clearly displaying his assault rifle. I retrieved my binoculars once more and focused in on what appeared to be an inmate still present in the weight-pile. What kind of game is this clown playing today? I thought to myself. My phone rang just as I turned to look at my wall clock. "Lieutenant Price." I paused for a moment to digest the incoming information. "What do you mean it looks stiff to you?" I repositioned the phone towards my ear and listened closely. Something grabbed a hold within telling me that this was definitely not my day.

"Hold your position, I'm on my way." Just as I hung up the phone, Officer Mulberry appeared at my door. "The two fighters are in isolation, I can bring them in for an interview any time you'd like." Hustling towards the door I said, "We've got a problem on the weight-pile, I need your assistance now." We both dashed from the office and headed hurriedly towards the weight-pile. Once we reached the grassy portion of the prison yard, our brisk walk quickly transformed to an accelerated jog.

As we arrived to the large rectangular pile of sand that was consumed by iron obstacles of weights in various magnitudes, we saw what appeared to be a lifeless body.

"Do you think he's dead T.P.?" said Mulberry. I shrugged my shoulders with uncertainty as I moved in for a closer look. "He's either dead or strung out on some bad dope."

By this time, Sergeant Little had arrived on the scene. "I see that you're right on time, why don't you do the honors," I said calmly. Several prison officers were now present on the weight-pile, watching the procedures.

Sergeant Little removed a pair of rubber gloves from a leather pouch on his belt. He placed the gloves on his hands and kneeled down beside the body that was face down in the sand. He grabbed the victim's shoulders with both hands and turned him over. "Oh my God, it's Newton Black! There's no pulse T.P., he's dead as a door-knob." I stood frozen in my tracks, unable to speak momentarily. The victim's blue, denim shirt was saturated with blood. A pool of blood had gathered under his body and formed itself into a reservoir in the sand. Without speaking a word to one another, it was an understood fact that this was a very serious situation. The leader of the BCMO (Black Confederate Movement Organization), one of the most powerful groups known within the prison, was dead.

Why me, I thought to myself. How could such a horrible event take place just a few weeks before I retire? This was unbelievable. Within the silence, I knew I had to exercise and take charge of the situation. I immediately ordered anyone who was now present in the weight-pile to carefully step out of it. Sergeant Little was instructed to obtain the tower officer's name and whatever information he could provide concerning the murder.

Officer Mulberry proceeded to secure the crime scene while being careful to preserve any evidence that could possibly be in our midst. Officer Jones, a medium-built, dark-skinned black man, who proudly sports a "jeri-curl," well after the fact of being told they were extinct, had arrived on the scene. Officer Jones is a genuinely likable guy. Both inmates and prison staff appreciate his humor and straight forwardness.

Officer Jones approached me. "I heard the call on the radio T.P. and thought that you might need a little assistance. Here's a sheet to cover him up, that is if you're going to leave him here until the Coroner's Office arrives." He unfolded the sheet and handed it to me as I stood on the edge of the weight-pile approximately four feet from the body. "Thanks a bunch Jones. I know it's not everyday that you have to deal with this kind of dead meat." I took the sheet.

Officer Jones responded, "Yeah, you're right about that, I just don't allow anything up in my kitchen." I proceeded to cover the lifeless body with the sheet. For a moment I thought, why would Jones have bed sheets in the kitchen. Who am I to complain, he's the best kitchen officer in the entire prison.

"Is there anything else you need T.P.?" asked Officer Jones. "Believe me, you've done more than enough," I said with a feeling of surety. "Call me if you need me T.P. I'm headed back to the kitchen before these fools with the gifted hands steal all my food." He tipped his black baseball-style cap and proceeded back to the kitchen.

Jones is a real good brotha and I really appreciated having his presence on the yard. I knew I'd miss these interesting, daily conversations of ours. There are other things that I'll miss, but for the most part, I'm glad I'm retiring.

My thoughts immediately focused back to the alleged murder victim who lay in front of me, knowing that a serious uprising could easily be generated from this incident. Why was I worried, I thought to myself. I remembered that I was currently in the process of completing my last investigation and my subsequent investigations would be referred to my replacement. An incident report would have to be completed first and an internal investigation would immediately follow. I didn't mind providing a preliminary report regarding what I'd witnessed today, but after that it was out of my hands, thank God.

The grim scene was now framed in front of a picturesque sunset, as my staff waited patiently for the arrival of the County Coroner. Once the task of removing the body was completed, a team of officers would be allowed to search the weight-pile for any alleged murder weapons. I was safe in assuming that the victim had been murdered based on the area of the apparent stab wound and also due to the manner in which the body was discovered.

The prison medical staff dressed in maroon smocks, responded to the scene and examined the body while awaiting the arrival of the Coroner. The medical staff is accustomed to treating sick and injured inmates on a daily basis. Death doesn't occur in prison, as often as many ordinary citizens would believe.

"Finally, the meat wagon's here," said Sergeant Little in a not so nice manner. The Coroner was being lead onto the yard by escort officers. A large, gray bobtail styled truck pulled into the facility and slowly pulled up to the kitchen area, just adjacent to the weight-pile. A short, older man with balding white hair walked slowly towards our location on the weight-pile.

"Howdy folks, is it true that someone requires my unique services?" He grinned softly and preceded towards the body with a look that said, "I've done this hundreds of times."

Murder never fails to amaze me. Each time I fall upon the opportunity to view a lifeless body shortly after a murder, it never seems to set well in my spirit. Immediately, I would wonder did this dead person ever know what his true purpose in life was and if that purpose was ever fulfilled. I would also think about the victim's family members and wondered if those family members loved the victim. Finally, I wonder if he had the opportunity to have his life back, would he make a change and do things differently in order to live a full, fruitful life? A life is a terrible thing to waste.

"He's been dead about two and a half hours, just for starters," stated Dr. Bishop. "There's a deep puncture wound located in the left chest cavity which could very well have lacerated the pulmonary artery, being that there's so much blood." He stood immediately to his feet stating, "Heck, you guys didn't want me to do the autopsy here in the weight-pile, now did you?" He raised his right index finger in an instructive manner. "I can tell you one thing, he's definitely dead and I think that's all you guys really need to hear." Dr. Bishop removed a document from his fifties-styled jacket and also grabbed a pencil, which was wedged behind his ear.

Doctor Bishop walked slowly away from the body as he approached two of his assistants who were dressed in white jumpsuits. The word "Coroner" could clearly be seen on the back of their outfits.

"Pack em' up boys, he's ready for shipping," bellowed Dr. Bishop. His assistants wheeled a stretcher onto the weight-pile. One of the men unzipped a large black bag and placed it beside the body. Doctor Bishop looked on motionless with his left thumb propped against his chin. The coroner's assistants picked up the ill-postured body and carefully placed it into the black body bag.

I anticipated the sound of the zipper being closed as a hanging, lifeless arm was placed into the bag. "Zzzzzzip." That's one sound I've grown to hate. The body was placed inside of the coroner's truck. Doctor Bishop informed me that his official autopsy report would be completed in less than a week. What an ending to a day that had already been filled with unwarranted excitement, I thought to myself.

Vowing not to become involved in this murder, somehow I was still prompted from within to initiate the investigation. Officer Mulberry was ordered to seal the crime scene until a formal investigation was formulated. Within moments, I received a radio transmission to report immediately to Captain Davenport's office. I looked down at my aching feet and wished I had worn my comfortable tennis shoes. Walking back across the institution at this time of day was not a picnic, unless I was on my way home.

The grueling journey had ended as I found myself standing in front of Captain Davenport's door. I could hear the Captain on the phone, so I went into the office and sat in the chair directly in front of him. The Captain didn't sound like he was in a good mood, based on the tone of the conversation. There was no doubt in my mind that he was irritated by the potential backlash that could be created by the situation.

"Thanks for coming so quickly," stated the Captain as he hung up the phone. Inwardly, I felt relieved. The Captain could have easily targeted his frustration toward me. "No problem Captain, the Coroner took the body away approximately fifteen minutes ago." I felt at ease momentarily and so proceeded on with a question. "How bad is the situation, Captain?" The Captain presented a magnetic stare as our eyes met. "We can't afford a major uprising within the prison. This matter has to be resolved in a short period of time. There's enough racial tension between the various races. But, to have blacks raging battle against one another could realistically turn this institution upside down." Captain Davenport stood up and strolled slowly to the dirt-stained window in his office. He appeared to have the weight of the world on his shoulders. I hoped to God that he was praying, as he stood silent, leaning against the window seal.

There was no doubt in my mind that the Captain was troubled. "You're the best man I've got, T.P., I realize that you'll be retiring in a few weeks, but facts are facts, I need your help." He clenched both of his fists and placed them on the windowsill. I could sense that he wanted to express himself further. I sat quietly, allowing him to verbalize his thoughts. "This is not exactly the type of good-bye present I had in mind. Of course, I understand your position if you choose to steer clear of the situation. Just the other day I thought about all the investigations that you've headed in the past and wondered, how did you do it? You're a natural." If this man only knew how much admiration and respect I had for him, I don't think he would be pouring on the compliments so thick. "The bottom line is, I'm in a bind and need the best man for the job." He'd never talked this much, I thought to myself. "T.P., it would be such a shame to throw someone new into an investigation task this serious. I'm tempted to do it myself but..." "Okay Captain, I'll think about it." "That's wonderful news, I knew you'd come through." Excitement was plastered all over the Captain's face. "Tonight, I'll give it some serious thought. You're asking me to lead an investigation in a very limited amount of time. But, if I do decide to immense myself in this matter, I will need full cooperation from the institution." The Captain placed his hand upon my shoulder, attempting to assure me I would receive his full support. "Anything you need, just ask," stated Captain Davenport.

Four

Opening my front door was the best thing I'd done all day. What an absolute joy to be present in the comfort of my own home. I've lived in this four-bedroom brick home for the last twenty years. Since my wife's death, I haven't changed a thing. The kitchen remains bright white, surrounded by black appliances. The living room is draped with gold curtains and two silk sofas to match. The dining table is made from richly carved cedar wood surrounded by six identical chairs. Both of my daughters live on their college campuses, but they usually come home every other weekend to visit. Their bedrooms are decorated with posters and pictures of their favorite actors, singers, and political leaders on the walls. Thank God this home is equipped with three bathrooms. Otherwise I couldn't have survived with three females in the house throughout the years.

I closed the front door and was greeted by another member of the family, Coco. Coco is our delightful poodle. I can tell that Coco misses the attention she received when the house was full of females. Coco and I are buddies and she's still worth coming home to every night.

"How are you girl?" I said. Coco looked up at me with her large, dark eyes and then shook her beautiful, shiny brown coat. She walked over to her dog bowl with a look of, are you going to feed me or not.

I hadn't planned on going in the kitchen, but for Coco's sake, I cooperated. Coco trotted over to the pantry and placed her paw on the tall door. I glanced down at her and noticed her little tail wagging from side to side. Coco frequently uses her nose to indicate which flavor of dog food she desires. She placed her nose against a can of beef-flavored chunks and waited for me to grab it. She saw that I was placing the can up to the electric opener and she began jumping up and down, anticipating the serving of her food. The sound of the can opener has initiated this ritual for the past five years. Coco is a good dog and she deserves the best. I would never disappoint my wife by neglecting to care for Coco.

I walked down the hallway leading to my bedroom and noticed a light on in my office. As I reached for the light switch, I couldn't help but notice my wife's brass-framed picture that hung on the wall just above my computer. The radiance of her beauty overshadowed all the many trophies. My wife's presence in spiritual form made all my work tasks that much more simplified. I loved that woman so much.

I flicked off the office light and continued down the hallway to my bedroom. The Victorian-styled setting was my wife's idea, and I have yet to change it. I've always considered my bedroom a place of peace and serenity.

Praying beside my bed each night is a privilege and not a ritualistic deed, as others may perceive it to be. Lord knows I'm in need of direction, so there's nothing better than talking to the master planner.

"Lord, I thank you for your many blessings that you've graciously bestowed upon me. Now Lord, you know the dilemma that I am currently faced with. I am asking for your guidance to make the right decision. You've brought me thus far Lord and you have never failed me yet. Thank you again for my forthcoming retirement and may you bless my future endeavors. Amen."

The next morning I hopped into my car and headed for Los Angeles. Traffic was appalling, but I tried to ignore it, realizing that I was on a serious mission. Unfortunately, there are three freeways I had to take before I was actually in the vicinity of Los Angeles. Thank God for the company of "The Steve Harvey Show." This morning drive time radio show kept me laughing many mornings while venturing to work.

Finally, I reached the interchange that led me from the 91 Freeway to the 110 Freeway, which led directly into Los Angeles. My appointment was scheduled for nine o'clock with the building manager of a location I was considering utilizing for my new company. The dream of operating my own business was a prospect I'd hoped for most of my adult life. The vague thought of a major investigation pending back at the prison was not going to hamper my business dealings, I hoped.

With the asphalt passing quickly beneath my vehicle, I could see the massive skyscrapers peeking over the layer of smog that covered the city. Los Angeles is an amazing city. The city is extraordinarily beautiful at night when the lights are twinkling.

My exit was approximately three miles away, so I flicked on my right signal and began to maneuver my vehicle to the far right lane. Within moments, I got off the freeway at the 6th Street exit. Pedestrians occupied the sidewalks to capacity on both sides of the street. I was protected from the hustle and bustle of noise and distractions as I kept my windows completely closed. I made a right turn and continued on to Hill Street.

After parking my vehicle, I walked towards the small, beige buildings, which were nestled in between two larger buildings. I wasn't impressed by the chipping paint and the cracked windows, but I was always told that what is on the inside matters most. The double glass door led to a staircase that creaked every other step as I galloped to the top level. Just beyond the dimly lit corridor was a large, brown door marked with the words, "Leasing Manager."

Just as I positioned myself to knock on the door, it opened. Much to my surprise, a young man who appeared to be in his twenties greeted me. His greasy, black hair was slicked back and he wore thick prescription glasses. He wore a striped shirt and plaid pants that might have been in style three decades ago.

"Greetings my friend, I'm Robin Keller, Leasing Manager. And you must be Mr. Price." Keller extended his right hand towards me and I noticed that he used a wooden cane to assist himself during his limited movements. We shook hands. "Yes, you are absolutely right. I hope you didn't have to wait long, downtown traffic was a mess." Keller turned around and began walking to a black, wooden workstation that included a computer, fax machine, and telephone.

"Come on in and make yourself comfortable, Mr. Price." Keller used his cane to motion towards a black vinyl recliner that appeared to be taped in several places. I imagined that the chair was possibly as old as the building.

"Would you care for some coffee or tea?" "No thank you, Mr. Keller, I've had my issue for the day." The room was poorly lit. The walls were decorated with pictures of fishermen and boats. The carpet was dark brown and easily capable of concealing dirt or stains.

Keller sat down at the workstation and proceeded to examine several documents that were lying before him. "Organization is not my forte. It's tough trying to be the manager and secretary." I nodded in agreement.

"Here we go," said Keller as his attention was drawn to a single document. "Now I remember, you were interested in opening a private investigation service." I nodded my head as he continued consulting his notes. "Let's see, you're a widow, you have two daughters, and you currently live alone." "Not exactly, I do have a dog." Keller adjusted his glasses. "Currently, you're employed as an investigative lieutenant at the California State Prison-South. In approximately three weeks you're scheduled to retire from your current position. You have over 29 years of law enforcement experience and you appear to have excellent credit." He placed the document face down on the desk. "Problem?" "No, not at all. I'm just excited to meet a man with so much experience in a field such as yours. You've probably seen lots of gory stuff, hmm?" His eyes bulged behind his bifocal lenses. "Well, I guess you could say that. My position has afforded me the opportunity to come across some very interesting situations. But for the most part, I have a knack for what I do and now it's time to do it for myself." Keller displayed a large grin. "Something wrong?" I asked calmly. "Not at all Lieutenant, I'm just intrigued by your investigative savvy. There's no doubt that you have hundreds of stories you could tell…" "Yes, but unfortunately I don't have time to even talk about one of them today." Keller stood up and walked towards one of the paintings hanging on the wall. "Just three years ago, I sailed the ocean blue. I was the best tuna fisherman this side of the Mississippi. No one could reel in the big ones like me. That was my life. Man, I miss it so much. One day my crew and I were caught in one of those serious pacific storms. The large tuna boat shifted suddenly and my leg was tangled between a rope that was attached to a wooden plank. Needless to say, I was practically ripped apart. After two surgeries, this is what I'm left to bear." Keller lifted up his left pant leg and reveals his prosthetic limb. I was temporarily lost for words. "Wow, that must have been a terrifying experience," I said. Keller had become very comfortable in my presence. "The ocean is so awesome. My dad would always take me out in his boat when I was a kid. I caught my first tuna at age five. I can't believe I got stuck doing a job like this." He peered out of a nearby window. "The ocean is nowhere in sight. All I see is a bunch of bums, drunkards and hoodlums. Do you actually want to lease an office in this dump?" This guy is really a piece of work, I thought silently. He could snap at any minute. "Listen Mr. Keller, I'm just a small, downtown businessman just getting started. Various business consultants advised me that setting up shop in downtown L.A. would be ideal for my type of services. The majority of my business dealings are conducted outside of the office anyway." Keller's face clearly read that he wasn't convinced. "Lieutenant Price, there are some very nice office spaces on Third Street and also in the Wilshire district." To avoid being rude, I took a deep breath and counted to five. "For your information, I've priced office space in the Wilshire district, Century City, Beverly Hills, and in West Los Angeles. I'm not opening a film company; it's a private investigation service. If my work record and investigation experience don't speak for themselves, then I should retire from the business completely. Money is something that I can't afford to throw away for the sake of a glamorous business location. My clientele will be solely interested in my skills in solving their problems." Keller shriveled in his chair, and then regained his boyish demeanor. "Mr. Price, please forgive me. Sometimes I get a little excited. We can go up to the fourth floor now and I can show you the available office space."

The office space presented by Mr. Keller was exactly identical to the office he occupied. The only difference was that the room was completely empty and there was a bathroom down the hallway, utilized by all parties on the fourth floor. It was just after nine-thirty and I was running slightly off schedule. My efforts were not completely futile as I had time to canvass the area for other possible locations.

Amid the sparkling tall buildings and the flashy advertisements lay a city filled with filth, overcrowding, and crime. I made my way back onto the freeway, on the Olympic Boulevard onramp. Cars, noise, and smog are the unfriendly elements I'm forced to encounter. The Santa Monica Freeway appeared to be moving steadily, so I maneuvered my vehicle into position and headed east.

The digital display of my vehicle clock flashed 11:42 a.m. as I pulled onto the prison grounds. I was fortunate to creep to my office without attracting attention. My office was peaceful and quiet. The clinging of the telephone startled me. "Lieutenant Price." I had a notion who it might be, causing me to exhibit a stifling sigh. "Yes Captain, I understand. But, what about my replacement, wouldn't this be a good opportunity for him to learn the ropes?" Why was I bothering to reason with a man who was convinced that I was the ideal candidate for the mission. "If that's the way you want it sir, I'm okay with your decision." I slammed the phone down and walked out of my office, directly to the edge of the weight-pile. Dried blood was still noticeable in a sand crater that had been formed by the body.

My entire career as an investigator could boil down to the outcome of this last assignment. All the credentials and accolades would mean nothing if I retired on a sour note. My anger quickly dissipated and my confidence was restored. The game plan was simple. Find the assailant and the murder weapon within three weeks.

In the real world, three weeks is a very short period of time in terms of solving a murder. The prison can be controlled and monitored more closely thus producing faster results.

A meeting was being held in the inmate kitchen. Officer Jones had prepared lemonade for all of us who were in attendance.

"T.P., I hope you're going to have some of this delicious lemonade I made," stated Officer Jones as he gulped down a cup. My attention was drawn to the participants in the room, hoping that all needed parties were present. "I'll have a cup a little later," I said. Officer Jones proceeded to pour lemonade in several plastic cups as everyone else in the room waited patiently for my comments. Present in the inmate kitchen were Sergeant Little, Officer Garcia, Officer Mulberry, Officer Jones, and one officer from each of the five units within the yard.

"First of all, I want to thank all of you for responding to my call in a timely manner. As I am sure all of you know, we have experienced a death within the weight-pile, which appears to be a murder. Much to my surprise, I have been given the assignment of investigating the alleged murder." Officer Jones abruptly cleared his throat. "Excuse me T.P., but I was just wondering if the administration remembered that you will be retiring shortly?" "Matter of fact, they do and that's all the more reason I need the full cooperation from all of you during this investigation." Much to my surprise, I had captured the crew's full attention as they sat quietly at the round, stainless steel dining tables.

"I will be meeting with the Associate Warden this afternoon. We will be discussing the possibility of allowing the yard to operate at full capacity within a week, whether the murder is solved or not." Sergeant Little stood up and boldly interrupted my verbal instructions. "So what point would that be proving T.P.?" I lowered my hands and arms, gesturing for Sergeant Little to have a seat. "The bottom line is, to achieve normalcy here as soon as possible. For the time being, we'll remain on full lock down. Within a day or two, I hope to be utilizing controlled movement procedures. This investigation will take a concerted effort from all of us working together hand-and-hand." I paused a moment to unfasten my necktie. "Now, the first order of business will be to establish our modus-operandi. Bottom line, people, we need to follow a game plan. The second order of business will be to have a team of S&E Officers on full search of the weight-pile. We need as many metal detectors as we can muster up around the prison."

Officer Mulberry displayed a half wave to gain my attention. "Did you have a question, Officer Mulberry?" "T.P., we have eight metal detectors in full operational condition and ready to go. My squad is ready to proceed." Confidence glowed on Officer Mulberry's face. I love a person who has confidence in his or her abilities.

"Thank you for that report, Officer Mulberry. I'm sure you won't have any problems gathering enough shovels and rakes." Officer Mulberry gestured with his head, issuing a "no" response.

"You have my permission to begin your task at the conclusion of this meeting." The other officers anxiously awaited their instructions. "How many housing officers do we have present?" Six individuals raised their hands. "With the assistance of all available staff, you will begin a search of every cell in your dorm. You will also strip-out all inmates down to their skins, no exceptions. Lieutenants' clerks, porters, administration clerks, and barbers will be searched as well." Sergeant Little's eyes practically jumped from his eye sockets. "What about our facility clerks, T.P.? They were obviously working their positions during the time of the murder." "I think I made myself abundantly clear, no exceptions." Sergeant Little's body language reflected a too little too late retraction.

"I plan to interview as many inmates as possible that may have been present in the weight-pile at the time of the murder. Within a day or two, I hope to have a complete list of all the victim's associates and enemies."

Pacing across the front portion of the dining area, I heard the obvious sound of tapping coming from my black, leather-soled shoes. The glossy-glazed concrete floor clearly reflected the shine of my shadow in direct view of my audience. "I expect to have a progress report of each of your findings by 1530 hours. Be sure to keep your ears and eyes focused. We will leave no stone unturned until this murder is resolved." The meeting was completed.

Five

Within an hour, the grueling task of searching the weight-pile had begun. Several officers were equipped with metal detectors and digging tools. The sun's heated rays were relentless as sweat pours from the officers' bodies. Sergeant Little stood idle approximately twenty yards adjacent to the weight-pile with arms folded. He peered closely at the officers as they worked diligently in search of a possible murder weapon. Sand was tossed and hurled into the air from all directions.

"I think I've got something," yelled one of the S&E Officers. Sergeant Little dashed towards the officer, displaying a hunger for excitement. "What you got young man?" bellowed Sergeant Little as he sucked in deeply, attempting to catch his breath. The young officer, dressed in his black task force fatigues, held the metal detector steady in a ninety-degree angle. Observing the officer's position, Sergeant Little walked within a foot of the officer and grabbed the metal detector.

"Sergeant, the spot is right here," the officer pointed directly down in front of his left foot. Sergeant Little motioned with his right hand to an officer standing on the opposite end of the weight-pile. "I need you to bring that shovel over here now," announced Sergeant Little. The startled officer trotted over to the Sergeant and handed him the shovel. The Sergeant snatched the shovel with anxious aggression and began to dig. He reminded me of a busy beaver in the midst of his digging. Many of the officers stood motionless as they studied the actions of Sergeant Little. The shovel hit an object that sounded as if it was metal. Sergeant Little got down on both knees and began to clear away the excess sand with his large hands. Officer Mulberry watched intensely, hoping that Sergeant Little had actually discovered the murder weapon. Searches are hard, demanding, and require physical exertion. The majority of officers despise having to fulfill the assignment of search duty. The obvious attitude amongst the rank and file is that if an issue or circumstance involves an inmate, it isn't worth their time to solve the problem. In other words, so what if one inmate is dead, it's no big loss to the uniformed staff.

Sergeant Little slowly pulled up his hand from the sand. He didn't bother to raise up the object he had dug up, knowing that it was far from being the murder weapon. Sheer embarrassment filled from Sergeant Little's face as he attempted to conceal the old, rusty dumbbell. Officer Mulberry held his hand cupped against his mouth in a diligent effort to disguise his snicker.

"Don't all of you just stand around doing nothing, get back to work now," demanded Sergeant Little. An undercurrent of laughter was felt throughout the entire weight-pile. As Sergeant Little began to head back across the grassy yard to his office, he looked a mess. His green trousers were tucked inside of his black socks. The back tail section of his beige shirt had escaped from the confines of his waistband and his collar was flipped up mimicking an 'old school' disco dancer. His backside was covered with dust from the sand as he scurried to remove himself from the yard.

Meanwhile, I made my way into the administrative building to meet with Betty Wilkins. Betty wasn't expecting my visit, but I knew she wouldn't mind me dropping by.

"What brings you over this way past the lunchtime hour? Wait, don't tell me, it must have something to do with that situation on your yard." I paused with a look that said, "What are you talking about. Situation, what situation?" "Oh, don't give me that T.P., the incident made the prison's front page news." I found myself rubbing my head in awe of the lapse of memory I just experienced concerning the murder. "Betty, I must be losin' it, I'm sorry. Of course, I realize that my yard is on the hot seat. I just want the situation on ice before I make my final exit. Pressure has never been a problem for me, but you know as well as I do that this incident could easily blow up in our faces." Betty sensed the seriousness of the situation from my face. "Relax T.P., it's going to be okay. Now, wipe off your forehead and have a seat." She handed me a blue handkerchief with nickel-size white dots. "Thank you, Betty. I don't know what I'm going to do unless I receive some strategic help from people I can trust." Betty focused directly in on my mouth as I mustered up a cheek-to-cheek smile. "Come-on now T.P., I've seen that smile before, what do you want from me?" After all these years she can still read me like a book, I thought to myself. "Now that you mentioned it, I can use some help." Betty put on a pair of eyeglasses and removed a large notepad from the center drawer of her desk. She removed a pencil from her salon-styled hairdo and assumed a writing position. "Boy, that was easy, I thought I would have to beg and crawl…" "Don't push it T.P., you haven't told me what you need yet." With hands clasped together, I felt modestly humble but I was well beyond being too proud to beg. "What I need, is a direct link to the records office. I know what you're thinking, that I already know several people in records. That's true and I agree with you. But, I need someone who can wait on me hand and foot. A real go-getter is what I need. This person needs to be strong, confident, and shrewd. This person never takes no for an answer and always gets the job done. I need a person who…" Betty slammed her notepad down on the desk. "What you need is a personal slave!" My eyes were fully open in response to Betty's comment. "No, no, Betty. I just need someone who can give me some special attention. Of course, it's not for me personally, it's because of the nature of this case." I gave her my lost-without-a-home look. "Believe me T.P. if you weren't retiring in a few weeks, I'd tell you which cliff to go jump off of. Fortunately for you, you're still my favorite officer around this joint and I'm going to miss you." She cracked a genuine smile. I breathed a sigh of relief. "Listen T.P., I need you to meet me in the cafeteria in about fifteen minutes."

Time was of the essence, keeping in the forefront of my mind the ensuing murder investigation. I made my way down the shiny-corridor heading north in the direction of the Associate Warden's Office.

Some of these administrators are actually able to speak once they loosen up the neckties that have them all choked up. Mr. Richard Chambers was the Associate Warden responsible for management operations on facility 2. He was best known around the prison for the various shades and styles of gray suits that he proudly wore around the facility. As I knocked on his door, clearly marked with his full name in white capital letters, engraved on a black plaque, I entered. Chambers was seated in his brown, high-back leather recliner, dressed in one of his familiar gray suits. It is no secret that Chambers enjoys coordinating his clothing attire to match his silver-toned, perfectly styled hair. He often brags to female employees concerning his blood ties to a famous British rock star, though his name is one I fail to recognize. His celebrity connection didn't help in preventing his three failed marriages. But, it's understood that divorce occurs for many folks who are associated with law enforcement.

Once I entered the office, I sat in a green-padded, steel-framed chair that was only a couple of feet in front of Chambers' desk. This was only the second occasion that I'd been present in this office. I prayed that the uneasiness I was experiencing was not obvious. The walls were covered with several pictures of various breeds of wolves. On the rare moment that I would look away from Chambers, there was always one vicious wolf staring in my direction. I often wonder if the saying, 'a wolf in sheep's clothing,' originated with Chambers. Deep down within myself I had always hoped that Chambers had some type of feelings encased within that frail frame of his.

"My, my, my, it's not often that I have the pleasure of having you present in my office. But, you're definitely on top of your job." "Well, Mr. Chambers, I'm sure you'd be the first to know administratively if something was out-of-order on facility 2." Chambers displayed no emotions as he put a large coffee mug to his mouth. Though I would be retiring in a short period of time, I was hoping to refrain from any outburst of arrogance. I sensed that Chambers might have perceived a tinge of arrogance in my initial statement. "Slurrrrrrrp, so what's on your mind, Lieutenant Price?" Chambers removed the coffee mug from his mouth and somberly awaited my answer. "My officers are all situated and are currently in search of the assailant and the murder weapon. We anticipate that our concentrated search should take approximately three to four days." Chambers flipped open a manila folder and studied the material momentarily without uttering a word. I attempted to study his body language in hopes of calculating his thoughts.

After two minutes of silence, Chambers gently closed the manila folder. "This murder situation has the potential to spill over into a major uproar. I'm counting on you to keep the order intact, Lieutenant. Captain Davenport assured me that you would have this situation resolved prior to your retirement." This man knew as well as I did that nothing is guaranteed in this world and definitely not in this God-forsaken prison. If I didn't know any better, it seemed as though Chambers was trying to taunt my investigation abilities in terms of solving this murder. "I plan to do my best just as always, sir. Captain Davenport has been thoroughly informed concerning the situation." I hoped that my strong inner confidence was clear. Chambers appeared to be listening close. "I was also assured by Captain Davenport that the administration has given me the green light to proceed as necessary." Chambers removed a stick of chewing gum from its foil wrapper and placed it in his mouth. "As long as you are following the procedural statutes of the institution, we have no problems in you having complete control of the matters" Is this man crazy, I thought. He doesn't know who he's talking to evidently. "No disrespect Mr. Chambers, but I've been conducting drug and murder investigations for years. Quite frankly, my record should speak for itself. I don't plan on leaving any stone unturned before retirement." Chambers nodded his head in a forward motion appearing to be offering his blessings.

An exhilarating feeling consumed me as I walked out of Mr. Chambers' office. I rested briefly against the corridor wall before proceeding down the hallway.

Upon entering the staff cafeteria, I noticed that Betty was standing in the food line beside a large, African-American woman. The woman stood approximately six-foot-two in height and weighed about two hundred and fifty pounds. She was fashionably draped in red. Her hair was bound in a bun secured by a red silk ribbon. Her lips were adorned with bright red lipstick that matched her two-piece dress and her polished fingernails. I didn't recognize the woman, but Betty seemed to know her very well. For a moment, I contemplated leaving the cafeteria immediately. The time was just beyond the fifteen-minute period in which Betty had told me to meet her here in the cafeteria. Oh, what the heck I thought to myself. I might as well talk to her. My apprehension was magnified by the presence of the woman in red whom I preferred not to know of my business dealings with Betty.

Betty glanced to her left while reaching for a napkin and observed that I was standing by the entrance. She displayed all thirty-two of her teeth and motioned for me to meet her at a table in the northeast section of the cafeteria.

As I walked over to the table, I kept my eyes focused on Betty, hoping that she was not going to invite the lady in red over to join us. Oh my God, I mumbled under my breath as Betty and the lady in red approached the table. "You're late T.P., I told you to meet me here in fifteen minutes," uttered Betty. "If you must know Betty, I was in conference with Mr. Chambers. Our meeting was a necessity." Betty didn't appear to be moved by my statement as she sat down and bit into her tuna sandwich. The lady in red smiled before taking a sip of her beverage. Food was the furthest thing from my mind and I hoped Betty would realize that. My only concern at the moment was to have some inside help in regards to the murder case. "I'm sorry Ethel, have you ever met Lieutenant Price?" Ethel shook her rosy red cheeks from side to side, gesturing that she hadn't experienced the pleasure of meeting me. "Forgive me you two, I thought that you guys had met prior to today." "Lieutenant Price, it's finally nice to have the pleasure of meeting you in person." She reached out and grabbed my hand. "I'm Ethel Williams, we've talked several times on the phone." "Why of course, you're the Ethel from records. After all these years, I can't believe we're just meeting." We were both elated with the opportunity of meeting one another. Betty sat quietly and continued to eat her lunch. She winked twice in my direction in hopes that I would receive her signal. I took a wild guess in assuming that Ethel was the person referred by Betty to assist me with the case. "Please tell me that you're going to help with the facility 2 murder investigation?" I pleaded genuinely. Betty nodded her head in a positive motion, unable to speak due to her mouth being full. "Betty informed me that you could probably use a helping hand. I'm not promising any miracles, but I'll do my best," stated Ethel. Relief suddenly flooded my senses. I was now convinced that I could realistically complete the investigation prior to my retirement.

Prior to leaving the cafeteria, I explained in detail to Ethel the information that I would need to assist me in my ongoing investigation.

The four o'clock hour was fast approaching as I made my way back to the facility 2 yard. Officer Garcia greeted me in a most professional manner as I was let through the plaza gate. "Will you be requiring an escort onto the yard, Lieutenant?" For a brief moment I considered the officer's thoughtful offer. "That won't be necessary Officer Garcia, the yard poses no threat at the moment." Officer Garcia locked the plaza gate as I passed through. In the distant foreground, I noticed that there was no movement on the weight-pile. This could be the break that I was hoping for if indeed the murder weapon had been recovered. My pace increased as I anticipated the good news. There were a few officers standing in front of the inmate culinary. There is no doubt that these officers had been working hard, judging by the grit and grime on them. The officers saluted me as I opened up the door leading into the inmate culinary. Once I entered the facility, Officer Mulberry and his security squad were seated, appearing to be exhausted from their grueling search. No one looked in my direction for any substantial period of time, which immediately sparked my concern. Officer Mulberry stood up from the stainless steel table that he was seated on and walked in my direction. "You guys look mighty worn out to me." "Can we step outside for a moment, Lieutenant?" Officer Mulberry spoke in a serious tone. "Sure, no problem at all." I didn't mean to leave a bunch of officers who looked as if they had run the Boston Marathon.

Upon exiting the inmate culinary, I felt a swift breeze, a much needed breath of fresh air. Officer Mulberry walked over to the location of the murder and kneeled down on one knee. Judging by Mulberry's somber actions, it was apparent that something must be heavy on his mind.

"So what's on your mind, Mulberry?" He turned and looked up at me. "Lieutenant, we searched for several hours and there was no weapon discovered. I'm sorry to disappoint you sir. If necessary, we don't mind devoting more hours to searching the weight-pile again." I like Mulberry. He's a young man who reminds me a lot of myself. His efforts, motivation, and dedication are a formula that I believe in every day of my life. "Son, let me tell you something, Rome was not built in a day. There are going to be some murders that will never be resolved. But, life must go on. As an investigator, as long as you've done your best and no stone has been left unturned, your job has been done." Mulberry pointed to one of the metal detectors. "That metal gadget probably cost a fortune.

Sometimes I wonder if it has a mind of its own. It would have felt good if we at least found an old piece of silverware from the inmate culinary buried in the sand." Mulberry was obviously bothered by the fact that he didn't find anything in the weight-pile. "Mulberry, you've got to stay focused. There is so much work that needs to be accomplished concerning the case and this is only the beginning." Mulberry commenced to retrieve the equipment and tools that were left lying within the weight-pile. The housing units were now my focus of attention, knowing that each inmate and his property were being thoroughly searched.

Six

My personal theory concerning the situation was that if the murder weapon was not present within the weight-pile, then it was removed. There were no bloodstains or blood drops leading away from the weight-pile. If this was the case, the assailant only had two options concerning disposal of the weapon. The first scenario was that after stabbing the victim, the assailant used a towel or an item of clothing and wiped the blood from the weapon. He then concealed the weapon in an unknown location on the yard. If this theory could be authenticated then there must be a blood-soiled piece of material somewhere on the yard as well. The second scenario was similar to the first, but only that the assailant wiped the blood off from the weapon onto the victim's clothing. The assailant then took the murder weapon back to his housing unit and concealed it in the day room or in his cell.

Well, I guess I'd better stop fishing for a theory without any possible clue of a motive, I said to myself calmly. Any information would help at this point although it was still early into the investigation. "Are you ready to go?" yelled Sergeant Little from across the yard. He was pointing towards the housing units, so I assumed that he was ready to check up on the officers' findings. As I began to walk, I waved back to Sergeant Little, acknowledging that I would be meeting him in front of the first housing unit. This segment of the job was one I wasn't fond of conducting; men being searched like animals or slaves during an auction, one thousand men having to be scrutinized due to the actions of one person or a small group of hoodlums. As Sergeant Little arrived, we both approached the housing entrance. The electronic door leading inside of the first housing unit creaked loudly as we entered. From what I could gather, the unit officers were conducting strip searches on the east tier, second level. Each inmate stood naked as a newborn as they waited. Several S&E (search & escort) Officers proceeded to probing the prison cells in search of any type of contraband or weapon. Another set of officers strategically searched each inmate. I peered closely as two officers searched an older man. One of the officers used his finger to ruffle through the inmate's hair. The other officer maneuvered a special magnifying glass, searching for any possible scrapes, cuts, or trace of blood that might be present on the inmate's body. Each body cavity, including his anus was closely searched to ensure that no weapon or contraband had been concealed within the body. After the inmate bent over and coughed, he was allowed to put on his underwear and enter back into his cell. There are approximately thirty more inmates who were standing naked in a military-style line for their individual turn to be searched. During these procedures, I tended to oversee the actions of the officers to reduce the possibility of any illegal or malicious behavior. Truth be known, some officers have been known to abuse their limited authority and that's one program I can't get with. I don't have a problem at all in writing a disciplinary report regarding an officer's unlawful actions. Of course, some of these inmates were the scum of the earth, but I had to respect the fact that they're human beings. There is a very thin line between right and wrong and all humans have the potential of breaking the law on a daily basis.

"How do you feel T.P., you think they'll find something?" My eyes remained focused on the second tier, not really concentrating on Sergeant

Little's comment. My voice managed to murmur a few words. "The killer is here, maybe not in this particular housing unit, but he's definitely on this yard." Sergeant Little hesitated with surprise before offering his sentiments. "Damn T.P., you're absolutely right. This murderous fool is living amongst everybody and probably acting as if nothing is a big deal. When we catch this nut I'm going to beat his..." "Save your energy Sergeant, the fight has just begun." He never ceased to amaze me. This man had been in this department for years and he still displayed rookie tendencies.

A six-three brotha named Blue approached the Sergeant and I. Sweat was shining on his clean-shaven, brown-skinned face. "My favorite supervisor. I bet I know why you're here." He removed a dingy handkerchief from his shirt pocket and wiped his face. "I'm definitely not here to keep you from sweating," I said, as we all forced a chuckle. "T.P., we haven't found anything. Usually we'll find some dope or some pruno (inmate-manufactured alcohol), but we're striking out. If I didn't know any better, it almost appears as if everyone was expecting this shakedown. I hate to say it, but this one really has me concerned." Blue looked cautiously from side-to-side, "The Brothas ain't sayin' nothin' to me or any of the other officers. I thought for sure I had a good rapport with the inmates." Blue was caught-up into the emotional pitfalls of an environment that functions solely on survival. Practically every inmate held their mood, thought, and conceived controversy in silent contempt. Ignorance is valued as gold and silver is the reward for suppressing a gut-wretched sentence. "When I was a little boy and there was a very serious situation that needed to be dealt with, my father would always say, let's handle this one with kid gloves. I honestly believe that we are in the midst of one of those situations." Blue formed a tight fist. He gestured in my direction with his fist, then immediately returned back to the top tier to continue his assigned duties.

There appeared to be approximately ten inmates present on the second tier, patiently waiting to be searched and examined. "What the hell is going on in this hell-hole," yelled an inmate of European culture. My attention was clearly focused in this individual's direction. Several officers hurried up the steep metal staircase, rushing to assist the officers already present on the tier. I grabbed Sergeant Little as he attempted to walk briskly in the direction of the metal staircase. Several officers restrained the inmate as the other nine inmates were ordered to place their knees to the ground and place their interlocked hands behind their heads. This real life scenario could easily develop into a situation that could warrant an internal investigation. I wasn't about to allow this housing unit to be turned into a circus.

"Everyone hold your position now!" Several sets of bewildered eyes were converged in my immediate vicinity. "Bring him down here now!" I shouted aloud. The inmate did not resist as he was brought down the metal staircase.

Approximately ten feet behind me was the unit office. The room is approximately 6' X 8' in diameter. Sergeant Little attempted to follow me to the room, but I motioned for him to leave me alone so that I could question the inmate in private. As the officers escorted him to the front of the door, I requested that they allow him to walk into the room on his own accord.

"Come in and shut the door behind you," I said softly. The inmate immediately followed my instructions and stood quietly by the door. "What's your name?" He appeared reluctant to provide his name, but within moments he complied. "Olson is my last name, Nick is my first," he pronounced slowly. "What seems to be the problem today, Mr. Olson?" He looked around the room, staring through the large glass windows that surrounded us on all but one wall in the office. Olson stood erect in front of me, clothed only in his white boxer shorts. His upper body was covered with several tattoos of various symbols. His muscular chest bulged, and jewelry hung from his pierced nipples. Several officers gazed into the office, to ensure that the situation between us was secure.

"I can't believe you're frontin' me off like this. Now every convict in this joint thinks I'm spilling my guts out to you just to save my neck. We didn't have anything to do with the murder." His blatant statements aroused my curiosity. "Now that you've mentioned it, what do you know about the murder?" "I don't know crap about no murder. Even if I did know something about it, who said I would tell you?" I pointed to the chair that was situated in front of the small, wooden desk that I was seated behind, instructing Olson to be seated. "Mr. Olson, I recall your statement just moments ago, saying 'We didn't have anything to do with the murder,' who were you referring to?" Olson stood up abruptly. "Sit down before I have your butt dragged down to Ad Seg." (Administrative Segregation). He immediately sat back down in the chair. I motioned for the on-looking officers to hold their positions. "This disturbance was brought on by you, Mr. Olson. Officers don't take too kindly to negative comments during a prison shake-down."

Olson positioned his lips to speak, but elected not to follow through. "If there's something you want to say or a comment on the situation that you need to get off your chest, I strongly advise you to take advantage of this rare opportunity." Olson stroked his beard and mustache and began to speak softly. "Well, I just don't think it's fair for us to be snatched out of our cells and searched like the rest of the folks. I'm nobody's snitch, but you know as well as I do that we didn't have anything to do with the murder." Olson's face showed signs of seriousness. "So what are you telling me, Mr. Olson, that no 'White' inmates had anything to do with the murder?" "Well I…" "Don't you think I know that, Olson? But, I guess you figure that we should go against prison procedures and search the "Black" inmates just because the murder took place on their side of the weight-pile. I've been investigating murders and other prison incidents well over fifteen years, so suggestions from you on how to do my job are not necessary." I took a moment to regain my composure. "Tell me something if you can, Olson, why are you so sure that 'we' as you stated, had nothing to do with the murder?" Olson sneered, illustrating his confidence. "If there was a hit out this serious, I definitely would have known about it. Someone didn't think about the repercussions associated with this type of hit." Olson folded his hands together appearing to be relieved of his frustration. "Believe it or not, I agree with you Mr. Olson, but situations such as this have to be handled a certain way." I motioned for Sergeant Little to enter the office. "What's up, T.P.?" "Would you kindly have one of the officers escort Mr. Olson to his cell," I stated while gesturing for Olson to stand up. "No problem," stated Sergeant Little as he tugged at Olson's upper arm. "He's okay Sergeant," I said as I picked up the office phone. I was waiting for a full report from another housing unit regarding the possibility of discovery of evidence linked to the murder. "This is Lieutenant Price, what information do you have for me?" The officer spoke rapidly as he provided me with information that did not lend itself to be promising. "Well, you've done all that can be done." I continued to listen to the officer's verbal report. "Keep your unit in lock-down status until you hear back from me." I hung up the phone in disgust realizing that my investigation had not yet produced positive results.

The afternoon had proved to be fruitless if physical evidence was the measuring guide for success. The sun was slowly creeping below the horizon and the prison yard was as quiet as a cemetery.

As I entered my automobile, I peered closely at the large; cement-colored structure that houses thousands of convicted felons. The majority of the inmates are more than likely guilty of the crimes that planted them within the criminal system. A small voice in the back of my mind seems to always remind me of that small percentage that are innocent and are being incarcerated unjustly. I've always dreamed that one-day a system of equality and fairness would prevail where all men would be tried on a level playing field.

The traffic was somewhat smoother than usual as I headed down the dimly lit highway towards home. Ever since I got the privilege to operate a state vehicle, my biggest complaint is that these cars don't have cassette decks. The State of California could care less concerning my listening pleasure, so I imagine I should be grateful to have a car radio.

Why was I worrying about this state car? Why was I worrying about the murder investigation? Was it really that important to know who the murderer was? Why should I care anyway, I'd be retiring in a few weeks. I'd receive a full pension and medical benefits. I'm about to open my own business and I'll be the real boss for once. I twisted the radio knob and blasted the radio to full volume. Who was I kidding? There was no way possible that I could ever consider my retirement as pleasant, knowing that I had an unsolved murder hanging over my head. I had to solve this murder.

The brakes screeched loudly as I pulled the vehicle into the driveway. Coco greeted me at the front door as I entered the entryway. "Hey Coco, you hungry girl?" I grabbed a can of dog food from the pantry and Coco followed me to the can opener. As I activated the can opener, Coco squirmed about the kitchen hopping up and down as I opened the can of dog food. "Here baby dog, come and get dinner," I said as I placed the food in the dog bowl. In the meantime, I walked over to the freezer and removed my favorite frozen TV dinner, Oriental rice with beef and broccoli. "Any phone calls for me?" I shouted towards Coco. Coco ignored my question and continued eating. The answering machine's light was blinking indicating that I at least had one message. This machine is the last electrical gadget my wife purchased prior to her death. Her voice is still present on the message greeting and I swore I would never erase it. Just as I proceeded to retrieve my phone messages, the doorbell rang. "I am definitely not expecting any company." Coco would normally beat me to the door, but due to her nose being planted in the doggy dish, I was left to answer the door on my own.

I carefully scanned the porch area through the small peephole on my door. "Man, what are you doing over this way?" I said with excitement, as I opened the door. "I was in a bowling tournament down the street, why didn't you listen to your phone messages?" I quickly motioned towards the kitchen. "Believe it or not I was just about to listen to my messages. If you don't believe me you can ask Coco." Coco walked up while wagging her little tail. My brother Peter reached down and gave Coco a pat on the head. Peter is my one and only younger brother. He stands about six-foot five and sports a clean-shaven head to match his boyish, smooth-skinned face. I always thought of Peter as being an honorary cowboy as he is rarely seen without his boots and jeans on. Peter placed a medium-sized paper bag on the kitchen counter. "What's in the bag man?" I bent over and sniffed the bag. "Come-on T.P., you know I had to stop and get some of Charlie's catfish." Charlie's is a small fast food restaurant on the south side of town that specializes in fried seafood. I remember nights when my mouth would water just hoping to get my hands on a fried shrimp sandwich on a French roll. The building looks a little shabby but their food is excellent. "Help yourself bro…" "I was just about to break-out with the paper plates." Coco looked up towards us with an expression of, I know I'm gettin' some of that fish. We usually save Coco a couple of crumbs. Good luck must be coming my way. Things usually happen for me when fish is somewhere in my diet.

During our finger-lickin' period, I waited patiently for Pete to bring up the subject of retirement. "Dad asked about you today," stated Peter in a less than enthusiastic manner. "The rest home seems to be agreeing with him, cause we both know how demanding he can be at times." Peter poured me another cup full of red soda pop. The bottle refers to it as being strawberry soda, but when we were growing up, it was red to us. Peter was preparing me for his anticipated barrage of questions as he continued to serve me cups of soda as if it was an alcoholic beverage that could have some affect on my reasoning and decision-making. "What is it that you need to know Peter?" He pretended to be choking on his soft drink. "Whatever gave you that idea? I'm just sitting here relaxing while enjoying a good meal." His sympathetic look was not meeting my approval. "For your information, I will be retiring as scheduled. The business plans are on line, but I still haven't decided on a location. Nevertheless, I do have two prospective locations in mind." I purposely placed my hand up to my mouth before speaking further. "Work's going good, and I only have one pending investigation and its maj—." Peter jumped up immediately, sensing that I was reluctant to spill my guts. "Did you say what I think you said?" Peter said cautiously. "Yeah, it's major, so what!" "Did anyone remind you that the clock is ticking and time is almost up?" For a brief moment, I remembered that when we were kids, Peter would always question my better judgment. That boy sure did have a mouth on him. The nerve of him to talk to his big brother that way. Moments such as this caused Peter to get his little butt kicked when we were kids. One thing about Peter, he never told Mom and Dad when I roughed him up. The boy took it like a man. "You know Peter, I had a brief thought, but I won't even go there right now. But, to answer your question, I know what time it is and I am well aware of what needs to be accomplished. I think you know my work record. I could never leave an investigation half done." I took a breather, knowing that he was eagerly awaiting his opportunity to jump in. "That's my whole point, you don't know when to call it quits. God forbid you fail to complete this investigation before your retirement clock ceases to tick. Haven't you ever heard of just taking a break?" Where does he get off speaking to me like this in my house, I thought to myself. "Peter, I think it's time to change the subject," as I reached in the freezer to remove a carton of strawberry ice cream. I reached for my favorite bowl, the one that my daughters gave me way back when, on Father's Day. "Big Daddy" was inscribed on the bowl in light blue writing. "Would you care for some ice cream?" "No thanks, I'm trying to cut back on sweets," said Peter. I immediately pointed to the carton label and stated, "It's all natural." "It may be natural but it's still sweet, I'll pass." When we were kids, Peter would always pretend to not be hungry when we were over at various friends' homes. Upon our friend's parents offering Peter food or drink, he would always pretend to not be thirsty or hungry. As soon as the parents would walk into another room, Peter would nag his friends into getting him food and drink. He would tell me that his excuse was that he was trying to be polite by not accepting anything. "There's some news that I think you should know," stated Peter. The hair on my head began to tighten up. "Okay, but if it's about my retire…" "No T.P., it has nothing to do with your retirement, for your information. Realistically, it's about when you immediately leave the job. It is supposed to be a surprise, but I wanted you to know so you wouldn't spoil your daughters' treat. They're planning on throwing you a party for your retirement and I'm responsible for your delivery. I've had my share of you skipping out on celebrations in the past, but this one is certainly not going to be ruined if it's up to me." "Don't be such a grouch, I wouldn't let my two little angels down. But no, you had to spoil it. You never could keep a secret." Peter balled up his large fist and pointed in my direction. "Please T.P., be serious, you wouldn't have been anywhere to be found if it were left up to you."

Deep down inside I knew for a fact that Peter was right. I was never big on celebrations no matter what the occasion. Somehow, some way I would attend this event. My biggest dream would have been to have my wife sitting right beside me at the celebration. My girls would be there and that was good enough for me.

Peter eventually left the house and I decided to turn in. One of my biggest challenges was to change the bed linen. I commenced to remove the floral comforter and the gray sheets from the bed. I walked to the linen closet that was located just outside the bedroom in the hallway. As I sorted through the various shades and print styles, I decided to go with blue. A man can never go wrong with blue. The sheets were folded gracefully, a trait I learned from my late wife. The bed took about fifteen minutes to prepare. Afterwards, I got down on my knees and beckoned the Lord with deep prayer to intervene in my current dilemma.

Seven

The next morning, Coco had gently found her way to the end of my comfortable bed. Who could blame a good dog that desires to be with her master? Instead of waking Coco up, I placed an extra blanket on her small, frail body.

The sun had begun to sneak through the partially closed drapes. The shower was always my best friend in the early morning hours. The gentle feel of hot water on my skin had an electrifying, yet soothing appeal.

An apple and a glass of orange juice usually satisfy my appetite for breakfast. When I was a kid, I don't remember Dick Tracy ever eating a heavy breakfast prior to starting his day. He was the best investigator in the world, in my opinion.

The freeway traffic was surprisingly light this morning. Complaining about the situation was the furthest thing from my mind, but it was just shocking to see the road clear from traffic. I wanted to listen to some music during my drive, but for some odd reason I was unable to relax.

Tension had overwhelmed me and I could not clearly focus on the investigation or my upcoming retirement. My stomach twisted and turned, though I had had a light, healthy meal. I recall this same problem when I first walked into the inner walls of Folsom State Prison.

There was a group of about twenty of us, rookies of course. We were all anxious and excited about viewing the inner guts of a prison for the first time. We took a bus from the academy in Galt, a small city in Northern California, about 20 miles south of Sacramento.

Upon our arrival at Folsom, we were greeted by uniformed personnel who were professional in appearance. Our group was split in half as we journeyed to the entrance of one of California's former leading, notorious prisons. I remember quite clearly entering the prison grounds and being consumed with fear. As the large gates closed behind us, I knew that we were in danger. We toured the prison grounds and witnessed several hundred inmates as they lifted weights and roamed the prison grounds. It was not the most glamorous sight that I've experienced, but for the most part I could handle the scene. The same feeling that I was experiencing now, occurred back then in the prison once we entered the cellblocks. The dark, dungeon-type atmosphere clearly illustrated within me a clear picture of doom and punishment. The feeling I experienced was not one that I like to talk about.

Today I was experiencing that same feeling and I didn't like it. Something had to break and I prayed that it wouldn't be me. Today had to be different, I thought to myself as I pulled into the prison parking lot. After hesitating for a short moment, I exited the car and headed for the administration building.

The landscaped grass in front of the administration building proves for once the saying, "The grass is greener on the other side of the fence." Well, at least the grass was greener on this side of the fence.

Upon entering the administration building, I noticed that Betty wasn't at her workstation. As I continued down the spotless corridor, a large red figure was fast approaching in the distance. "Oh my God, it's Ethel Williams!" I said aloud. Ethel proudly slung her large, red dress from side-to-side while high stepping towards me with her red, snake-skinned high heels.

"T.P., I've got a bit of news for you, and I felt I should deliver it to you myself." What could be so important, I thought to myself. "Thank you for your diligence in this matter Ethel. Good help is hard to find these days." She handed me a document. "When I say I'm going to help somebody, that's exactly what I mean." She brandished a large smile, displaying her pearly whites and her cherry red lips. "Notice the names on the 812" (enemy sheet). "All I see are two names, and quite honestly I'm shocked that it's only two names. I expected this 812 to be filled with names." I studied the names for a brief moment. "Tuck Williams is the only name I'm familiar with. I don't recognize the other gentleman." Ethel gave me a look that clearly illustrated that I should check into this matter. "For your information T.P., Tuck Williams is housed within the same facility as the murder victim. Craig Battle is currently housed in Riverside County Jail. Get this, he's being detained on murder charges." "Hmm, interesting." Finally, a small break in the case, I thought silently. "You've been lots of help. Keep up the good work." Before I had the opportunity to extend my hand, Ethel had already grabbed it and began shaking firmly. "It was a pleasure T.P., I'm glad to be of service." I gently snatched my hand back from Ethel, hoping not to appear rude. "Well, I guess I'll be on my way." Ethel replied, "If you're still around the administration building at lunch time, stop by my office. Last night I went a little crazy and cooked a bunch of black-eyed peas, macaroni and cheese, baby-back ribs and some corn bread. You're welcome to join me, I have plenty to share." What was this woman trying to do to me, I pondered briefly. "Maybe another time when I'm less pressed for time!" I said. There's no doubt at all in my mind that this woman can throw down in the kitchen.

My grandmother was exactly like Ethel, when it came to cooking. That woman could really burn some food, in a good way. From childhood to my adult years, I loved going to my grandmother's house after church for some fantastic meals. I sure miss those good old days.

My nose flared as the smell of food floated down the corridor. Of course the smell was no match for my late grandmother's cooking and I doubt if it could compare to Ethel's. I decided to go to the cafeteria, but not for the food. Coffee is the ticket for me. Manny greeted me with his signature smile as he poured me my usual large cup of coffee. As I commenced to add sugar and cream to my coffee, I observed Captain Davenport sitting in the far west corner of the cafeteria. God must have heard my silent prayer as I looked up towards the ceiling, demonstrating a small gesture of thanks. I was pleased that I had this opportunity to meet with Captain Davenport on neutral grounds. He was sitting with his back in my direction as he faced a wall covered with floral wallpaper.

"Hello Captain, what's new?" Captain Davenport twisted around towards me while seated on the round steel chair. "Lieutenant Price, a man who always has a plan. Come have a seat and join me." Things were going smooth so far, I don't know why I was so nervous, except that this was a man whom I admired and respected. The question that I was about to ask of the Captain might not leave our relationship in the best of light. A man has to do what a man has to do.

"Captain, can I be up front and frank with you?" I squirmed momentarily in my seat while awaiting his response. "Sure Lieutenant, what's on your mind?" "The investigation is on-going as we speak and unfortunately I have no strong leads. I've received some information, but for the most part I'm clueless." Captain Davenport nodded his head as he listened closely to my report. "My experience as an investigator tells me that the prison yard should be opened and all facility operations should be returned to normal. Believe me, I know this sounds crazy, but in this particular case, the murder will probably not be resolved until I can maneuver throughout the facility and interview various inmates at will. I will have a full report completed by the morning. The report will illustrate all my actions taken thus far." Captain Davenport peered directly into my eyes momentarily before uttering a word. "Prison life is definitely hell on earth and I'm sure you know that just as well or better than I do. This is a very serious situation that can easily blow-up into something very major. Though you're leaving soon, you're still the best I've got for this situation. I don't know what plan you've been working on, but I'm trusting that it's a winner. I can't promise you anything, but I will be speaking with Richard Chambers in regards to your request." That would be a very big mistake, I thought to myself while absorbing the Captain's sentiments. I really wished that he didn't have to confer with an Associate Warden that was unconcerned to say the least. Nevertheless, I did understand that the chain of command was the command that unlocks the chains. In other words, someone else other than me held the key in making the decisions that I was proposing. "Thanks for all of your help Captain, I'll be waiting for your call."

Thank God for understanding people. The meeting was much better than I had anticipated. All I could do was hope and pray that the Associate Warden would cooperate with my investigative strategy. What was the worst thing that could happen by opening the yard too soon?

Just around the corner from Captain Davenport's office was an empty office that had just been painted, judging by the strong odor of fresh paint and a half full can of paint sitting in the corner, near a large paintbrush. The office was clearly unoccupied and this would be a perfect opportunity for me to make some important calls. A small black chair and a computer desk were the only items in the office besides the phone that was on the floor under a white sheet. The old, brown tweed carpet was still on the floor. I'm sure that the next task would be for the maintenance crew to replace this worn-out carpet. My real concern was not to let loose paint get on my brown, snake-skinned shoes. I promised myself that I would dress sharp each and every day prior to my retirement. I pulled my leather reminder pad from my inner coat pocket and flipped through the pages. Within seconds, I located the phone number I needed. As I punched in the numbers on the phone, I anticipated hearing some type of news regarding the case. "Hello, I'm Lieutenant Price, an investigator with the Department of Corrections. Would you know if Dr. Bishop is available?" The female on the other line placed me on hold as she proceeded to locate Dr. Bishop. Usually, I only allow a person 20 seconds to pick up the phone when I'm holding the line. After 18.5 seconds, the female returned back to the phone and informed me that Dr. Bishop was busy in the midst of an autopsy. "Would it be possible for you to take a message for him?" She gave her approval. "My phone number is 785-3249, and again my name is Lieutenant Price with the Department of Corrections." I hung up the phone, glanced at my watch, made a few notes in my reminder pad, and exited the abandoned office.

Eight

The administration hallways were free of traffic as I made my way outside the building.

Once I was in the privacy of my office, I felt a bit energized. I began to study all of my written notes and subsequently formed a strategic plan for interviewing all potential murder suspects. My mind was immediately drawn to the two individuals who were present on the murder victim's enemy sheet. These hot leads needed to be tackled quickly, but ever so carefully. Interviewing the wrong inmates could possibly disrupt future communications with other inmates. My plans were to proceed with caution, but when a lead proved worthy, I'd proceed full blast with the investigation.

Tuck Williams was an inmate who was no stranger to prison fights, riots, and officer confrontations. When Ethel provided me with his name as a possible suspect due to his name appearing on the victim's enemy sheet, it seemed too good to be true. As an experienced investigator, I knew from training to proceed with extreme caution, even when names and evidence seemingly falls in your lap. For the most part, I knew that

Tuck Williams wouldn't be going anywhere due to the length of his current prison term. I was convinced that suspect number two, Craig Battle, should be my first custody interview. Craig Battle was an inmate on this yard just three months prior to the murder. He was now on parole and currently facing alleged charges of robbery and assault. He was being housed at the Riverside County Jail facility in the City of Riverside. Riverside is a well-populated suburban city located approximately 60 miles from Los Angeles. If there was a situation on the yard, Craig Battle might be able to provide some information that could help me discover the murderer. Mr. Battle was still considered a suspect although he had been out of prison approximately three months. Gangsters are known to order hits on individuals they want dead for various reasons. Hits can be ordered from outside of prison, especially when there is unfinished business present within the prison. I was quite curious to know what information Mr. Battle was willing to share with the Department.

I decided to place a call to the Riverside County Jail authorities. "Hi, this is Lt. Price with the Department of Corrections. I need to check on the custody status of an individual by the name of Craig Battle." The jail staff responded favorably. On many occasions, the jail staff will react as though I'm bothering them when conducting a necessary function of my job. "His birth date is 7-24-65." She recited his booking number and I jotted the information down on a yellow stick'em on my desk. "What time is your feeding period over for lunch?" She stated about noon, which was what I figured anyway. "Thanks a bunch for your help." Eleven o'clock would be a good time to leave the prison in order to arrive at the county jail right after lunch. An hour drive is no big deal during the middle of the day. My thought process was interrupted as Officer Mulberry walked into my dimly lit office unannounced. "How's it going T.P.?" My mouth dared a rude comment, but my mind reminded me of the young kid standing in front of me who was here to do his job. "I'd be doing a lot better if I could solve this murder in the next few days. Investigations never get easier throughout the years, contrary to what others may believe.

One thing is for certain, a person has got to keep on keepin' on or no investigation would ever be solved. I'm an old man now, and it's safe to say that I've paid my dues. I started in the department at about your age. Each year has definitely proved to be a learning experience. Use your time wisely Mulberry, opportunity usually comes around once in life and you have to be prepared. So, what's going on with your end of the investigation, any talk leaking out?" Mulberry appeared relieved that I was finished speaking. "Things are quiet on the yard T.P., I imagine we won't learn much of anything until the yard re-opens." Mulberry's sentiments matched mine completely, in terms of the murder, that is. "My thoughts exactly, Mulberry. I'm trying my best to get the yard back open. Hopefully, I'll have some word before the day is out." Why was I venting to this young officer, I thought to myself. "My squad are keeping their eyes and ears open for any information that may provide proof of who may have committed the murder." "Tell me something Mulberry, is the tower officer who was present during the time of the murder on the yard today?" Mulberry reached for his hand radio and activated a radio call to the officer presently on duty in the yard tower. "I'm not sure T.P., but I'll find out in a matter of minutes." The static-filled voice response responded on Mulberry's hand-held radio. "That's him!" I shouted. "Officer Parker, Mulberry have Officer Parker 10-19 my office immediately." Mulberry nervously spoke into the radio. "Officer Parker, 10-21 Lieutenant Price's office immediately." Why is he telling Parker to phone my office, I want him in front of my face, I thought to myself. "Why the 10-21, Mulberry?" "Sir, Parker is in a tower, he can't just up and leave." Who does he think he's talking to, I know that a gun tower can't be left unmanned. Due to the circumstances, I kept my harsh thoughts to myself. "Either you go up into the tower and relieve him or feel free to get someone else to cover. All I'm concerned about right now is having Parker in my office."

Parker was a pretty good officer from what I've heard around the yard. He was going to be shocked out of his pants wondering why he was being taken from his assignment post right in the middle of his shift. The interview would probably go a lot smoother if I was calm and if Parker was left at ease. For a moment, I considered bringing Sergeant Little in on the interview, but my conscience advised me differently.

"Come on in Officer Parker, have a seat." Parker nervously sat in a chair that was directly in front of my desk. "Do you have any idea why you're in my office today, young man?" Officer Parker hesitated before speaking, as he slowly wiped the sweat that was dripping from his clean-shaven head. His face was also free of hair, which allowed his dark brown freckles to be illuminated by his Carmel brown skin. "These days Lieutenant it could be anything, so I'm not even going to attempt to guess." "Well, I'll do the honors and cut right to the chase. It's about the murder." Parker glared out the window, responding confidently, "I figured that." "That's good perception on your part, Officer Parker, and I hope to know how clear your perception was on the day of the murder." I took the liberty of handing Parker a paper towel to absorb the sweat that was continuing to drip from his forehead area. "Go ahead and wipe your face," I instructed him in a gentle manner. "This is very important, so I need you to take your time and think carefully before you answer my questions." He nodded in agreement. "How long have you been assigned to this tower position?" "I would say approximately seven months." "So would it be safe to say that you're pretty well-versed in the operations and procedures mandated by this particular job post?" "Yes, I would say so." "Out of all the job assignments that you've been assigned to at this institution, how would you rank your performance at this particular position." Parker raised his eyebrow. "My nickname is 'Hawk', and it's not because of that television show in the past where that ball-headed brotha would always assist the white guy who was in trouble. It is because my eyes are as sharp as a hawk on the hunt. The officers up at Folsom gave me that name since I seemed to spot most of the fights on the yard." Parker appeared calm and relaxed. "Not everyone has the gift to spot trouble before it gets too far out of hand." "Tell me something Parker, how do you remain alert for eight hours stuck in a boring tower with nothing to do but stare out at an open yard, filled with hundreds of inmates and a half-dozen yard officers?" Parker's face was free from any emotion. "My job is to survey the yard inch-by-inch and minute-by-minute. There's no time for games up there, sir. My fellow officers' lives are in constant jeopardy. Believe it or not, I feel for inmates who are being attacked or victimized by other inmates as well. I realize that I'm commissioned to protect them also." "Tell me what you saw on the yard prior to the discovery of the murder victim." I reached for a pen in my desk and prepared to document notes within my green-colored murder manual. Parker proceeded to speak. "The weight-pile was full as usual. I remember seeing the south side of the sand pit packed with several black inmates. The north side was filled with Hispanic inmates and about two-dozen whites. Everything appeared normal until the disturbance began." I was filled from head-to-toe with excitement. Maybe this is the break I'd been hoping for. "So, there was a scuffle prior to the murder?" Parker gestured with his head and proceeded to explain the situation. "The brothas on the basketball court, Lieutenant, don't you remember?" My brief moment of hope quickly changed to disappointment. "Of course I remember the basketball court incident. I just thought that there might have been a notable problem in the weight-pile prior to the murder." "There was nothing out of the ordinary. The only thing that stood out slightly was seeing some of the brothas standing around laughing and apparently having a good time." "Do you suppose they might have been causing this distraction to enable the murder to occur?" "To be honest with you, Lieutenant, the scene looked pretty genuine to me. I really believe that the basketball court incident was meant to defray attention away from the weight-pile." My mind was burning with questions at this point. "Do you remember the black inmates whom you're speaking of, who were joking on the weight-pile?" "Oh yes, I know who the gentlemen are. Well, I know who they're referred to around the yard by other inmates. I remember C-Dog, Tuck, and a skinny brotha named Coke." "Matter of fact, they're all housed in building six if I'm not mistaken." Parker appeared relieved as he wiped the sweat from his hands onto his green trousers. "You've been a great help Parker. I'll be sure to put in a good word for you before I leave." Parker stood up from his chair. "By the way, Lieutenant, there's two other guys that always hang around the group of inmates I just mentioned, Ronnie Phillips and Todd Henderson-a.k.a. BOO. They weren't present on the weight-pile, but then again from what I've seen and heard, the weight-pile is not a place they choose to frequent too often." I jotted down the cast of characters in my notebook as Parker promptly exited my office. "Thanks a bunch, Parker, I'll probably see you real soon." I wasted no time in picking up the phone and calling the building six floor officers. It was my lucky day, the officers knew exactly which inmates I was inquiring about.

My first inclination was to interrogate Tuck Williams extensively. Besides, I knew this guy's reputation wasn't the best within the prison grounds. Also, Ethel pointed out that Tuck Williams was one of two names that appeared on Newton Black's enemy sheet.

"This is Lt. Price, I need you to pull the bed cards on five inmates. I'll be down to check'em out towards the end of the day." I provided the officer with the names in question.

Nine

The sun was still shining bright as I made my way across the prison yard, headed towards the parking lot. I flicked on the radio to a local talk show as I headed out of the parking lot. My trip would lead me to the Riverside County Jail facility, approximately sixty miles from Los Angeles. Better Riverside than Los Angeles, I thought to myself. Los Angeles County Jail is the pits. The housing conditions are horrid. Honestly, I wouldn't wish these living circumstances on my enemy's worst enemy. Of course I'd only made it as far as the interview rooms, but I was able to sense what the conditions must be like. Also, to this day, I have never met one inmate who has said one positive thing concerning Los Angeles County Jail. The facility is overcrowded and one's safety is considered bleak and not of importance. Every drug dealer and gangster still seems to find an avenue to conduct his or her corrupt business from within the gruesome jail. Just the thought of L.A. County Jail puts a bitter taste in my mouth. By no means am I promoting other county jails as the place to be, but L.A. is literally in a class of its own.

I recall an incident in one county jail that I won't mention by name, but I will say it is known by its popular citrus fruit name. About two years ago, I needed to go to this particular jail to interview an inmate who happened to be on parole. Even in my initial contact with the lobby officer, I was given the cold shoulder. The presentation of my peace officer credentials were acknowledged with disbelief. After speaking to the officer, no words were spoken in return. Instead, the officer proceeded to phone in my request to interview the client who was being housed on the third floor of the jail. This was one of the nicest jails that I've ever been in. The visiting lobby was practically spotless as well as free of noise and confusion. After waiting patiently for just over fifteen minutes, I was slowly becoming impatient, wondering why a peace officer would be forced to wait this long to see a client on an official visit. I heard the black, old-fashioned phone ring and the officer reached to answer it. "I'll send him on up," I witnessed the officer state in a less than pleasant voice. "Thanks for all of your help," I said as I walked in the direction of the chrome-plated elevator doors. I pressed the number three button. The doors closed and the elevator began to move upwards. Once I exited the elevator, I journeyed down a seventy-five yard cement-walled corridor leading towards the housing unit that my client was housed within. I arrived at a wooden door with a window in its upper portion. A buzzer was activated within the door; I pushed it and it automatically opened. I entered the small, 3' x 4' interview room and sat down on the small, circular, steel seat. Two of the walls in the room were plain and painted light blue and were evenly proportioned on my right and left. To the rear of me was the door that I entered and directly in front was a large glass window leading to a less than scenic view of a room identical to mine. The only difference was that the two walls on the left and right that were in my direct view were covered with a multitude of graffiti.

The room was fairly warm and I had been waiting just over thirty minutes when I became physically upset. I left the room and went back down to the first floor with the hopes of speaking with the duty sergeant. The duty officer behind the counter had the same attitude that he'd displayed earlier in our dealings. He reluctantly contacted the duty sergeant by phone and I waited patiently for his presence. There were no civilian visitors present in the lobby. Due to the circumstances, it was probably a good thing that no one from the general public would be witnessing the negative interaction between law enforcement officials.

Within moments, a tall, thin, browned-haired gentleman sporting sergeant's strips on his beige uniform top, strolled into the lobby. His presence could not go unnoticed as his patent-leather shoes sounded off as they tapped against the shiny concrete floor.

"Was there someone looking for Sergeant Kline?" stated the sergeant pretending that there were others present in the lobby other than myself. "My name is Agent Price, with the Department of Corrections," I boasted with confidence. "What seems to be the problem today?" He had an expression of concern on his face as he inquired about my unfortunate situation. "Today has been quite an experience, Sergeant. I've been here almost an hour and I still haven't seen my client." "I'm sure you know as well as I do that unforeseen situations take place in any institutional setting," he stated while forcing a stiff grin. "Point well taken Sergeant. It would have been nice to have just one officer explain to me that they were experiencing some inmate problems within the jail. But unfortunately, no one bothered to provide me with any information." The sergeant was apparently not impressed as he stood with his arms folded. "Well Agent Price, sometimes things get a little bit hectic around here, but we do our best." My God, I thought to myself silently, I'm not getting anywhere with this idiot.

"I appreciate your time, Sergeant." "Don't mention it, I'll have your client waiting on you when you get back upstairs." I nodded my head in agreement. The sergeant removed a two-way radio from his black leather belt to contact the third floor officers. Again, I waited patiently hoping to be given the opportunity to interview my client. "You're clear to go up, Agent Price." My legs reacted quicker than my mind did as I found myself standing in front of the elevator in a matter of seconds. Once I arrived at the interview room, I noticed that my parolee was sitting nervously behind the thick glass window that separated us. Normally, this particular parolee would be in an upbeat mood and have something positive to say. I could clearly see as well as sense that something was wrong. The words of the parolee were graphic to say the least. I was told that due to my actions, airing my concerns, the parolee was punished severely. By the way, the parolee was a female and she personally told me while crying that the officers kicked her butt. I felt so bad that day, knowing that sworn peace officers had taken their frustrations out on an individual who had nothing to do with the situation at hand. Needless to say, I did not allow that situation to fade away without informing upper management of the entire ordeal. For what it's worth, I did receive a phone call from the jail captain. Thank God I never experienced a situation like that ever again.

After crossing a major intersection, I saw an available parking space in front of the Riverside Jail Facility, so I took it. The green and white posted sign on the sidewalk listed the curbside-parking limit as one hour. I removed the official law enforcement business placard from my glove compartment and conveniently placed it in the front window of my vehicle. I grabbed my black leather notepad, opened the door, stepped out, and began walking towards the jail entrance. I slowly approached the uniformed officer seated behind a large glass barrier. After reaching into my back trouser pocket for my badge and identification credentials, I placed it into a small opening between the countertop and the glass barrier.

"May I help you," bellowed the portly, blond-haired officer. "I'm Lieutenant Price with the Department of Corrections." He peered closely as I retrieved a document from my inner coat pocket, placing it gently into the slot. "Here's the inmate that I need to interview." He gazed momentarily at the name on the document before picking up the beige telephone to check on the inmate's whereabouts and availability. Silently, I wished that the inmate would not be in court. There's nothing worse than a wasted visit when an inmate is unavailable for an official visit. On numerous occasions, I've experienced the unpleasant situation of not having inmates available to be seen after traveling several miles to see them. Sometimes, I believe that a few officers don't put forth the effort to inform an inmate that he or she has a visitor. This theory is based on the various attitudes that I have encountered during my attempts to visit inmates. The officers seldom smile and they usually question me concerning the size of my inmate-visiting list. On some occasions, the officers claimed that the inmate was about to be served a meal or was in court. I wonder how many of those claims were actually true.

"Okay Mr. Price, your boy is here. Just take the elevator to the fifth floor." "Thanks a lot," I said as I glided quickly towards the elevator, which is just to the left of the visiting reception area.

The aluminum-plated doors opened before I entered the elevator. No one else was present on the elevator. I noticed a small, black video camera in the right corner just above me. Am I being watched, I thought to myself? "Who cares," I mumbled. The light above me illuminated the number five and the elevator stopped. As I ventured down the long, empty corridor, I noticed the mangled pipes that were sprawled just above my head. This huge, beige-colored corridor separates the various visiting areas in the jail. Once I arrived at the visiting area, I opened the windowed door that separated the corridor from the visiting room. I glanced at the general population visiting area and observed that some of the inmates were involved in visitations with family and friends. Warm conversation filled the air as families and friends were temporarily reunited. To my left was a door clearly marked with the words "ATTORNEY 1."

After a brief moment, the door was electronically activated and I immediately entered. I placed my black leather folder onto the stainless steel countertop and sat on the round, wooden seat.

The interior of the attorney's booth was lined wall-to-wall with brown tweed carpet. What a change, I thought to myself, from the other jail visiting rooms where graffiti covers the walls. During the short period of time that I would have before the inmate enters the visiting booth, I took a few moments to examine my paper work. Prior to any interview that I participate in, I attempt to pre-determine the manner in which the inmate might respond to my various questions. I studied the 812 (confidential information sheet), hoping that there might be some hidden information that I may have missed earlier. The door suddenly opened on the opposite end of the glass and inmate Craig Battle entered the visiting booth. He peered through the glass directly at me. He wore an orange jumpsuit; his face and neck were covered with several razor bumps. His hair was short and kinky. For some unknown reason, Inmate Battle remained standing.

"Please have a seat, Mr. Battle," I stated calmly. Inmate Battle paused for a moment, but eventually sat down. "Who the hell are you?" said Battle. It's going to be one of those interviews, I thought to myself. "My name is Lieutenant Price and I'm with the Department of Corrections. I'm conducting a murder investigation..." "Murder investigation! Man, you trippin', I'm not in here for no damn murder, fool." Inmate Battle appeared quite upset as he pushed his right hand flush against the glass barrier that solidly separated us. "Calm down Mr. Battle, no one implied that you committed any murder. I simply want to question you concerning a murder that took place in prison." "Alright man, you need to come correct with your game, 'cause I don't have no time to waste with no bull," pronounced Battle. Inmate Battle was extremely hostile for some unknown reason. I'm sure that I can't say that I know how it feels to be in his position, but I don't believe his attitude should have been that hostile. "Mr. Battle, I only have a few questions for you and I'll be as brief as possible." A permanent frown seemed to be plastered across Battle's face. I took a short breath and continued to communicate with inmate Battle. "The reason that I'm here today Mr. Battle is because I'm investigating the murder of Inmate Newton Black..." Inmate Battle's eyes bulged as he interrupted my sentence. "The leader of the Black Confederate Movement Organization! Is that the Newton Black you're talking about?" Battle appeared anxious to receive my response. "That is exactly who I'm talking about Mr. Battle." I was curious to find out why inmate Battle was so happy. "Let me tell you something Lieutenant Price, it's a good thing to me when bad things are eliminated. Newton Black wasn't good for nothin' but a bunch of bullshit. Day in and day out all he talked about was uniting all the niggas together for some kind of revolution. You would think that he had enough sense to know that any time a bunch of niggas were seen together bunched up on the yard, it would launch an immediate investigation. All he was doing was causing a lot of problems for the brothas. I ain't gonna let no nigga mess up my visits with my woman. And you think I would lose my store privileges for him? Nothing matters but me when I'm doing time, everybody else can kiss my black ass." I didn't mind letting Inmate Battle voice his concerns regarding Newton Black and his own personal issues. Some of these guys have so much anger and hostility built-up within them that they take the opportunity during an official visit to air their emotions. "How well did you know Newton Black?" I asked softly. "We played dominoes together amongst other brothas a couple of times, but for the most part we knew each other from a distance. People like that I have no interest in knowing." I continued to question Inmate Battle, though the air was still thick with hostility. "Did Newton Black ever do anything to you or threaten you in any manner?" "Hell naw! I wish that fool would touch me in any manner, I'd kill that punk..." "He's dead, Mr. Battle, remember?" Battle relaxed his clenched fists and bowed his head with a slight touch of embarrassment. "Yeah man, I remember, but you just told me a few minutes ago that somebody took'em out, remember?" Battle smiled, a brief sign of human emotion. Most guys in jail or prison could care less if a person lives or dies. Values and morals are only things considered in the wee hours of the morning through the minds of those who envision it within their sleep. At this point, I took the opportunity to put Inmate Battle to the test. "Mr. Battle, I want to show you some photographs of Newton Black for identification purposes to know if we're speaking about the same brotha." I removed a white envelope from my black leather notepad and carefully took out the photographs. "I'm going to show you one picture at a time." The first picture was placed against the glass as Inmate Battle looked on. The lifeless body was pictured in a position lying face down. No blood could be seen in this photograph. The second photograph held to the glass revealed the body lying in a position horizontal to the camera. The third photograph I held up to the glass clearly illustrated the victim's upper body area, which was fully covered with blood. Battle squinted, but he continued to view the photographs. The fourth photograph, which was held to the glass, was a close-up of the victim's face. I could sense that the photographs disturbed Inmate Battle. "Is this the person you remember as Newton Black?" Battle refrained from speaking, choosing to nod his head in an up and down manner. Battle appeared calm. I wondered if this would be my opportunity to obtain any information that might pertain to the case. The possibility of obtaining any leads from Inmate Battle seemed hopeless. Why am I even here, I thought to myself. This guy couldn't care less about my investigation, not to mention the actual murder. "Just a couple more questions if you don't mind, Mr. Battle." "I'm listening," stated Inmate Battle. "When was the last time that you saw Newton Black alive and do you remember anything about that particular situation?" Inmate Battle hesitated, appearing to be pondering the answer. "The last time I saw homeboy alive was about nine months ago before I got out on parole. He was having a meeting in the day room telling some of the brothas that they need to chill-out on gettin' into confrontations with the S.A.'s (Spanish Americans). He was good for talkin' about the problems that were happening, but he never had no real solutions." Inmate Battle sounded sincere with his concerns. "Tell me something Mr. Battle, do you have any idea who may have wanted to see Newton Black dead?" I cringed as Inmate Battle began to display his sinister smile. "Now isn't that the million dollar question Lieutenant? Answering that question would set a lot of people's minds free, especially if I knew the answer. I'm sure if I provided you with the answer you probably would get a promotion and a pat on the back from your boss-man." Oh boy, he's at it again, I thought to myself. Inmate Battle continued with his sarcasm. "Do you really think I would tell you if I knew? I'm facing twenty-five years to life in prison, something you could care less about. My life is on the line and you come up here talking about some fool that's dead. Miss me on the dumb shit man." "You're absolutely correct Mr. Battle, I'm a firm believer that if a person makes his bed, he must sleep in it. I didn't put you in jail, you apparently don't need any help in doing that." Battle chuckled as I began placing my documents and photographs back into my black leather notepad. "Sorry I couldn't be much help to you today Lieutenant, maybe next time," said Battle in a joking manner. I had one more trick in my bag and I hoped it would work. As I stood up to leave, I blurted out an impromptu question to Inmate Battle. "You've helped me more than you could imagine. By the way, I was wondering, did you ever associate with a guy in prison by the name of Tuck Williams?" Inmate Battle immediately stood to his feet and carved right through me with his piercing eyes. It was my turn to smile back at Inmate Battle and it felt real good. He continued to glare at me without blinking an eye. He jerked his right arm upward, bending it at his elbow, while displaying his isolated middle finger. I really don't believe that he was telling me that he was number one.

Thank goodness that fiasco was over. I entered the elevator hoping to reach the first floor as quickly as possible. Once I reached the lobby area, I checked out with the duty officer and left the building.

As I drove out of the jail parking lot, many thoughts began to clutter my mind. I pondered over the manner in which I had conducted the interview with Inmate Battle. The interview was fruitless until the point when inmate Battle reacted like a guilty man or like a man who knows who might be guilty in this matter. I was determined to discover the obvious connection between Inmate Battle and Tuck Williams.

Ten

By the time I arrived back at my office, there was a written message on my desk instructing me to call Associate Warden Chambers. The message was marked urgent, but that did not change my mind from tossing the message aside. There was something more important that held my attention, Inmate Tuck Williams. I had this strong feeling that Tuck Williams knew something about the murder. Just as I was about to phone Ethel, Officer Mulberry entered the room. "Excuse me T.P., I didn't mean to bust in on you, but I wanted to make sure you received the message I left you." "Thanks a lot Mulberry, I got your message. Anything new happening on the yard?" Mulberry's face was dimmed by disappointment as he attempted to mutter a response. "Unfortunately, there's no new information to report." My fatherly instincts consumed me as I provided Officer Mulberry with a word of encouragement. "Don't lose any sleep over this situation Mulberry, it's not that serious. Life is always full of surprises, so we must keep on going while doing our best. Remember this, Mulberry, life is everything that happens that we don't plan." Mulberry appeared relieved as he stuck out his chest and presented a boyish smile. "Give me a second to call Ethel in records," I said. Mulberry leaned up against the wall nearest the door, waiting for me to complete my call. "Ethel, it's Lieutenant Price, how are you doing?" I awaited her response. "Well, I'm glad you're doing fine. I was wondering if you could pull some C-files for me." She responded with an immediate yes. "Would it be okay if I came by before you left for the evening?" Again, she responded with an immediate yes, but added an additional statement. "Of course I can come right now, I'm on my way." I didn't know Ethel's intentions, so I hoped to bring Mulberry along for back up. There's nothing wrong with a little interference to keep everything on the up and up, if you know what I mean.

My mind was on another planet for a brief moment, but I quickly regained my composure. Mulberry was staring at me out of the corner of his eye, as his body remained draped against the wall. "Mulberry, I need your assistance for about an hour." "No problem T.P., I'll be glad to assist you." I picked up my black leather notepad and headed for the door. Just as Mulberry was about to close the door behind me, the telephone rang. My first thought was just to allow it to ring, but with all the recent problems here at the prison, I figured I should answer it. Mulberry moved quickly to the side as I dashed back through the door for the phone. "Hello, Lieutenant Price speaking. Hey Ethel, what's up?" By this point, Mulberry was possibly wondering what was up with Ethel and me. Mulberry's a bright young man, he wouldn't think such a thing, I hoped silently to myself. "The C-files, I almost forgot. I'm sorry Ethel, let me give you their names." I flipped open my notepad and thumbed through the pages searching for my investigation notes. "The first name is Corky Price, CDC number V75894. The second name is Todd Henderson, CDC number V63309. The third name is Bobby Nelson, CDC number V41126. The next name is Ronnie Phillips, CDC number V28317. And the last name is Tuck Williams, CDC number V39675. Thanks a bunch Ethel, we'll be right over." I hung up the phone and headed for the door once more. Mulberry followed behind me without saying a word.

It was an incredible sight for me to walk across an entire prison yard and not see a single inmate. A murder had occurred, and ruined normal operations within the prison. There are approximately a thousand men on this yard and at least one was guilty of definite premeditated murder. Patches of grass that were once brown were now turning green due to the fact that no one was sitting, walking, or playing on the isolated turf. The only company that the grass has had for the last several days are the water sprinklers which easily soaked the thirsty soil in several areas on the yard. There was no doubt in my mind that Mulberry was anxious to get the prison back on track. Officer Garcia greeted us as we were let through the plaza gate, headed towards the administration building.

As we entered through the doors of the administration building, we witnessed Betty Wilkins, as she was busy working at her regular post. We overheard Betty on the phone giving someone directions to the prison. As Betty completed her phone conversation, she removed the telephone ear set that was around her head. "And what brings you over here to my neck of the woods?" "My job is never done Betty, you should know that." "I know something else as well, you better not let anything interfere with your retirement." Betty pointed her finger directly at me. Her hand gesture was done in fun, but her statement was meant to be serious. "I will retire Betty, I just can't guarantee you on what day." "T.P., you have got to start thinking about yourself. You know as well as I do that nobody in this department cares if you work yourself to the bone. Whether you solve this recent murder case or not will make no difference to the powers that be," harshly whispered Betty. Mulberry pretended not to be listening to the admonishment by Betty.

"How rude of me Betty, I'd like you to meet Officer Mulberry. He'll probably be the next warden at the rate he's going." "We can start by giving him your job. I'm Betty Wilkins, good to meet you." Betty extended her hand towards Officer Mulberry. "It's good to meet you too, Ms. Wilkins," stated Mulberry. They shook each other's hands as I looked on, hoping to divert the conversation away from my retirement. "Mulberry is one of my best men. He's reliable, trustworthy, and efficient. I don't have any sons, but if I did I would want them to be just like Mulberry. Matter of fact, Mulberry is my lead man on the investigation." Oh no, I thought to myself, Betty is probably going to get back on my case regarding my retirement. "That's the best news I've heard all day. You stick right on in there Mulberry. Your boss needs to kick back and let you do your thing," said Betty. "I'll keep that in mind, Ms. Wilkins. I'm not making much headway so far, but hopefully something will break real soon," Mulberry said. Betty's telephone rang and she was quick to take the call. Mulberry and I began to walk down the corridor and Betty gestured with her hand, wanting us to stop. She immediately placed the caller on hold and turned her attention towards us. "I'm praying for both of you, different prayers of course," announced Betty. She waived goodbye as Mulberry and I continued walking down the corridor.

As we entered the room, we passed several individuals seated at desks, conducting various duties. Ethel's small cubicle was located in the back east section of the large records room. Once we reached Ethel's area, we could clearly see her gold engraved nameplate on her desk. Ethel's desk is always neat and presentable. There were no files or other documents sprawled across her desk. We stood around hoping that someone would ask us if we needed some assistance since Ethel was not present. A thin woman with short, sandy-colored hair approached us. "Are you gentleman looking for Ethel?" "Yes, we are thank you," I said politely. "You must be Lieutenant Price," stated the woman. She apparently knew that I was there to see Ethel. "Your guess is correct, I'm Lieutenant Price and this is Officer Mulberry." Mulberry and I exchanged handshakes with the woman. "I'm Ann Banks, pleased to meet both of you. Ann pointed towards two brown folding chairs. "Please have a seat right over here, Ethel should be back in about five minutes." We accepted Ann's advice and sat down waiting for Ethel to return. Phones continued to ring and various individuals were walking with stacks of files in their hands. "Well, well, well, fellas, you made it over here," bellowed Ethel with a Kool-Aid smile. She was fashionably dressed as usual; sporting a blue linen dress, blue Kenneth Cole pumps, blue sheer stockings and blue eyeliner. Her arms were full as she carried a stack of C-files (central files). She slammed the files onto her desk and flopped down into her comfortable gray office chair. "Dressed to kill Ethel, what's the special occasion," I inquired. "There's two things I love to do, one is to dress nice whenever possible and the other is to eat good home-cooked meals." If she only knew how much I could use one of her good home-cooked meals. One day I'll just have to break down and beg for a meal, I thought silently. "Ethel, this is Officer Mulberry, he's my lead S & E officer on the yard." Ethel extended her hand across the desk and Mulberry stood up to reach Ethel's hand. "It's a pleasure to meet you, Officer Mulberry," said Betty. "Good to meet you as well, Ethel," stated Mulberry. We all sat back and relaxed prior to the task of examining the C-files. "Mulberry has been instrumental in assisting me with the investigation, so I asked him to come along to help peruse the C-files." Ethel nodded while listening closely. "That's no problem, Lieutenant, it's your thang, do what you want to do." We all chuckled for a brief moment as Betty separated the C-files in preparation for review. "May I make a suggestion, T.P.?" "Sure Mulberry, tell us what's on your mind." "How about you and I take two C-files a piece to review and have Ethel examine one of the files, if that's okay." "That's fine with me, Lieutenant, I'll be glad to help, that's what I'm here for," boasted Ethel. Mulberry's timing was perfect, just the suggestion I needed with time being of the essence. Ethel shuffled the files within her hands and chose one. I reached over and grabbed two files and handed them to Mulberry. Ethel was kind enough to hand me the remaining two files. "I've got Corky Price," blurted Ethel. "I've got Todd Henderson and Bobby Nelson," stated Mulberry in a professional manner. This is a great match I thought to myself, "I have Ronnie Phillips and Tuck Williams." "Let's not leave any stone unturned. We need to check each section of the C-file thoroughly. Please read the entire probationary report, and when reading the medical section check out the psychological reports for any weird diagnosis. Also check to see if they've ever received any stab wounds or gun shot injuries." This is unbelievable, I'm talking as if we were involved in a war and I was providing them with the battle plan. "Forgive me you guys, I don't mean to be blunt with my instructions, I'm just anxious to catch this cold-blooded murderer," I said plainly.

Approximately forty-five minutes had passed and no one had murmured a word. The annoying sound of shuffled paper was driving me nuts. If there was a faster process, I was definitely open to all suggestions. I must admit that we were being subjected to some of the most lengthy criminal rap sheets and probationary reports that I had ever seen. These guys could have easily made the 'Who's Who Book of Criminals.' Just prior to my mind going off on the deep end, Mulberry blurted out, "I think I've got something." "According to this Los Angeles Probationary report, Bobby Nelson and Tuck Williams belonged to the same street gang, 'The Plum Town Crips', prior to them going to prison. This gang is reported as being one of the most vicious, brutal, notorious, and uniquely sophisticated gangs on the West coast," Mulberry spoke with a satisfied tone. Another small piece of the puzzle had fallen into place. I was pleased, but I knew there was a multitude of ground yet to be covered. "It doesn't appear that Bobby Nelson was a co-defendant with any of the other suspects during the latest crime that sent him to prison," said Mulberry. The mere fact that he and Tuck Williams associated with one another on the streets was connection enough for me. As I continued to thumb through the material, Tuck Williams' probationary report revealed that Craig Battle was his co-defendant in the crime that sent him to prison. "My, my, my, what do we have here? It appears that we hit the bulls-eye with one of our boys. Craig Battle is a name you provided me with a few days ago," I directed to Ethel. "Well, as you may recall, Craig Battle's name appeared on Newton Black's confidential information sheet. And wouldn't you know it, Craig Battle was a co-defendant in the case that brought Tuck Williams to our prison facility." Ethel appeared pleased with the information. She immediately asked about my recent meeting with Craig Battle. "Whatever happened when you went to visit Mr. Battle at the county jail," asked Ethel. Inwardly, I knew it was one of the worst contacts I had ever experienced with an inmate. "Do you really want to know?" I stated reluctantly. Both Ethel and Mulberry expressed the, you better tell us something, look. "Okay, well, the meeting didn't exactly go as planned. Quite frankly, it was a fiasco. This guy was indignant to say the least. He's one of those guys who puts all law enforcement individuals in the same basket. In other words, he hates us all. The guy refused to talk for the most part, and his point of view was the only one that mattered. When I mentioned Tuck Williams' name, he practically had a heart attack. I don't think he'll be providing too many people with any information in the near future." We all continued to canvass our files, hoping to find other pieces of the puzzle that could possibly assist us in solving the murder.

The wall clock clicked into the four o'clock position which symbolized the completion of our task. Ethel gathered up the files in order to place them back on the records shelves. "Thank you so much for your help Ethel. Mulberry and I are gonna head on back to the war zone." "The pleasure is always mine, Lieutenant. It was good meeting you Officer Mulberry and if you ever need some assistance, don't hesitate to call," said Ethel.

As Mulberry and I exited the records room area, we bumped into Captain Davenport in the administration hallway. "Hey Captain, tell me some good news, I could definitely use it." The Captain looked dumbfounded. "Did you get my message?" Mulberry was quick to cut into the conversation. "Lieutenant, the message that was on your desk is the one the Captain is talking about. I meant to tell you about it." Mulberry turned and walked away to avoid direct eye contact with me. I realized that everyone makes mistakes; I just hoped that the message wasn't important. "Richard Chambers called this morning," stated Captain Davenport as he looked in my direction. "Believe it or not, Chambers agreed to give in to your demands. You're lucky that I've believed in you throughout the years." Boy, was my attention cranked to the highest level. "Please tell me that Chambers agreed to allow the yard to open," I said in a hopeful manner. "At 0800 hours tomorrow you're clear to commence with normal feeding procedures, Lieutenant." Captain Davenport had just delivered some of the best news I'd heard all day. "Captain, I really appreciate your support on this one. The murder will be solved before I leave this prison, and you can bank on that." Captain Davenport nodded his head in agreement. "I know you'll do a good job, Lieutenant."

Eleven

The murder had yet to be solved, but for some reason I felt the need to celebrate the events of the day. It was approximately six-thirty in the evening and I decided to place a call to my brother on my cellular phone. After searching my cluttered glove compartment, I soon located my cellular phone. I felt that I needed the company of my brother, Peter, so I commenced calling. "Peter, I'm glad I caught you at home. How would you like to go out to dinner with me?" I waited quietly allowing Peter a moment to respond. Peter was receptive and I was pleasantly pleased. "I'll explain what we'll be celebrating once we get to the restaurant. I have a taste for Earl's Bar-B-Q, and since I'm treating, I'm sure you won't have a problem with my choice."

Earl's Bar-B-Q is located on the outskirts of downtown Los Angeles. Whenever I have a taste for Bar-B-Q, Earl's is definitely the place to eat. The approximate thirty-mile drive from home is never a problem.

After traveling approximately two miles down Crenshaw, I could see the dimly lit neon sign displaying Earl's Bar-B-Q. I've been enjoying Earl's Bar-B-Q for over five years and I still haven't seen the 'a' in Earl's sign ever illuminated. The food is excellent and that's all that really matters. I parked my vehicle on the street's curbside instead of entering the small parking area attached to the Bar-B-Q shack. Once I exited my vehicle, the smell of home-cooked Bar-B-Q lifted my spirits. An older gentleman was walking out the front entrance just as I was about to enter. We spoke to one another as I held the door to allow the gentleman to pass by me. There were four other customers already present in the small restaurant, waiting to place their orders. No one was seated at the five small tables that were nestled in the dining room area, which is only about four feet away from the order counter. The two wood-paneled walls on opposite sides of the room are plastered with various colored sheets of paper, displaying various lunch and dinner specials. The counter is without any type of elevated barrier, which allows the customers to view the cooking as well as the preparation of the food. Most customers tend to order their food and take it home.

Peter hadn't arrived, so I took my time studying the menu. Tonight would be the first time in two years that I would actually eat within the small restaurant. Peter's a bachelor, so I was sure he wouldn't mind eating here. The clock above the counter told the time as seven-thirty sharp. I grabbed one of the pink paper menus off the front countertop and retreated to one of the nearby tables to be seated.

As I sat quietly, I looked over the menu, wondering which dish I would order. Pork is not the meat that I delight myself in these days, but of course the menu was covered from back to front with various pork dishes. After carefully scrutinizing the menu, I spotted a Bar-B-Q chicken special priced at $5.25. The meal included baked beans, potato salad, corn bread, greens, and three hefty pieces of chicken. My mouth watered briefly. A complete meal for $5.25 wasn't a bad price and I would only have to purchase something to drink separately.

This restaurant has been known to make a mean glass of lemonade. Matter of fact, pink lemonade has always been my favorite.

As I turned my head to gaze outside the large storefront window, I observed as well as heard Pete's large, blue Lincoln Continental pull into the parking lot. That car is so loud, it's a wonder he hasn't gotten a ticket for disturbing the peace. Since Pete first started to drive, I've never known him to own anything but large vehicles. But then again, the brother is over six feet tall, and he needs that extra leg space.

Pete entered the restaurant sporting his usual attire of cowboy boots and jeans. Pete walked over to the table, removed his jean jacket and placed it onto the back of his chair before taking his seat. "Thanks a lot!" I said. Pete's eyes bulged. "For what!" shouted Pete? "I'm sittin' up here, havin' to smell this food, waitin' on your slow butt to get here, and you've got the nerve to say for what," I said. Pete buried his face within the pink menu, which he held in front of him.

"It does smell good in here, doesn't it?" He appeared to be studying the menu, but I wasn't buying it. "So what are you going to order Mr. Wise Guy?" Pete looked up at me, displaying a large, boyish smile and stated, "The chicken dinner special sure sounds good, I think I'll try that. You get three pieces of chicken, potato salad, baked beans…" "I read the menu three times Pete, while I was waiting on you."

We happened to be sitting by a jukebox, and wouldn't you know it, some teenager walks over, puts a quarter in and plays some rap jam. We found ourselves shouting at the top of our lungs just to communicate. "Have you talked to mom and dad lately," I stated aloud. Pete responded saying, "Yes, I spoke with them last week and they both were doing fine." "How are my favorite nieces doing?" asked Pete. "Your favorite nieces are your only nieces and they're doing quite fine, thank you." I found myself isolated in sound as I was shouting at the top of my voice when suddenly the rap song was over. Pete looked over at me and laughed, knowing that I felt like an idiot. "Okay, big brother, what's the deal, you usually don't invite me out to eat unless you've got something on your mind you want to talk about. And, I know it's rare when you want to talk to me about something," said Pete. "You know what I'm trying to do, and you know what's standing in my way. All I want is for you to tell me if you think that I'm doing the right thing." Peter appeared to be astonished, as he reclined back in his chair and just stared right at me. "You're asking me for advice, brotha? I feel privileged. You know I'm here for you if you need me." "I can't retire on a sour note, I've got to solve the murder first. Come on Pete, how's it gonna look. I've invested the majority of my life into this job. I'm the best investigator they have. They rely on me for every serious investigation, so how's that going to look, me walking out on one of the most controversial murder cases that the prison has ever experienced prior to my retirement. I personally think it's kind of selfish for me to just leave. But, on the other hand, what gave them the audacity to assign me the case, knowing that I would be retiring in less than three weeks. Needless to say, I'm caught between a rock and a hard place, if you know what I mean." "Brother please, don't let your dilemma be your downfall. Man, you've given these people well over twenty years of your life, you owe them nothing, and I mean nothing. Take your retirement money and get to steppin'." I chuckled a bit at Pete's carefree attitude; he's right in many ways, I thought to myself. But then again, pride has always been one of my downfalls. You're absolutely right Pete, but that still doesn't solve my problem. There has to be a way for me to get out of this thing smoothly and still maintain my dignity, if you know what I mean. I just want to make sure that this investigation is handled properly in hopes that the right criminal or criminals are apprehended. It all boils down to the fact that I'm too heavily involved, even though the murder just took place a few days ago." Pete bit his bottom lip with his upper teeth and clenched his right fist against the table. "Man, I love you, and you're my big brother, you've always been there for me and I can honestly say that I don't know where I would be without you. It's been a long time, but do you remember the tree house we had in the backyard?" I nodded my head in agreement. "The tree house was always the place to be when things weren't going our way. It didn't matter if we lost a baseball game or if we got a bad grade in school, we could always retreat to the tree house for peace of mind. We would sit up there for hours talking over our various problems. We would actually believe that we could create solutions, thinking that we could actually change the world. So, when it was time to come down from the tree, we felt good. Reality soon kicked in when mom or dad was waiting for us at the back door. I know all of this may sound crazy, man, but I say all that to say this; no matter how much you want to change the world, no matter how much you want to do for people, and no matter how much pride and dignity you may possess, the world will continue to turn. There are never any guarantees that any of our ideas or opinions will ever be implemented. Just keep praying. If the murder is not solved by the date that you are set to retire, my advice to you is to just walk away. It will be alright, and you know as well as I do that the prison system will continue to function well beyond your retirement."

I was touched deeply by the sentiments expressed by Pete. He has never been a touchy-feely type of guy and he really surprised me with his words of encouragement. I extended my hand across the dinner table and Pete reached over with his hand to meet mine half way. We embraced one another momentarily as the warmth of brotherly love electrified the setting.

"Thank you for meeting with me little brother," I said solemnly. For a moment, I thought we were back in the old tree house. Of course that was wishful thinking on my part, but I've always been a dreamer.

The timing couldn't have been more perfect as the waitress walked up to take our food orders. Her head was covered with a minimum of a hundred mini-styled braids and she was dressed in a tight fitting denim jumpsuit. "Are you gentlemen ready to order?" she stated in a girlish voice. I took the initiative to order first. "Yes, I'll take the chicken dinner special with a lemonade on the side." The waitress looked in Pete's direction. "And for you, sir." Pete gazed at the waitress from head-to-toe before placing his order. "Everything looks good," stated Pete as he smiled at the waitress. "I'll take the chicken dinner special as well, and your phone number on the side." The waitress immediately stopped writing on her order pad. "Excuse me." The sistah didn't seem to be receptive to Pete's untimely come-on, as she rotated her slender neck from side-to-side. "I was wondering if there was a phone outside," stated Pete in a not so confident tone. She pointed towards the right side of the building with her order pencil. "The closest pay phone is on the corner," she stated plainly. She continued to write down our dinner orders. "I'll be back shortly with your orders." We both held our breath in an attempt to conceal our laughter until the waitress left the area. We chuckled a bit and Pete was the one who regained his composure first. All of a sudden, he turned serious on me. "What are we celebrating anyway?" "Oh that's right, I did forget to mention that small little detail. Well, the associate warden has approved my recommendation and agreed to open the yard," I said. Pete offered his congratulations. "You know you have my blessing old man as long as it doesn't interfere with your retirement." I simply acknowledged him with a nod of my head, knowing that I didn't want to discuss that topic any longer.

We had a ball eating and conversing the remainder of the evening, prior to returning to our homes.

Twelve

The next morning, I took a detour while on the way to work. I had an urge to venture back to Crenshaw Boulevard, but this time a few miles south of Earl's Bar-B-Q Shack.

I was on the prowl for a good location for my investigative service. The location of 6th and Hill wasn't bad, but I didn't really feel at home there. Robin Keller tried his best, but it just wasn't working for me and I knew that. The whole restaurant thing last night meant a lot to me. Peter was instrumental in bringing many things into perspective in my life, whether he knew it or not. That story concerning our old tree house really brought things into the light for me. I knew for a fact where my mission in life would end and I had to prepare properly for the journey. There was a city of people who were in desperate need of my help. The majority of them are black and some are Hispanics. I don't know how many whites would want my help, but I told myself that I would be there for them too if they needed me.

This particular section of Los Angeles that I was cruising through was quite different than that of 6th and Hill. There were no high-rise buildings and sprawling streets filled with prosperous businesses. There were mostly storefront businesses such as beauty salons, nail shops, and various fast food joints. No banks, jewelry stores or manufacturing facilities.

The bible states that the people perish 'cause they have no vision. Not only do the majority of my brothers and sisters have no vision, they also have no one willing to show them the way. I knew for a fact that I could make a difference in a few lives if given the opportunity. These people down here need an abundance of help, but oftentimes they can't afford it.

I had been on one side of the law for well over twenty years. All that expertise had to amount to something positive, in my opinion. Money is no longer my motivation. My wife has gone on to be with the Lord and my two daughters are now receiving a quality college education. I really do want to give back to the community and hopefully my efforts will be appreciated. I really do believe that I should set up shop amongst the brethren in the inner city. Whatever I decided to do, I knew I had to do it quick, realizing that my retirement was just around the corner.

I noticed a few vacant places nestled between the storefront businesses that appeared to be doing fairly well. I pulled my car over to the curbside and parked in front of the empty space. There was a large plate glass window surrounded by red brick. After exiting my car, I walked up to the large window, placed my face against the glass and peeked inside. The building was long and narrow and appeared to have a back entrance, which was something I liked. The inner walls were semi-gloss white and the floor was covered by a dark gray, blend carpet. The facility had a lot of potential and my interest was sparked. I could envision my name sprawled across the front of the building.

I removed a pen from my shirt pocket along with a piece of paper, and jotted down the phone number of the property manager. This could really be the one, I thought to myself.

As I made the long journey back towards the prison, I had the realization that the yard would be open once again. My thoughts were mixed to say the least. Was I just anxious to open the yard simply to fulfill a selfish ambition or did I really care about the victim's rights being served? Sometimes the whole ordeal of investigations seems frivolous. The guy is dead and no one can change that fact. No one really cares about an inmate getting murdered. In the words of the people, he wasn't contributing a darn thing to society anyway. Even more so, he was just another nigga. Was he really going to be missed? I don't think so. Why was I placing so much emphasis on this case? Why did I care so much about this prison crap? All I should be thinking about was my retirement. I could be lying on any beach in the world, gazing at beautiful women in skimpy bathing suits. I could be at home everyday, sitting in bed watching television from dusk to dawn. I could very easily live off of my retirement money and not have to do anything else in life. Who am I kidding; daydreaming was never one of my biggest past times. I'll continue to be old "T.P.," the man with the never-ending investigative mission, retired or not.

Just as I pulled into the prison parking lot, all my ethical sensibilities seemed to have returned to my inner thoughts. I took my usual journey through the various security checkpoints, before arriving at the plaza gate, leading into my yard.

"Good morning T.P.," stated Officer Garcia, as he unlocked the plaza gate. "I guess 11:30 is still morning, and believe me Garcia, I'm glad to be here," I said happily. I gave him a bright smile and kept right on walking to my office. While crossing the prison yard, I gazed pointedly at the green grass beneath my feet, realizing that it would soon be trampled once again. They can play softball and trample all over the newly grown grass to their hearts desire. I had no problem with allowing the inmates access to the basketball court and the racquetball court. But, the weight-pile was an entirely different issue. I had elected to keep a portion of the weight-pile off limits to everyone until the investigation was completed.

Once I arrived at my office, there was an inmate roster sitting on top of my desk. This inch thick set of documents had all the movement information pertaining to all the inmates present on the yard. Of course, I wasn't concerned about any movement on the yard since we were operating on total lock-down status. As I thumbed through the information, I could see that our inmate count totaled 998 men. We were operating at just about capacity, shy of two men. I immediately picked up my two-way radio and summoned for Officer Mulberry to report to my office. I was sure Mulberry would be happy to hear the good news. The time had come to get things back rolling into full swing, and Mulberry was going to be my usual lead man. Mulberry and I shared the same sentiments that the only way this murder could be fully investigated was by allowing the inmates to operate on the yard with normal movement, with exception to the weight-pile of course. We wouldn't be pressuring anyone for information, but we were definitely not going to leave any stone unturned.

"I came as quickly as possible," blurted Mulberry as he dashed into my office. "Are you ready to do some work?" Mulberry appeared surprised at my statement. "Sure, is there something for me to do?" Mulberry appeared eager to get the ball rolling, just as I knew he would be.

"I will be giving the order to open the yard in approximately one hour," I said with authority. Mulberry attempted to clap his hands together, but instead he reverted to a gentle hand rubbing motion. I was probably even more excited than Mulberry, but of course as Lieutenant; I had to maintain my composure. "Please meet me in the culinary in about ten minutes and be sure to bring the rest of your S & E officers with you."

Upon my entrance into the inmate culinary dining area, I saw Sergeant Little, Officer Jones, Mulberry and his crew, and also officers from each housing unit on the yard occupying the room.

"I'm sure that all of you have heard by way of Sergeant Little or Officer Mulberry that the yard will be opening within this hour. The purpose of this little gathering is to let you know briefly what will be taking place today. The first order of business is to open up the yard by commencing feeding of each housing unit separately. This procedure will cause the lunch period to be extended, but this is necessary due to the circumstances.

Inmate workers at the evening feeding will relieve the civilian kitchen staff. Your job is to watch closely for any unusual movement or contact amongst the inmates. Also, keep your ears open for any conversation directed towards the murder. Are there any questions?" Officer Jones raised his hand. I gestured towards him, "Yes Officer Jones."

"T.P., I was just wondering if I could have some of the S & E officers assist me with kitchen duty this evening. I'm sure that you know just as well as I do that those inmates are gonna try their best to rob me blind tonight." Sergeant Little stood up to address Officer Jones' statement. "I've got you covered Jones, I figured them boys would be hard-up for all kinds of goodies since they've been locked down for the past several days." I was pleased to know that one concern had been taken care of, in light of the many problems that we were still faced with.

"Are there any other questions," I stated in a less than sincere fashion. I glanced to my right and then back to my left side, and no one was raising their hand to speak. Thank goodness, I thought inwardly, as I was more than ready to move into operation feed. "Well gentlemen, I suggest that we all position ourselves at our assigned posts and wait for my instructions to proceed."

Officer Mulberry, Officer Jones, Sergeant Little, and myself remained in the inmate culinary as the other officers peacefully filed out. Sergeant Little watched in anticipation as the last officer exited the culinary. He said, "I kind of like the yard being on lock-down myself. Who in their right mind would want to criticize kicking back, it doesn't bother me one bit." I almost wanted to tell Sergeant Little that he was one of the few officers walking around the yard with a uniform that was three sizes too small. I also wanted to remind him that he got paid a hefty salary that was not given for him to sit on his huge butt all day. I was not going to allow this man to ruin my day. "Sergeant Little, I'm sure you remember that someone was murdered on this yard not long ago. As I stated to you earlier, it would be more beneficial to conduct an uninhibited investigation while the yard is up and running. No inmate in their right mind is going to give up any information while they're locked down. Furthermore, some people just enjoy their job and working doesn't seem to bother them one bit." Sergeant Little removed a Butterfinger candy bar from his inner jacket pocket and commenced to remove the wrapper. "T.P., you know I have no problem with anything you want to do, I'm simply here to serve," stated the Sergeant in an unconvincing manner. Sometimes, certain people just have to be ignored.

"Let's do this thing men, but remember we must proceed with caution," I said. "I've got a feeling that everything is going to be just fine," stated Officer Jones.

"Well, if you don't mind men, I need to tend to a couple of personal business matters in my office before we get this thing rolling. More than likely, I will be calling you guys in about a half-hour." I walked out of the inmate culinary and headed for my office.

Thirteen

Motive and opportunity is the key to murder. Someone had both elements and took advantage of it. Newton Black was more of a threat to the whites and Hispanics, if the entire situation was to be evaluated at face value. White inmates don't like black inmates and black inmates in turn don't care for white inmates. The vast majority of Hispanic inmates don't like black inmates and therefore most black inmates don't care for the Hispanic inmates. It's a vicious circle of hate and somehow the black inmates are always in the middle. Both white and Hispanic inmates hate them. What makes the scenario even worse, is that the black inmates are widely divided amongst themselves, which makes for an even more horrific situation. I removed a large manila envelope from the dark-gray file cabinet, located in the east-west corner of my office. The envelope was full of graphic photographs of the murdered victim's body. I placed each photograph one-by-one on my desk. There were approximately 24 color photos. There appeared to be no trail or traces of blood other than the blood that was pooled around the body. The body was lying face down in the sand. This would mean that the victim was stabbed and fell forward or the victim was stabbed and placed face down in the sand by the assailant. My investigative instincts told me that the victim was possibly stabbed and then placed face down in the weight-pile. If the victim was stabbed and the body was simply left to fall to the sand face forward on its own, more than likely there would be traces of splattered blood. Maybe there were traces of splattered blood and they were just too minute to spot with the naked eye. Who knew what really happened, I was just fishing around without any real bait.

After placing the photographs back into the manila envelope, I reached into the third file cabinet drawer and removed a diagram of the weight-pile. I was quite curious to find out how many inmates could possibly fit into the section of the weight-pile where the murder took place. Of course I wasn't a mathematician, and calculating measurements to bodies was not my cup of tea either, but I still gave my self a shot at guessing. I figured between 10 or 15 men could fit in that area. This posed the question of whether or not each of the men in question were involved in the murder, or if someone acted alone.

My brain hummed with various scenarios that could have accounted for this murder. But, the fact of the matter was, that there was no murder weapon found. The murder weapon was undoubtedly a very important piece of this investigation. I've always believed that a murder weapon somehow and some way more than likely leads to an assailant. One thing was for sure, whoever committed the murder knew that they were the one and this same killer knew he was being sought.

The wall clock clicked into the 12:15 p.m. position and I decided that the time had come to move. First, I picked up the telephone and contacted Officer Jones in the inmate culinary and informed him that I was about to send over the hungry, caged-up masses. Subsequently, I contacted Officer Mulberry on my hand-held radio and instructed him to commence with feeding.

At approximately 12:25 p.m., I observed Mulberry and a host of other officers leading a group of inmates from the first housing unit. I made it my business to steer clear of the inmate culinary, allowing Sergeant Little, Officer Jones and Officer Mulberry to coordinate the feeding procedure. As the men ventured across the yard walking towards the culinary, I was somehow reminded of the bible story of the people of Israel being led out of Egypt. This same scene was repeated three additional times until eventually all the housing units were served lunch. The Officers, who were staffed within the security-housing unit, served the inmates their food within the unit.

As I sat in my chair, my eyes were glued on the yard watching the situation from afar. Once the last groups of inmates were escorted back to their housing unit, I left my office and began to walk towards the culinary. Imprints of shoe tracks covered the grassy infield area where the inmates had crossed to enter the culinary. I must say that it was good to see signs of life back on the yard.

"Congratulations Officer Jones," I said proudly as I entered the culinary. Officer Jones was sweating from head to toe as he wiped his face with a handkerchief. "T.P., this was rough. I can't wait to get my crew back in here working." "They'll be back sooner than you think. Matter of fact, your crew will be clear to help you serve dinner." "Now that's what I'm talkin' 'bout, T.P., gettin' this place swinging in full operation. I'm tired as hell." I couldn't help laughing after seeing Officer Jones' pitiful face. By this time, Officer Mulberry and his security squad had entered the culinary.

"Everyone is locked-up and accounted for, T.P.," said Mulberry. Everything was going too smooth and that has me a little concerned. The murderer was present in one of the housing units as we spoke. It was somewhat weird to know that the murderer just ate in this same dining room not long ago. I wanted to get this guy so bad, and I didn't know why and that scared me.

"Everyone is to stay on lock down until dinner time. The only inmates that will be allowed out of their cells will be those assigned to work in the culinary and also those who are assigned to clean the housing units. There is to be no inmate doing any sort of yard duties at this time. Inmate clerks assigned to the program office will be permitted to report to their positions at the conclusion of this conversation. Keeping in mind that the program clerks work directly with us, it would behoove you to be very careful of what you say in front of them. This investigation is too valuable to allow any pertinent information to leak out. Remember, clerks are inmates too; they just have a slightly upgraded prison stay. Even when the yard is allowed to open after dinner, we must make certain that no one comes within 20 feet of the weight-pile murder scene." Everyone seemed to be receptive to my instructions.

Officer Blue raised his hand to get my attention. I nodded my head acknowledging him.

"T.P., practically all the inmates have been bitchin' and moanin' concerning using the phone. Do you have any idea when you want the phones to be cut back on?" Blue was a seasoned officer to say the least. I was quite curious why Blue cared about cutting the phones back on. Supervising the phone list is a pain in the butt. Inmates try to sign their buddies up on the phone list without them standing in line to do so themselves. Some inmates attempt to take advantage of the rules by staying on the phone beyond their allotted times. Inmates who are intimidated by their fellow inmates who are violating the phone privileges usually stand silent and wait for their turn. The housing unit officers eventually discover what's going on and end up cutting off the inmate's phone call. "Blue, I'm surprised that you aren't happy with the recent peace in the unit. But, if you're willing to put up with the headache, be my guest, you're welcome to conduct sign-ups at your convenience," I stated in a soft manner. Blue wasn't bothered by the statement, and responded with a head gesture. "I'll see you all at dinner time, gentlemen," I announced just as I turned to exit the inmate culinary.

My office telephone rang, just as I was beginning to doze in my comfortable office chair. I glanced up at the wall clock knowing that the phone call probably had something to do with the fact that it was now dinnertime. The meek, mild-mannered voice on the other end of the telephone was that of Officer Mulberry. He said without any hesitation that it was time to feed the inmates. "Rock and Roll," I said confidently. My mind hadn't played any mental trips on me, so I thought this was a sign from God that the whole food venture would go smoothly.

Almost an hour had passed and I continued to sit patiently in my office until the food ordeal had come to a complete finish.

I worried that if I did not carefully scrutinize the questions I would be asking the inmates whom I would be interviewing, I could easily blow the case. Inmates are shrewd, and on most occasions it is like breaking into a bank vault to get any information from them.

As I consulted my black notebook, I spent the remainder of my time formulating questions that I would ask each inmate present on my investigation list. This of course was the most difficult task to perform. Good questions are cardinal, but being able to evaluate body language can prove to be significant. A person's eyes can tell a whole story. I've been able to capture a great deal of useful information that was proven to be true just by studying an individual's eyes. Hands are also an important part of the human anatomy to study. An individual's hands can very easily display signs of nervousness, eagerness, calmness, and many other emotions. The tongue is one of the smallest parts of the human body, and more than oftentimes proves to be the most dangerous. The tongue can spew multitudes of filth and can destroy lives in an instance. The tongue can also offer a gentle fragrance of joy. The tongue can cut as well as comfort.

Just as I wrote down my last question, the telephone rang once again. This time Sergeant Little was on the line. He informed me that feeding had been completed about twenty minutes prior to his call and the yard was clear to open.

"Before the yard opens, I need two inmates pulled and brought down to my office separately." Sergeant Little didn't question my request and offered to assist in bringing the inmates to my office. "That'll be fine, I'll see you in a bit."

The inmates that I requested were each respected leaders of well-known gangs within the prison system. It was important to me to know that none of these gangs had a legit hit called on the murder victim, Newton Black. Gang shot-callers usually don't have a reason to lie, as they know in prison, authorities would have a difficult time proving that a specific individual from their gang actually committed a murder.

Before I allowed the yard to open, it was imperative that I speak with these gang leaders to establish if the crime in fact was gang related or if one individual was responsible for the cruel act of violence.

Sergeant Little and Officer Mulberry walked into my office with the leader of the Sun Brothers gang. Billy Baker was a large 300 pound white male with a clean-shaven head and a thick brown beard and mustache. His thick body was covered with a multitude of tattoos, which were partially hidden by his enormous amount of body hair. The joke around the yard was that no one really knew if he had any teeth since no one had ever seen him smile. He modeled a stoic expression, as he stood quietly handcuffed in the doorway of my office. "Bring him on in." I grabbed a folding chair that was amongst a set of three other chairs placed in an unoccupied corner section of my office. "Have a seat over here, Mr. Baker." He slowly responded to my instructions as Officer Mulberry carefully guided him to the chair. Sergeant Little stood behind Inmate Baker on his right side, while Officer Mulberry placed himself on the back left shoulder of inmate Baker. Both men stood firmly at attention watching every move made by inmate Baker. "Go ahead and remove his handcuffs, gentlemen," I said to Sergeant Little and Officer Mulberry. "Are you sure T.P.?" pleaded Sergeant Little. "It's okay, Sergeant Little." Sergeant Little shrugged his shoulders and promptly followed my request.

"Mr. Baker, I won't beat around the bush with you, I'll get directly to the point if that's alright." Baker nodded his head with approval. "As you probably know, the entire yard has been on lock-down for the past several days due to the murder that took place on the weight-pile. We plan to find the person or persons who committed this murder and prosecute the responsible party as deemed by the law. I'm quite aware of the numerous racial problems that are present in the yard, and I'm sure you have no love lost for the person who was murdered." I consulted my notes prior to continuing my questioning of inmate Baker. "Did you have occasion to know the victim Newton Black?" Baker cracked a kid-like smile without exposing his teeth. He leaned forward exposing his huge biceps that rippled beneath his short sleeve prison shirt. "We never had tea together, but I knew who the dude was." At least he was talking, and that was a good sign. "Have you ever had a negative encounter with the victim Newton Black?" I inquired. "I've never had a personal beef with the man, but there's no secret that he wasn't liked by my people," he stated cool and collected. "So, are you saying that your gang did have an unsolved problem with the victim?" Baker glared directly into my eyes as he narrowed his focus prior to speaking. "Can I save you some time Lieutenant?" It was a treat just to know that Inmate Baker desired to lead the conversation. At this point, I concealed my notes within my black notebook and sat back comfortably in my chair. "Sure, Mr. Baker, the floor is yours." Baker cut his eyes at Sergeant Little and then stared back in my direction. "No disrespect to you and the Sergeant, but wouldn't it be foolish for my people to kill this guy on the nigger side of the weight-pile where we're not welcome nor do we have business there? If we were going to kill him or someone else in this joint, we have a lot more interesting ways to get the job done." Inmate Baker was serious concerning his statements, and he definitely had me convinced. "Thanks for your time, Mr. Baker, and make sure you take care of yourself." Inmate Baker nodded his head, but refrained from speaking again. Sergeant Little and Officer Mulberry instructed Inmate Baker to stand and exit the office.

Within ten minutes, Sergeant Little and Officer Mulberry had returned with another inmate. It was Mario Vargas. He is known as the head shot-caller for one of the most powerful Mexican gangs in the prison. Mario looked at us suspiciously as he entered my office. His jet-black hair was greased and slicked back towards his neck. He displayed a uniquely styled mustache that curled upwardly on each respective end. His left eye was adorned with a series of teardrop tattoos that trickled downward on his face. His light blue denim shirt and his blue jeans were creased and ironed to a stiff perfection. Sergeant Little pointed towards the empty chair that was placed in front of my desk. Inmate Vargas slowly sat down. No prison gang relishes taking the heat for a beef that they did not commit. Vargas was considered a true convict. An "O.G." (Original Gangster), he was from the old school and he knew all the ins and outs of prison life.

"Mr. Vargas, so we meet again." Vargas massaged his curly mustache and nodded his head. I decided to hit Vargas with a blatant question. "Do you know who murdered Newton Black?" An obvious smirk filled Vargas' face as he took his sweet time answering my question. Patience is my specialty, so I was prepared to wait as long as Vargas took. He cracked three of his fingers on his left hand before he decided to speak. "Life is just a moment in time, Lieutenant, and evidently my man's moment was up." What a smart-ass, I thought to myself. Why should I be surprised? Being a king jerk is what this guy lives' for. "Am I to assume that you do know something about this murder?" His lips thinned and his jaws puffed. "Assume what you like, Lieutenant, and prove what you must. My motto has always been not to speak on subjects that I know little or nothing about." For some reason Inmate Vargas was attempting to throw me a line without any bait. He was too proud to state that he didn't have anything to do with the murder, yet he embraced the fact that he and his boys could be suspects. Nothing but a "Fear Kite". In other words, a public relations statement amongst the prison population that their gang should be feared more than others. I didn't know for certain if this was Vargas' motive, but I certainly wouldn't put it beyond him based on his criminal history. Inmate Vargas is serving a 30-year sentence for murder. He is currently in his twelfth year of incarceration.

"Vargas, you might as well admit that you don't know anything about the murder. Because if you did know something about it, I would be on your butt like white on rice. Matter of fact, I'll be watching you and your boys real close." Vargas appeared fractionally uneasy as he squirmed a bit in his chair.

"Just do your job, Lieutenant, nothing more and nothing less. If we have issues or problems that need to be resolved, we simply handle our business. We don't go around cryin' about the situation. I'll tell you another secret, Lieutenant..." "I'm listening Vargas," I said in a less than enthusiastic manner. "If we did have a hit list, and I'm not saying we do or don't, but for your information, the dead dude didn't make the list. If you think I didn't have anything to do with the murder, why in the hell am I in here?" I got up from my chair and approached Inmate Vargas. For some unknown reason, I bent down in front of Vargas face to face with a five-inch gap separating us. "Sometimes you just got to be sure, if you know what I mean. Furthermore, I get a kick out of talking to you sometimes, Vargas. Now go on back to your unit and keep the peace." Vargas didn't respond verbally. Sergeant Little and Officer Mulberry escorted Vargas back to his housing unit.

I sat silent in my office contemplating if I was going to interview the leaders of the two remaining black gangs on the yard. There was no ongoing rivalry between the black gangs in the past eight months but that still didn't excuse the fact that Newton Black was dead. Newton Black was the most well respected gang leader on the yard, which may have caused some serious internal jealousy between the black inmates. Being able to call the shots on a prison yard is a serious position of power. The question I had, was would this type of power cause someone to kill to have it? Of course, someone would kill for power, given the right opportunity.

Fourteen

The static of my radio crackled as I heard Sergeant Little attempting to contact me. "Ten-nine that last transmission Sergeant." I placed the radio up to my ear. "Inmate Vargas is secured, please advise on the next inmate to be seen." "Lieutenant Price copy, please 10-23 that last request." "Ten-four lieutenant." What should I do, I thought silently to myself. Time is of the essence. "Lieutenant Price to Sergeant Little." "Little copy." His voice was much clearer now. "Please be advised that the yard is to be opened now. Inform Mulberry that his team of S & E officers is to visually observe each unit during yard release procedures." "Ten-four Lieutenant," announced Sergeant Little.

I stood patiently by my window gazing onto the yard awaiting the initial release of inmates. Within a matter of twenty seconds, the doors of building ten slowly opened and a bunch of anxious inmates hurried out towards the yard. The scene was a classic example of how good freedom feels after being locked behind closed doors for several days. Although the inmates' freedom was limited to the yard, they still appeared to be happy to enjoy that bit of luxury.

Officer Mulberry and his S & E crew went on to the subsequent housing units excusing the inmates to the yard in the same manner. The operation appeared to be going smoothly. I watched as the basketball court was filled in a matter of minutes. Two inmates who were engaged in a bout already occupied the handball court. A large group of inmates were quickly forming teams on the softball diamond. Also, the available area within the weight-pile was quickly filled. The yard was back in full operation and I must admit that I felt good.

There was no doubt in my mind that the killer or killers was probably standing right in the weight-pile right at this moment just as sure as my name is Price. The responsible party had no fear at this time and possibly gloated, knowing that the murder was successful. My personal desire would be to run over to the weight-pile and detain everyone who was standing in the sand. I would interrogate all of them and deny them all privileges until someone confessed or turned over the killer. As good as that may sound, I knew as a professional that it was not the way to pursue a credible investigation. Furthermore, some inmate would probably write the governor's office reporting accusations that I was utilizing unlawful practices to conduct an investigation.

In less than two weeks I would be retiring. I made a vow to myself as well as my family that I would not let anything in relationship to this job interfere with my well-deserved retirement. But deep within, I know that I must solve this murder to have peace of mind. My motto is, don't take an assignment if you're not willing to finish it.

The phone rang and I casually walked away from the window to answer it. "Lieutenant Price speaking." "This is Mulberry, T.P. Just wanted to let you know that the yard release is complete. How would you like us to proceed from this point on?" "If possible, I want you to take note of which black inmates are present on the weight-pile. Of course I don't expect you to document them all, but I do want to know if Inmate Tuck and his boys are hangin' out in the sand." "I got you covered T.P.," said Mulberry in an eager voice. "One other thing, Mulberry, I may be walking the yard in the next few minutes which would probably divert some of the attention away from you so you record the black inmates on the weight-pile." "Ten-four T.P., I'll see you out there."

Once I made my way to the yard, Sergeant Little immediately joined me. I was pleased to see that his shirt was completely tucked in and his mouth wasn't covered with crumbs from his last meal. He appeared to be in a good mood and quite frankly I didn't mind his company. "The kids are back on the playground, hmm, T.P., a lot sooner than I had hoped." And the lazy man spoke. He hadn't had to do anything in the last week, and he had the nerve to complain. Some folks seem to forget that this is a real job that pays real dollars for real work. "Sergeant, I'm kind of glad that the yard is finally open. I think my investigation will go a lot smoother with the inmates going about their normal operations. Besides, a little work never hurt anybody." Sergeant Little sucked his large teeth and refrained from commenting. We continued to walk the yard and I was pleased to see a group of Hispanic inmates competing against a group of black inmates. The other half of the grassy infield was occupied by a large group of soccer players. Just as we were about to pass the soccer area, a ball came bouncing in our direction. Sergeant Little galloped about ten feet in front of us to retrieve the ball. I was hoping that he wouldn't embarrass himself by attempting to kick the ball back. Inmates love to get their clown on (laugh) at an officer's expense. I was relieved to see that Sergeant Little gently threw the ball back to an inmate who was already running after the ball. "T.P., I should have kicked it, I was a heck of a player in my day." "You use to play soccer?" I said, surprised. The sergeant's eyes bucked wide open as he responded to my question. "Naw T.P., I didn't play no soccer." "Well what in the heck are you talking about then?" He held a jolly smile as if to say I had just asked him the million-dollar question. "I use to kick field goals, I was a football player. Can't you tell from this old body of steel?"

Oh my God, I thought to myself, this guy is really a character.

We continued to walk the perimeter of the yard observing the various activities of the inmates. As we came upon the basketball court a black inmate who was dressed in the assigned prison blues drenched in body sweat questioned me. "Hey Lieutenant, why were we locked up so long?" he shouted this disgustedly with his hands on his hips. I gestured with my hand, for the inmate to come to where we were standing. "What's your name young man," I said politely. "David Cox." "Well David, I don't know if you are aware of the fact that there was a serious crime that took place last week on the yard. Prison personnel including myself, needed an opportunity to check out the scene and make sure that we had all the information we needed before opening the yard. Did you know anything about the situation?" For some reason, suddenly Inmate Cox wasn't so talkative. "I don't know nothin' about no murder, or how many times he got stuck, I'm just trying to do this time and get the hell up out of here." "Well, it was nice talking to you Mr. Cox." Cox turned and walked back to the basketball court. "You were certainly nice to that little nappy-headed punk. You should have read him the riot act." Sergeant Little can't stand the fact that I talk to the inmates like they're humans. I don't raise my voice, I don't curse at them, I simply give them respect as men. "Do you want me to get that smart ass back over here T.P.?" Little said angrily. "Definitely not, he already told me everything I wanted to know." "I was standing here too Lieutenant, and that punk didn't say much of nothing." A satisfied smile covered my face as I cheerfully responded to Sergeant Little. "You said that you were standing here Sergeant, so that means you heard what he said also." Sergeant Little gestured with an up and down nod of his head. "When I asked Inmate Cox about the incident and what he possibly knew about it, I never mentioned what the situation was. I never said it was a murder by way of a stabbing. Also, there was no official word given to any inmate that a stabbing was the mode of murder. I'm willing to bet that the majority of the inmates on the yard know about the murder incident. And a certain percentage of inmates probably know who did it."

The sound of percussion beats could be heard just ahead in our pathway. As we got closer to building six, I could see that Dread-lock Freddie was up to his old usual behavior. He had a number of cardboard boxes positioned in the manner of a drum set. He was utilizing tightly rolled newspapers as makeshift drumsticks. A small crowd of inmates had gathered around Dread-lock Freddie to hear his latest song. He has a heavy Jamaican accent that could be easily detected as he sang.

His thick brown, mangled dread-locks were flopping back and forth over his face. His clothes were wet with sweat as he looked towards heaven singing at the top of his lungs.

"You know that girl did not love me, she told me that so many times. So why you think I went so crazy, committing all those crimes. Ohhhhh, she didn't love me, no, no, no, she left me all behind. Well, I'll tell you my brother, it's all right, cause she can get on with her big fat ass behind. Yeah, yeah, yeah!" Dread-lock Freddie was in rare form, I must admit. I noticed Sergeant Little patting his foot as we stopped behind the small crowd that had formed in front of Dread-lock Freddie. The inmates really enjoyed Freddie's yard show, which he usually performed three to four times a week. Freddie kept to himself for the most part, and none of the inmates or the officers bothered him. Freddie's the kind of peacemaker that every prison yard needs. He doesn't cause any internal problems, he goes to work every day, he keeps his cell spotless and I've never heard him complain about the food. But, when he sings, he lets it all hang out, the truth, that is. To be honest, I like the guy.

Sergeant Little was really into Freddie's song, so I tapped him on the shoulder before he got too emotionally involved. "Let's keep moving sergeant," I said in a stern manner. We continued walking, as we had not yet journeyed the complete circumference of the yard. As we approached the inmate canteen facility, I was amazed at the number of inmates that were gathered in the line that stretched back beyond the weight-pile. The inmate canteen is probably one of the most popular places for the inmates to go. The canteen is considered a mini store to the inmates, and they are allowed to purchase items with money that the inmate notably possesses on the institutional accounting books. All sorts of goodies can be purchased, such as soft drinks, candy, cookies, soup and a few other food items. Also, toiletries and other pertinent items are available for inmates to purchase. All inmates who have received notification for first draw, second draw, and third draw, etc., are allowed to utilize their recorded credit to purchase needed items. Inmates must remain in their allotted group to be eligible to spend their credit.

Surprisingly as we passed in front of the anxious inmates, many of them spoke to Sergeant Little and myself, referring to us as T.P. and Sarg. We acknowledged each of the inmates who greeted us, but we refrained from getting into any one-on-one conversations with them. We continued to walk in the direction of the weight-pile. I didn't see officer Mulberry but I was sure that he was somewhere on the yard gathering a complete glimpse of the weight-pile.

The inmate culinary was just ahead of us on the right hand side so I decided that we would enter. The dining area was clear but I could hear pots and pans being slung around in the back portion of the culinary. The door that separated the dining area from the kitchen suddenly swung open. It was Officer Jones. "So you got me working hard again, hmm T.P.?" Officer Jones flopped down on one of the stainless steel tabletops and waited for my response. "Well I'm glad to see that someone's actually doing something for their paycheck. A little work never hurt anyone." "That's a lie, the corns on my little toe are killing me." We all chuckled a bit and Sergeant Little and myself sat down on top of two stainless steel tables, which were adjacent to Officer Jones' table.

"So what's going on with the investigation," inquired Officer Jones. This question was going to drive me crazy if I'm not careful. But it was normal for everyone to want to know what was going on. I just wished I had some answers. "Come-on Jones, I came over here to get some answers from you brother, don't tell me you don't know nothin'!" This was not really a time for joking around but for some reason we all kept laughing and that's a good thing under these circumstances. "T.P. you know I'd give you the shirt off my back if I had to," laughing while speaking. "Something smells good back there, what you cookin' man?" Sergeant Little would be the one in the group to discover there was food in the vicinity. "I can't take you anywhere without you wanting to eat something," I said jokingly. "Hey, you guys are the big brass, I'm just the kitchen man. Be my guest and help yourself to whatever you like," offered Officer Jones. Sergeant Little rubbed his hands together and started to walk towards the door leading to the kitchen. "Whoa, whoa, Sergeant, we don't have time for that right now. Matter of fact, I need you to contact Mulberry and find out his present location." I handed Sergeant Little my radio, as I walked towards one of the culinary windows to take a glimpse of the weight-pile. Sergeant Little sat down while attempting to contact Officer Mulberry and Officer Jones followed me over to the window.

The weight-pile was packed. There were whites and Hispanic inmates occupying the north end of the weight-pile. The black inmates occupied the middle as well as the south end of the weight-pile. I placed my forehead against the window in search of any obvious inmate who might be taking an interest in the murder location. A short portion of the weight-pile was roped off to preserve any elements that still may be present at the murder scene. My main interest was focused on the black inmates who were to the right of my focal point. It's amazing how most of the guys look similar while they're slinging weights up and down and side to side. Everyone seems to be in a hurry to pump back up their muscles. Inmates have a notion that their muscles shrink tremendously during times of lock-down. They all look like they're related to Hercules, as big as they all are.

Officer Mulberry entered the dining room area accompanied by two officers. I left the window area and joined Mulberry, Sergeant Little,

Officer Jones, and the two officers that walked in with Mulberry. "Tell me something good Mulberry," I said with a degree of hope. "Everything looked pretty normal in my opinion. No one seemed to pay too much attention to the murder scene. There were looks here and there, but no one appeared to be overly interested. I did keep an eye on Tuck Williams and his boys. Tuck Williams, Corky Price, and Bobby Nelson were all together inside the weight-pile. Bobby Nelson a.k.a. C-Dog, was spotting Tuck as he bench pressed a stack of weights. Corky Price, a.k.a. Coke, just stood around and talked and didn't participate in weight lifting. Ronnie Phillips and Todd Henderson, a.k.a. Boo, were outside of the weight-pile but not far from Tuck. Ronnie was busy placing rollers in Todd Henderson's hair. I didn't detect anything abnormal on the yard." "So Tuck and his boys were basically on the weight-pile except for the two sitting outside the weight-pile," I said. "That's correct, T.P., no one appeared nervous or suspicious," Mulberry said reassuringly.

The murderer was clever to say the least. No confessions or signs of guilt were apparent amongst the inmates. My mind constantly reminded me that the murderer wanted the victim dead. The majority of inmates aren't college scholars and they tend to spill the beans concerning their actions when they've done wrong. The perpetrator in ninety-nine percent of cases desires credit for the crime that they've committed, especially when it's murder. No one usually wants to surrender the status of committing a murder behind bars. Just based on this hidden rule alone, I knew something was very different concerning this hit.

"Tomorrow I want Tuck Williams and his crew brought to me one by one. Either one of them committed the murder, or one of them knows who did." Mulberry had the strangest expression on his face as if to say, "That would be too easy to blame the murder on one of those five punks."

Fifteen

Prior to sunset, I drove my vehicle down the 60-freeway west to the 57-freeway south. After passing Disneyland and the renovated stadium that the Anaheim Angels call home, I turned onto the 5-freeway momentarily before exiting at Broadway. The city I just entered is Santa Ana. This particular city is known for several hundred gangs, drugs, and a fair amount of illegal alien activity. It's probably no accident that the city houses the county jail and several courthouses.

I received a phone call earlier in the day from a parole agent who currently supervised the murder victim's brother. During a routine visit, the parolee made mention to the parole agent that Tuck Williams more than likely had his brother killed. Time was of the essence, and I dare not leave any stone unturned.

The sun continued to peak above the skyline but was slowly losing its brightness. I was running out of time if I wanted to reach my destination before darkness consumed the day. As I continued south on Broadway, I made a right turn once I reached McFadden Street. Upon traveling several blocks eastbound, I made a right turn on Jackson Street and quickly located the home address of the parolee.

A medium built man with very dark skin answered the door. His head was clean-shaven and his muscular chest showed through a light-colored, fishnet shirt.

"Who you lookin' for?" bellowed the bass voice through a slightly torn screen door. I carefully reached into my back pocket, pulled out my state-issued wallet, and brandished my gold plated badge against the screen. The parolee didn't appear to have a problem with my presence and immediately invited me inside his home. The living room was sparsely furnished with only a brown vinyl couch and a badly scratched coffee table. An old ceramic lamp that contained a bulb that illuminated less than 25 watts lit the room. I glanced briefly to my right side towards the dining area and saw an old green, ripped, card table surrounded by three rusted chairs.

"My name is Lieutenant Price, and I was fortunate to have a conversation with your parole agent. I'm in the midst of an investigation that involves your brother's murder." "Yeah, I know, Agent Combs told me that you might stop by. I just didn't think it would be so quick. We just buried my brother two days ago." The guy didn't look too disturbed to me, but of course everyone handles death differently. I remember when my wife passed away, something always prevented me from crying in front of others. But once I was at home in our bedroom, I cried uncontrollably. One never knows the confines that can be placed upon an individual who is experiencing a loved one's death.

"My sympathy goes out to you and your family. In no way am I trying to intrude on you and your folks during this unfortunate time. I simply need your help and I need it now. If tonight is a bad time, maybe I can speak with you tomorrow or the next day." Jason took his time in responding to my request. "Go ahead and ask me your questions man, I guess it can't hurt nothin'." I silently agreed and proceeded with my question. "Your parole agent informed me that you think you may know who killed your brother, did you make such a statement?" Jason nodded his head slowly prior to speaking. "I said it, and it's true. He's lucky that I haven't had a cap busted off in his ass already," he said abrasively. I moved to another question pretending not to hear his threat. "What proof do you have that this individual you're speaking about committed your brother's murder?" "My brother kept records of every little issue. His foot soldiers kept their ears open concerning any information that might affect the movement. The movement meant everything to Newton, and he wasn't gonna let anybody get in the way." He still hadn't answered my question, but patience is a luxury that I have been able to cultivate over the years, so I waited. "When you speak of the movement, are you talking about the organization which he led within the prison?" "That's right, the Black Confederate Movement Organization," he said confidently. "Were you a member of the organization?" "Of course I was, it wasn't a gang or nothin' like that, we were doing some positive things. Newton was gettin' all the brothas together. He would teach us about our African roots and other valuable information. He taught the inmates about finances and a whole lot of other business stuff." A shadow consumed a small portion of the hallway that was just adjacent to the couch that I was sitting on. From the shadow appeared a small boy who walked just to the right of us, headed for the kitchen. "Hello young man." He smiled at me and continued walking into the kitchen area. "That was Newton's pride and joy. His only son." Now I was beginning to feel touched by this situation. I don't like seeing any kid growing up without a father. I imagine that kid didn't have much of a father with Newton being locked up for so many years. "How old is the kid," I inquired. "He's eleven years old. He was born three months after Newton went to prison." I didn't want to stop Jason from airing out his feelings, but I was now in the frame of mind to just deal with specifics.

"Who do you think killed your brother, Jason?" "Tuck Williams is the one responsible for my brother's murder." My ears perked up and my brain was now operating at the capacity of a computer's maximum megabites. "Can you prove that Tuck Williams committed the murder or is somehow responsible?" "He hated my brother and everybody on the yard knew it. That punk was jealous because he knew that Newton had most of the brothers looking up to him. Believe me, word would always get back to us concerning things that were said by Tuck and his boys. During his little meetings with his boys he said on more than one occasion that he was gonna get rid of that militant nigga, Newton Black."

Did Jason have any hard-core evidence, or was he just exhausting some built-up anger? I really didn't know the answer to my inner thoughts concerning this situation, but it was definitely worth looking into. "Do you know anyone that I might be able to speak to that can substantiate this information?" "Hell yeah, you can talk to Master J, P-Funk, Puddin' and also Scrooge," he blurted out. Jason sounded like a high-priced promoter putting on a rap concert. "Do you know the birth names of these gentleman?" I said. "Nope. That's a trip, hmm?"

The next morning I arrived at the prison earlier than usual. My goal was to have everything in place prior to conducting the interviews with Tuck Williams and his closet prison partners. I carefully stacked each inmate's documents into five separate piles. I positioned a small cassette recorder on the right corner of my desk. On the front center portion of my desk I carefully placed a clear plastic pitcher of water. I reached into my bottom right drawer and removed a pack of Styrofoam cups that I immediately placed beside the water. Ice-cold water is a valuable commodity within prison walls. Besides, I wouldn't want any of the interviewees to choke from a dry throat.

The inmate breakfast had been completed around 7:30 a.m., and I left instructions with Officer Mulberry for the interviews to begin at 8:00 a.m. sharp. The thought of having one of the nicknamed inmates that Jason Black mentioned last night, interviewed, vaguely crossed my mind. I wanted to first deal with the initial interviews at hand.

Static was projected from a hand-held radio that sounded like it was in the immediate vicinity. As the sound became stronger, Mulberry soon appeared at my door.

"Everything is in place T.P., your first subject should be here shortly if he adheres to the time posted on the ducat." A ducat is a small document similar to a ticket, which summons an inmate to a specific place on the yard, such as the dentist, legal library, program office, medical doctor, etc. This document further permits an inmate to walk the yard during unauthorized times without an escort. In this particular set of circumstances, fabricated ducats were issued to prevent any suspicion of the ongoing murder investigation. This particular precaution would possibly prevent any of the suspects from suspecting that they were being singled out to provide potential information concerning the murder. This method should also lessen the chances of the prison population knowing about the situation until well after the interviews were conducted.

"As soon as you see the first inmate approaching this area, intercept him and bring him directly into my office. I won't need any assistance; I want to interview each of them in private. I've instructed Sergeant Little to remain in the Ad Seg. building until the interviews are completed." Mulberry displayed a gumball smile and exits my office.

Meanwhile, I decided to place a call to Ethel Williams in the records office. The phone rang twice before I heard Ethel's bubbling voice answer. "Ethel, how are you doing?" "I'm fine, Lieutenant, and to what do I owe this pleasure on such a nice day?" "Well Ethel, it's the nature of this wicked business which unfortunately causes my job to never be done. I was hoping that you could assist me with a small task since my time is tighter than normal." She didn't hesitate to offer her services. "What ya' got for me Lieutenant?" "Recently, I began interviewing possible suspects in reference to the ongoing murder investigation. I came across the victim's brother who informed me that he and many other individuals could substantiate that a particular individual had a concrete motive to commit the murder. I was provided with four names, but they're all prison nicknames. My question to you is if there is any way to access factual legal names from prison nicknames." It is a common practice for prison officials to document nicknames beside an inmate's legal name. I honestly didn't know if I was asking for too much, but if anybody could do it, Ethel could. "I'll definitely give it a go Lieutenant, my computer is usually pretty good to me." "I feel better already," I said. Ethel seemed to be in her usual upbeat mood. This woman is always pleasant and willing to lend a helping hand beyond the scope of her normal assigned duties. I consulted my black notebook, which contained the nicknames of the inmates that could possibly implicate Tuck Williams. "Okay Ethel, here are the names, Master J, Puddin', Scrooge and P-Funk." "My, my, aren't they creative," she snickered while repeating their names. She did have a point, the names do sound ridiculous. "Thanks a lot for your assistance Ethel." "No problem Lieutenant, glad to be of help. I'll call you as soon as I have something." We both hung up, and I patiently awaited the arrival of Corky Price, who was scheduled to be interviewed first. This particular inmate has my last name.

The long arm on my wall clock clicked into the twelve position just as a knock sounded from my door. It was nine o'clock in the morning. "Come on in," I shouted. Mulberry opened the door allowing the tall, slender Corky Price to enter my office. Mulberry closed the door and left us alone. Inmate Price came in and sat down in the brown folding chair that was positioned directly in front of my desk. I planned on spending no more than fifteen minutes with each inmate on my interview list.

"Have a seat Mr. Price." "My ducat says that the Psych Doctor wanted to see me, why you got me up in here?" he said angrily. "I have no problem with you seeing the doctor, I just need to see you first. I'm investigating the murder of Newton Black." "Oh here we go, like I know something about the murder." Inmate Price was irritated, to say the least. "Relax Mr. Price, no one is accusing you of murdering the victim. But my sources do tell me that you were in that particular portion of the weight-pile when the murder was committed." "So what if I was, that doesn't mean I know anything." "Do you know anything Mr. Price, concerning the murder of Newton Black?" He began to rub his hands together in a circular motion. "The only thing that I remember was that me and my boys were lifting some iron when we heard a commotion happening on the basketball court. Before we knew it, the gunman was telling everybody to hit the ground. We were all just as shocked as everybody else. Don't you think I would know if one of my boys stabbed somebody?" I thought for a moment before responding to Inmate Price's question. "That may be true Mr. Price, but who's to say that they wanted you to know? Furthermore, what if you killed Newton Black and didn't want any of your boys to know?" "Man, I didn't kill nobody!" Inmate Price hopped out of his seat and stood in front of me with the palms of his hands planted firmly on my desk. "Mr. Price, take your hands off my desk and kindly sit your butt back down in that chair." Inmate Price sat back down without incident. I was surprised that Mulberry didn't rush in to see what the problem was. Quiet as it's kept, the fool could've hurt me. Maybe not, I still have a few good punches in me. "Since you say that you didn't kill Newton Black and you doubt very seriously if your boys committed the murder, who do you think did?" "I don't know." "Did you know Newton Black?" "Yeah, I knew him, but it wasn't like we hung out or nothing." "No, I didn't think that you guys hung out together, matter of fact, didn't you and your boys despise Newton Black to the point of hate?" "We didn't like the dude and we couldn't get with his little nice Negro program. Homeboy was so busy trying to brainwash brothas into believing his crap." I could sense that Inmate Price had no love lost for the victim. "What can you tell me about the relationship between Tuck Williams and Newton Black?" Inmate Price began coughing almost to the point of choking. I offered him a cup of water but he waived off my offer with both hands. "I'm all right, it's just a little cough. And to answer your question, Tuck never talked about Newton Black." "One more question, Mr. Price, does it bother you that

Newton Black is dead?" "I'm not bothered one bit." "I want to thank you for your time, Mr. Price. Officer Mulberry is going to escort you to a holding area until it is clear for you to return to your housing unit." I removed my two-way radio from the leather pouch that is attached to my black leather belt. "Lieutenant Price to Officer Mulberry." Mulberry immediately opened my office door and motioned for Inmate Price to exit. "Where am I going?" asked Price. "Don't worry about it, just follow me," instructed Mulberry. Boy, I hope he's not related to me somewhere down my family line.

Ten minutes had passed, and I quietly prepared myself for the next inmate, Todd Henderson. He is better known around the yard as Boo.

The jingle of Mulberry's prison keys could be heard as he approached my office. The door was partially open so I took the liberty of instructing him to bring the inmate inside.

"Come on in, Mulberry." A large-framed, chubby young man slouched his way across the floor in front of me. His cheeks were round, and his hair is neatly braided. His small beady eyes were unable to hold continued contact with mine.

"Sit down in the chair right there," stated Mulberry. As I flipped through some documents, I could sense the nervousness that Inmate Henderson was experiencing. Maybe I would play with his mind a while, I thought silently. Or maybe I would sit here and watch how long it would take for a man in his position to sweat all over himself. But, reality reminded me that it was time to get down to business. "Mr. Henderson, I understand that your nickname is Boo, is that correct?" Inmate Henderson squirmed in his seat for a moment before answering my question. "Just a few people call me that," he said in a soft, uneasy voice. This guy reminded me of someone who just moved into a neighborhood and is unsure of his surroundings. He's the type of guy that needs to be handled with kid gloves, to ensure maximum information is obtained. Henderson continued to look downward towards his lap. A part of me wanted to laugh, as I remembered duplicating his same actions as a kid when I was called into the principal's office on a few occasions. "Mr. Henderson, the ducat that you received is for you to see your counselor. But, as you can clearly see, you're here in front of me. I need to ask you some questions about the recent murder of Newton Black. You are not a suspect at this time; I simply need to ask you and some other inmates questions concerning the murder. First of all, how well did you know Newton Black?" Inmate Henderson slowly raised his head and looked into my eyes. "I knew him just like everybody else did." "Mr. Henderson, I'm not concerned about everybody else, I want to know about your personal encounters with Newton Black." "I just knew the guy for a short period of time, but I didn't kill him." This guy was either extremely mentally slow, or he was scared to death. "Listen close, Mr. Henderson, before you answer the next question. Have you ever had an opportunity to speak one on one with Newton Black?" Inmate Henderson displayed a puzzled expression, but I wasn't buying it. "We spoke a few times, it wasn't anything big. He was an alright dude to me." "Do you remember the kinds of things that you two discussed?" Inmate Henderson swayed from side to side prior to speaking. "He would talk about a lot positive things, like education and money management. He was a good dude, I don't know why anyone would want to kill him." "Speaking of the murder, do you have any idea who would have wanted Newton Black dead?" A slight grin escaped from Henderson's chapped lips as he mumbled his response. "Probably a lot of people." "I couldn't understand you clearly, Mr. Henderson." "I said, probably a lot of people would want him dead." "Really," I said with surprise. Henderson appeared more relaxed at this point. "People talk, and I listen. Some brothas just couldn't stand his philosophies, I guess. He was outspoken, he was smart, he feared no one, and he had a lot of influence over a lot of people." "It seems as though you really respected Newton Black, but according to my research, you are not apart of the B.C.M.O., is this correct?" "That's right, I'm not. But I did respect him." So far, it appeared that Henderson was being honest. Now I was about to throw some questions at Henderson that I knew to be facts. "Do you know anyone affiliated with the Plum Town Crips?" I could tell I hit a sore spot as Henderson bit his bottom lip and looked momentarily towards the ceiling. "I know a lot of guys in gangs, that's just the nature of being in prison. You can check my prison jacket (file), I'm not a gangbanger." This guy was good at sidetracking my questions with his own spiced-up answers. He's correct, I knew he wasn't a gangbanger, but he darn sure hung out with one. "Tell me about some of the guys that you hang out with on the yard," I said softly. "Ronnie, Coke, C-Dog, and a few other guys." He seemed relieved. "Are you sure that's everybody you hang out with?" "Oh, oh yeah, I almost forgot, Tuck Williams is one of my partners too," he said smiling. "Just a moment ago, you made no mention of your affiliation with Tuck Williams, who is a known member of the Plum Town Crips. In fact he's the leader of the gang. Are you denying your connection with Tuck Williams?" "No, no, we hung out, but it wasn't a gang thing, we just hung out with the fellas and talked about life outside the prison." This guy is really good, I thought to myself. "Correct me if I'm wrong Mr. Henderson. Just a moment ago you spoke about your dealings with Newton Black, but on the other hand, you openly claim that Tuck Williams is one of your partners. Are you aware of the documented fact that Tuck Williams hated Newton Black?" "Not really." Uh, huh, he was finally lying to me. "Oh please Mr. Henderson, even the prison roaches knew that there was no love lost between those two. Do you expect me to believe that you didn't know about the obvious hostility that existed?" "Hold on now Lieutenant, I never said that they didn't have a problem with one another, I simply stated that I didn't know if Tuck hated the guy or not. I would say that they were more in competition with each other. Tuck had his theories and beliefs that he threw at the brothas while Newton had his own set of philosophies. I understood exactly where both of them were coming from." "But yet you chose to hang out with Tuck and his boys verses Newton." "Tuck is from the hood, so we kind-of hung tight, you know how it is." "I can't say I do, Mr. Henderson, but for now, I'm through talking to you. Please escort him out of here Mulberry." Henderson stood up, nodded his head in my direction, and exited the office.

Sixteen

Things weren't going as planned, but that's the nature of this business. No one is obligated to cooperate and game playing becomes a treasured art.

Inmate number three was on his way to my office and I braced myself for another uncooperative jerk. Ronnie Phillips is one of the rare guys who hangs out with Tuck Williams and doesn't have a nickname. I doubt if that makes him different from the rest of the gangsters that are a part of Tuck's chosen few.

My office was stuffy so I reached for a cup and poured myself some cool water. I remembered that I had a pack of Red Vines in my bottom drawer, so I reached down, opened the drawer and indulged myself in the sweet taste of licorice.

My mouth was full of my third piece of licorice when Mulberry escorted Ronnie Phillips into my office. "Go ahead and have a seat," I muttered, pointing to the chair in front of my desk.

"Please accept my apology, Mr. Phillips, you caught me in between snacks." "Oh that's okay, I know how it is when you're hungry and it ain't lunch or dinner time." This guy was obviously filled with a truck-load of energy. As he smiled I could clearly see all thirty-two of his teeth.

His mouth was probably the biggest portion of his frail structured, brown toned body. His hair was jet black, and neatly styled in a straight perm that lay neatly down his back. If I didn't know any better, according to Ronnie Phillips' appearance, and voice tone, he could easily pass for a female.

"Would you care for some water, Mr. Phillips?" I believe in killing guys with courtesy. Most inmates aren't used to being treated hospitably, so it's a tactic that works fairly well with me.

I started to offer the guy some of my private licorice stock, but of course that crazy thought left my mind quite quickly.

"Oh yes Lieutenant, I could use some cold water. It has been so hot." He frantically fanned himself with his left hand. His feminine mannerisms were overt. "I'm not complaining, I'm just happy that the yard is back open," he said with relief. I handed Ronnie a cup and proceeded to pour him some ice-cold water. "This is so delicious. My momma used to make cold water just like this," he said while gulping another mouth full. Is this guy serious, I thought to myself. Ronnie began to laugh, "You know what I mean Lieutenant, it wasn't like she really made the water, she just knew what to do to make it really cold. Damn, I miss my momma." He slammed the empty cup down on my desk. "So what can I do for you, Lieutenant, I know you didn't invite me in here to just shoot the breeze, especially when there isn't one." "You're absolutely right, Mr. Phillips," I said politely. "Oh please, Lieutenant, call me Ronnie." "Okay Ronnie, as I was saying, you're absolutely right. I brought you in here to ask you some questions about the recent murder of Newton Black." Ronnie shook his head in agreement. "Where were you on the yard when the tower officer told everyone to hit the ground?" "Can I ask you a question first?" "Sure Ronnie, what's on your mind?" "The ducat I received was for the dentist, y'all must have tricked me in to coming in here." Ronnie was starting to go off on the deep end, but I decided to give him enough rope so that he could hang himself, or one of his buddies. "Yes Ronnie, we needed to talk to you first, but I promise you you'll get to see the dentist real soon." He sat back and relaxed in his chair. "That's cool, 'cause I've got to keep these pearly whites shining, you can't fault a brotha for that." This guy could talk me into next week. I wondered for a moment if it was safe to proceed with questioning.

"Ronnie, you can proceed with answering the question." "No problem. I remember the day was real warm and there wasn't a cloud in the sky. There was a big commotion going on at the basketball courts. Of course I don't know why the brothas were fighting, but they were fighting nonetheless. I was checking out the action just like everybody else was, but it was too far to see the situation up close. Just as I started to make my way towards the basketball court, one of your boys blasted everybody over the P.A. system telling us all to hit the ground." "And did you hit the ground immediately at that point?" He slapped the floor with the palm of his left hand. "Like a pancake Lieutenant, I don't challenge anybody with a gun that big. The only thing I didn't like was that I got my clothes dirty. Ain't nothin' like having sand in all your clothes. How would you like it, Lieutenant, if somebody made you lay on the ground like a dog?" "You're right, I wouldn't like that one bit, but if I was in prison such as yourself, I guess I wouldn't have much of a choice." Ronnie choked momentarily on the water that he had just swallowed. "Man, Lieutenant, you're a cold brotha, I was just trying to make conversation." "No disrespect, but I'm in the middle of a serious murder investigation. I just have a few more questions and you can be on your way." Ronnie now appeared more somber. I just hoped that I didn't put too much of his flame out. "Was there anyone near you when the tower officer announced for everyone to hit the ground?" "Probably Boo, 'cause I was still braiding his hair." "You mean Todd Henderson?" Ronnie shrugged his shoulders, "Yeah, that's his real name." "So you recollect that he was on the ground beside you at the time that the murder may have taken place?" "From what I remember, Boo was right there." Ronnie dipped his fingers inside his cup and raised them to his face to pat water around his cheek area. "Did you see anyone around Newton Black prior to the basketball court commotion?" "I wasn't even looking in his direction." "Did you see anyone around Newton Black's lifeless body after everyone hit the ground?" "Lieutenant, there were people laying everywhere, I didn't notice anyone in particular laying by the victim." "Did you know Newton Black?" "I knew him a little bit, we weren't partners or anything like that." "You do realize that he and Tuck Williams, your buddy, did not get along with one another?" He smirked slightly. "Yeah everybody knew that. But, I didn't make a big deal about somebody else's business."

"Tell me something Ronnie, did you kill Newton Black?" Ronnie sighed aloud, "Please." "Do you know who may have wanted him dead?" "No one in particular, Lieutenant."

"Thank you for your time, Ronnie, and I'm sure we'll probably talk again." Ronnie stood to his feet and neatly tucked his shirt properly into his pants. "The pleasure was mine, Lieutenant." Ronnie extended his hand with a slightly bent wrist towards me and we shook hands.

Unfortunately, I was now running behind schedule. I spent longer than I expected with Ronnie. Bobby Nelson was next on my list, alias C-Dog. Bobby Nelson, and Tuck Williams were noted as being closer than any of the other individuals whom I had interviewed earlier.

Bobby Nelson was a documented member of the Plum Town Crip gang, the same gang that Tuck Williams led. I really didn't expect to receive much information from Bobby Nelson, A.K.A. C-Dog, but I was going to give it my best shot. Sometimes fellow gang members will provide a multitude of information in hopes that it will assist in the defense of their homeboy (friend).

As I waited patiently in my office, I could hear the voice of Mulberry in a dispute with another party. I assumed that it was Bobby Nelson, since he was the next inmate on my list. By the time the two of them entered my office, there was silence between them.

"How are you today Mr. Nelson?" He looked at me without expression as veins began to bulge from his clean-shaven head. His large muscles seemed to be escaping from every inch of the clothing that he wore. He is truly a big brotha. "How am I doing? Shit, man, I'm in prison, how the fu..." "...Hold on Mr. Nelson, all that cursing is not necessary, at least not in my office. If you don't wish to share your feelings with me then I can accept that." He crossed his left leg onto his right knee and stared without expression. "Mr. Nelson, I brought you in here to ask you some questions about the recent murder of Newton Black."

"I don't have a damn thang to say!" I stood abruptly and pointed in his direction while speaking to Mulberry. "Get him out of here now," I shouted.

"I want a 602 (inmate appeal form) so I can write your ass up," shouted Inmate Nelson.

"Be my guest, you can have as many copies as you want," I stated in a less than eager manner. I grabbed a few 602 forms from my desk drawer and placed them on the top edge of my desk.

"Good day sir," I said. He snatched the forms from the top of my desk and abruptly turned and walked out. There was obviously no love lost between the two of us. Despite the negative attitude and actions of Inmate Nelson, I knew for a fact that he was not the murderer. There's a certain flavor that a murder portrays and Nelson's demeanor was too genuine to be attempting to cover-up for his actions if he were the murderer. I would honestly say that the feminine Ronnie Phillips would be more a likely suspect than muscle-bound Nelson. It pays to be suspicious of overly friendly, talkative, and slick individuals.

The obvious murder suspect was about to enter into my office. I am quite ready and eagerly awaiting his arrival. All of my early investigation information has led in the direction of Tuck Williams. Inmate Williams definitely had a motive. The fact that he hated the victim should be considered a very strong motive, in my opinion. He also had the opportunity to commit the crime. Officer Parker reported that Inmate Williams was one of a handful of inmates who were in close proximity to the victim before his death.

I honestly believed that Tuck Williams was connected to Newton Black's murder. Either he committed the murder himself or he ordered the hit through one of his henchmen. I am rarely wrong on a gut feeling.

The juices were flowing, and I was ready to get deep into Williams' business.

I heard staggered footsteps in the hallway as they approached my office. The footsteps ceased, as Tuck Williams and Officer Mulberry stood at the door. I motioned with my hand instructing the men to enter. My decision at the moment was to keep my eyes pointed down in the direction of my desk. I purposely wanted to avoid eye contact with Inmate Williams until the verbal iceberg was broken.

"What is your prison number, Mr. Williams?" "V-39675," he stated without hesitation.

"My name is Lieutenant Price, and I'm conducting an investigation concerning the murder of Newton Black. I regret that we had to summons you with a ducat, it was a procedure meant to lessen the attention brought about by the murder investigation." "We all have to do what we have to do. I wasn't looking forward to seeing no drill happy dentist anyway," he said jokingly. The iceberg was clearly broken, and I decided to raise my eyes from my desk. Tuck Williams sat proud and erect in front of my desk. His clean-cut appearance didn't tell me he was the type of a guy who would murder another individual. But, in many cases, these are the suspects who are historically known to commit cold-blooded murder. His hair was short and neatly cut, his face void of any facial hair, and his clothes were clean and neatly creased.

Judging by his appearance, he didn't appear to be the type that would want to get his hands dirty. Moreover, that was another reason why it is likely that Williams ordered the hit on the victim. The brother is smooth, to say the least.

"Your cooperation is appreciated, Mr. Williams. You have not been charged with Newton Black's murder but you are considered a suspect. I want to take a moment to tell you your Miranda rights before we get started." Inmate Williams sat quietly as I spouted-off his Miranda rights. Officer Mulberry sat in a sparsely varnished, wooden chair, placed just to the right of my desk. Mulberry obviously sensed that this last interview was going to be lengthy. He stretched his legs forward and relaxed in the chair.

"Can you tell me as best you can, where you were when the tower officer demanded everyone lay on the ground." Williams gazed his eyes up towards the ceiling before speaking.

"The weight-pile is usually my spot to chill, on the rare occasions when I'm on the yard. I don't actually remember the tower officer telling us to hit the ground, but I did eventually end up on the ground after seeing everyone else there. The fact of the matter remains that I was just as shocked and surprised as everyone else."

"At the time you stood up to return to your housing unit, did you notice the victim laying face down in the weight-pile and if so did you notice any blood?"

"No, no, no, I didn't see a body or any blood. Blood is not a thing that people usually forget seeing. Matter of fact, a dead body is nothing nice to see either," he eagerly boasted.

"So your testimony is that you did not see or have any contact with the victim during the time the yard officer announced for everyone on the yard to hit the ground," I asked hoping for some clarity on the situation. "That's correct Lieutenant, I didn't see the victim prior to his death. The first time I heard about it was when all the brothas were talking about the murder in the housing unit."

This guy must have really thought that I was an idiot or something worse. Williams was right there beside the victim when the murder took place. He was obviously hiding something. His face revealed a unique glow of confidence that his secret was safe.

"Tell me about, as you refer to them, Coke, Boo C-Dog, and Ronnie." He gave me his, I wonder where you're going with this question, look. "They're some of my boys. What do you need to know about them?" I want to know which guy you ordered to murder Newton Black, I thought to myself. "Did any of these men have occasion to hang out with you in the weight-pile," I said plain and simple. "Sometimes all of them would hang out with me in the weight-pile and at other times only one or two of the guys would hang out. Wait, wait, wait, I take that back, Ronnie wasn't the type of guy who lifted weights. Matter of fact, he usually hung just outside of the weight-pile doing folks' hair."

This guy was difficult to read but I did like the fact that he was answering my questions. "So Williams, you will agree that it was possible that these same gentlemen could have been at your side during the murder." "Anything is possible, Lieutenant. But if you want to know any intricate details about the murder, I can't help you because I have no answers. And as far as my boys are concerned, I doubt very seriously if they had anything to do with killin' that dude," he boasted with confidence.

Tuck Williams was very impressive to say the least, and no question that I'd posed seemed to ruffle his feathers.

"If you were me, Mr. Williams, and having the knowledge of your strong feelings towards the victim, how would you proceed with the investigation?"

Inmate Williams smiled a bit before answering. "First of all, I would order all fiber and blood work from the coroner's office, and I would have the pathologist conduct a thorough autopsy.

Secondly, I would have to determine the type of weapon that caused the fatal wound. Finally, I would interrogate all known enemies of the victim, whether they be black, white or Hispanic."

His views were well taken and I agreed with most of them. "Tell me something Mr. Williams, why would you concentrate your time on interviewing alleged suspects who had no obvious access to the victim?" I said pointedly. "If you're talking about the white boys and the Mexicans, I can agree with that theory. That is the darkest section in the weight-pile if you know what I mean. That makes a lot of sense, Lieutenant," he said sincerely.

Williams had conducted an A-1 interview but it would be foolish of me to rule him out as the murderer. I couldn't forget the fact that Williams hated the victim beyond measure and he was near the victim during the time of the murder.

"That's all the questions I have for you today, Mr. Williams. Don't be surprised if I need to question you again in the future."

"I understand that you have to do your job, Lieutenant, I have no problem with that," he said with an obvious expression that he was indeed pleased with the interview.

Approximately fifteen minutes after the interviews were completed, I gave Officer Mulberry the okay to open the yard. From the viewpoint of my office window, I could see that the yard was fully occupied. There was an on-going basketball game, a group of white inmates challenging some Hispanic inmates in a softball game. The open grassy area of the prison yard was trampled as the soccer players ran up and down the field. A bunch of blue balls were smacked back and forth as several inmates engaged in two on two handball games. And last but not least, a large majority of the black inmates crowded themselves within the area of the weight-pile that had been shortened due to the area cordoned off for the murder investigation. The environment appeared non-threatening and the inmates appeared to be happy to be out of their cells. For once I really felt as though I could relax but of course that was just wishful thinking on my part, knowing that the murder had yet to be solved.

Seventeen

That night as I drove home, I remembered that I was supposed to meet my two daughters for dinner. I immediately hopped on the 10-freeway west and headed for the 405-freeway north. The restaurant that we were meeting at is located in a seaside city called Marina del Rey, which is less than 10 miles north of LAX. The restaurant is named Uncle Mizzy's. It's a seafood restaurant with a down-home Southern flavor.

I pulled my vehicle into the busy parking lot located directly in front of the restaurant. After approximately three minutes, I was able to find a parking space.

Upon exiting my vehicle, I walked towards the small storefront structure that is nestled comfortably between two other restaurants. The front is plain to say the least, as the carved words "Uncle Mizzy's" can barely be seen on the wood-grained structure.

Once I entered the restaurant, I was instantly reminded of the unique clientele that frequent this well known restaurant. A number of celebrity photographs are neatly hung wall-to-wall throughout the cozy restaurant. The curtains are beige and outlined with a beautiful array of kente cloth colors. The ceiling is encased by thousands of miniature clear Christmas lights. The view is spectacular.

"Do you have a reservation sir?" asked a beautiful brown-skinned young lady with extremely long braids. She smiled at me, and I casually smiled back. "No, I don't, but I know two people that do," I said jokingly. Just as I stopped laughing, my daughter Carmen walked up to the counter.

"Hi Daddy, I'm glad to see you made it safely." She gave me a bear-like hug. "We're sitting in the back, so follow me," she said happily. I smiled and followed after her like a proud papa should.

As we approached the table, my older daughter Cathy stood up and greeted me with a hug and a kiss. We sat down comfortably at our table while waiting to be served.

"I hope you brought a healthy appetite with you, Daddy, 'cause we're about to throw down," announced Cathy, with no obvious shame in her game. "I'm a little hungry, I think that I can muster up some type of appetite." I gently rubbed my stomach and smiled at my gorgeous daughter. Each of my daughters are rapidly taking on the traits of my late wife. I have no doubt in my mind that my girls will be extraordinary wives, mothers and citizens.

"Tell us about work Daddy." Cathy looked over at Carmen, with a less than pleasant glance, hoping for her support. "Yeah Dad, tell us about that place that's soon to be history," said Carmen in support of her sister. What are they up to, I thought to myself. Since the passing of my wife, my daughters have watched over me like I was a naked newborn in a hospital nursery. It is definitely a blessing to know that they care dearly for me, but sometimes they take it a bit too far.

"The job is busy as usual. Matter of fact, I'm in the midst of a murder investigation as we speak. This case is more difficult than I expected. No murder weapon was ever recovered and the suspects aren't budging on the information tip. And before you ask your next question, I'll answer it for you. Yes, this case is driving my crazy and I want some answers. And yes, I know you guys could care less about my job, you're interested only in my retirement date. God willing, I'm going to try hard to retire on the date that we're all expecting. I can't leave this situation hanging, because the matter is too serious. Besides, the murder victim was a controversial figure…" "But Daddy…" "No buts, Cathy, we all came here to have a nice dinner together." "Let it go, Cathy, Daddy's still Daddy." Carmen glanced over at Cathy and shrugged her shoulders. "Daddy, can I ask you a question unrelated to work?" pleaded Carmen. Carmen knows just where to pierce a daddy's heart with those beautiful puppy dog eyes. "Sure Carmen, go right ahead." "Once you do retire, which we pray will still be very soon, do we have the okay to continue with the plans for your retirement party?"

My stomach was just beginning to grumble, not to mention that this would be a perfect opportunity for the waitress to interfere with our ongoing conversation. I would never do anything intentional to hurt my girls. "Now Carmen, you know there is nothing in this world I would do to hamper you and your sister's efforts to organize my retirement party." Upon finishing my statement, I could see clearly that Cathy was anxious to speak her mind. "Daddy, invitations have to be mailed and food and other items have to be ordered. We don't want to plan an event for a phantom guest. Daddy, it's time to let it go. I'm sure you'll get enough action in your own private business. You've given those people enough years of your life." "Cathy, chill-out," whispered Carmen. Cathy appeared to be serious. "We are giving you your retirement party right on time, as scheduled. This is it, Daddy…!"

A middle-aged black woman with short wavy hair, wearing a white apron covered with green and red gum drops approached our table. "Hello this evening, would any of you care for anything to drink?" "Yes thank you, we'll all take water for starters," said Cathy. Cathy is the family's health fanatic. Just after she graduated from high school she fell in love with vitamins and herbs. This was a rare occasion for Cathy to be eating out. She refrains from eating red meat and pork. Broiled fish tends to be her favorite meat. On the other hand, Carmen is a girl after my own heart. She loves those beef ribs just as much as I do. She has a hefty appetite to be such a petite thing.

"The special for tonight is chicken and dumplings. Here are your menus, and I'll be back to take your order shortly," stated the waitress.

I just love admiring the menu at this restaurant. The outside cover is uniquely decorated with the names and faces of great historical African-Americans. There is also a small quote stating the accomplishments of the African-American right beside their names. The menu would make a great souvenir to take home.

The restaurant is quite noisy tonight as the patrons at the next table are being greeted with a loud birthday song by the restaurant staff. All of the restaurant's patrons usually join in with the singing festivities to help celebrate the person's birthday. If I wasn't so tired I would probably join in with the singing myself. Carmen and Cathy begin to sing along with the other patrons, which doesn't surprise me.

"What a blessing to see another birthday. I'm so happy for her." "You don't even know her Carmen," shouted Cathy. The timing is perfect, as our waitress was walking towards our table. "Ladies, ladies, can we just order our food please." They both looked at me and smiled.

"Are all of you ready to order?" I'm more than ready to order, I thought to myself. "I'll take the broiled salmon and a baked potato," said Cathy. "Anything to drink?" "I'll just have water, thank you." The waitress proceeded to take Carmen's order. "And for you ma'am?" "The special is fine for me. And to drink I'll have a pink lemonade." "And for you, sir?" "I'll take the same exact dish as my daughter, including the lemonade," as I gently pointed at Carmen. The waitress smiled, walked from our table, and left us to chat.

My mind drifted momentarily to the murder scene on the weight-pile. As I closed my eyes a montage of events flashed before my mind displaying possible scenarios of how the murder took place. Suddenly, I see lots of blood, a lifeless body, and a black crow. Several voices call out to me, but their origin and substance cannot be detected.

"Daddy, don't be such a mood spoiler," shouted Cathy. I was a little startled but quickly regained my composure. "Forgive me sweetheart, it's been a long day. But, I'm truly honored to be having dinner with my two most favorite ladies in the world." They both blushed and that pleased me.

Peace among the family is an element that I treasure. I decided to allow my girls to discuss the plans for my retirement. Maybe this was the ticket I needed to relieve my stress concerning the case. There comes a time in life when the pilot needs to relinquish his duties and accept the duty of co-pilot. My girls wanted to do something positive for me and out of respect I owed them that opportunity. "Well, tell me the plans for the retirement party?" Cathy and Carmen's smiles were larger than sunshine. Cathy reached down for her purse and struggled to remove a notepad. She flopped the notepad on the table, Carmen handed her a blue ink pen, and Cathy began to write. "I'm going to take a few notes, just to make sure that we're all on the same page. First of all, it is imperative that we place a date in stone as soon as possible. I've already reserved two Saturday nights at the Triple Tree Hotel, but they need a final answer by next Monday." My pupils dilated, as I peered over at Cathy. "The Triple Tree Hotel is, is, is…" "What Daddy, too much? We don't feel that there's any problem with the Triple Tree Hotel. And no Daddy, we're not sparing any expense for your party." "But honey, the Triple Tree is a very luxurious hotel. You guys can't afford a place like that on a student book store salary," I pleaded. "Daddy, let me put it another way for you if you don't mind. The party is happening, we've got the money, the location, and you need to chill out," Cathy gently instructed. Is this my baby girl addressing me in this manner? I thought to myself. She looked up at me with a smile, "No disrespect intended, Dad." "Okay, okay, but I'm going to go along with this situation under protest." "We love you Daddy," the girls bellowed in unison. I reached over, grabbed both of them and gave them a tight bear hug. "First things first Dad, we need to get the remainder of the guest list together, so get out your phone book," stated Carmen.

Eighteen

As I turned my key to enter the front door, I received a warm welcome from Coco, as she jumped up and down like a ball of energy. The evening had been pleasant, but my weary body was not accepting the treat. I dragged my legs slowly down the hallway heading straight for my bedroom. Coco led the way to my room, with a strut that revealed that she had witnessed my tired and weary state on other occasions. Once I reached my room, I flopped face forward onto my bed and stretched out. Coco tried desperately to remove my shoes, attempting to provide that extra added comfort that she felt her master needed. I wanted to get up and brush my food filled teeth but I couldn't. The pores of my face cried out for clean, fresh, hot water, but I couldn't get up. I would give anything to take off these sweat-drenched clothes, but I had no energy to remove them. There is one thing that I knew I could do well and I could do it now. I slowly closed my eyes and fell asleep.

After a short period of time, I felt the warmth of Coco's furry body rubbing up against my right arm. Sleep never felt so good, as I began to fall into a deeper sleep. Several colors began flashing within my head. The ocean suddenly appeared and a large dark cloud formed above. I knew I must be dreaming but the setting looked so real. A bright light shot across the sky and landed into the ocean causing a large splash. The ocean continued to roll, without any clear explanation. As I began to analyze the setting, the scene immediately changed.

The sun was shining bright and clear, while set in the background of a beautiful blue sky. I saw my grandmother's white two-story wooden house, nestled between several large trees. What am I doing here, I wondered. I ran to the front door as quickly as possible and began knocking. After several knocks, the door was suddenly flung open. The room was so dark; I was unable to see anything. As I turned to my left, I could see a glimmer of light slowly getting brighter. I decided to walk towards the light. As the light became clearer, I could see what appeared to be a lifeless body. Something forced me to continue walking towards the body. The body was less than a yard in front of me. I slowly reached down and turned the body towards me. It was Tuck Williams. His upper body was completely covered with blood. I desperately wanted to yell but I couldn't. I wanted to run out of the room but I couldn't. Within a matter of seconds, the room instantly turned pitch-black. My fear was now in control and I could feel the after-effects.

My concern turned immediately to my left ear that I felt was bleeding because of the enormous wetness. As I opened my eyes, I found Coco nestled by my head licking my ear. I had just experienced a terrible dream. What was the significance of the dream, I wondered to myself. The scene was so vivid, leaving me dumbfounded. All I wanted was a good night's sleep and I couldn't even get that. This was the second time that I'd experienced such a weird dream. I would be fooling myself if I didn't admit that I was now leery to even close my eyes to get a good night sleep.

Maybe these dreams were a sign or a message. It's quite possible that my mind could be trying to communicate a message to me. Tomorrow was a new day and a new opportunity to solve the mystery of this murder.

The loud buzz of my alarm clock startled me as I jumped out of bed. The time was six-thirty, and I planned to be in my office by eight. I quickly pulled off the clothing that I had on the day before and headed straight for the shower. Coco dragged my dirty clothes to the hamper located in the hallway next to the door leading to the garage. Little Coco works as hard as a mule, I guess that's why I love her so much.

Within twenty minutes, I had showered, shaved, brushed my teeth, ate breakfast, brushed my teeth again, fed Coco and walked out the front door.

Upon pulling my car into the prison parking lot, I noticed Betty Wilkins exiting her vehicle. I could sure use some inspirational talk, and Betty is usually the person blessed to deliver such sentiments. "Hey Betty, it must be my lucky day seeing you first thing in the morning," I boasted happily. She walked over to me and gave me a warm hug. "Darling, how are you doing?" "I'm hanging in there, Betty." She rolled her eyes towards the heavens. "Lord, forgive him, 'cause he's talking like a fool. I beg your pardon; you better count your blessings. You're about to retire from here and then live your dream as a private investigator. You must be crazy, saying, 'I'm just hanging in there,' you better be thankful." Betty won't ever allow me or anyone else she encounters to get down on ourselves. She is always upbeat and to the point. "No problem Betty, I'm just tired and a little disappointed. The murder investigation is still ongoing, and it appears that my staff has not made any significant progress." Betty grabbed my arms and pulled me closer to her. "Don't let anything or anyone keep you from your dream." As I nodded my head in agreement, Betty released my arms and walked towards the administration building.

Just as I sat down at my desk the phone rang. I allowed the phone to ring a second time before answering. "Lieutenant Price speaking." Much to my surprise, the voice on the other line was someone I thought I would never hear from again. It was Robin Keller, the leasing manager from the building on Sixth and Hill. "Things are going quite well, thanks for asking." He questioned me concerning my search for a business location. He's obviously the type of guy that can't take no for an answer.

"Yes, I'm still searching for a location slowly but surely. But to be quite frank with you, Mr. Keller, your leasing fee is a bit steeper than I want to commit to at this time." He countered my statement with a so-called "offer that I can't refuse." He has just offered to lower the monthly leasing payment by twenty-five dollars. "Thank you for the offer, but I'm still going to keep my options open at this time. Who knows, if my budget can be adjusted in the near future, I may be giving you a call." Keller rambled on for the next five minutes about the advantages of being at his particular location in the high rent district. My attention span had lapsed as I unintentionally began to daydream. I closed my eyes for a moment while Keller continued speaking. My eyelids began to flicker and all I could see was blackness. Suddenly, a lifeless body covered with blood appears in my mind. My eyes popped open-wide and I could still hear Keller spouting off information about his building.

"Keller, I don't mean to cut you off, but I need to take care of some important issues before my day really gets going."

These dream episodes were starting to take a toll on my mental state of mind. I refused to discuss this matter with anyone. People would think that I was old and senile, if I let on to what had been going on. My mind was playing tricks on me, but I was sure it was just the stress of my retirement being right around the corner. Life has its challenges, and this seemed to be one of those moments.

As I shuffled through some documents within my desk drawer, I came across Dr. Bishop's business card. Maybe I needed to pay this man a visit. He might have the answers that I was looking for. It's a fact that he was in possession of the body after the murder. At this point in the investigation I wouldn't leave any stone unturned. From this point on I was willing to work night and day to solve this murder.

Just as I attempted to dial Dr. Bishop's phone number, Mulberry entered my office carrying a large cup of coffee. I immediately hung up the telephone. "Good morning T.P., I thought you might like a hot cup of coffee." This guy was a Godsend. "This is exactly what the doctor ordered, you just don't know how bad I needed some coffee," I said. Mulberry placed the coffee on my desk along with some packets of cream and sugar. "What's on the agenda today, boss?" "Have a seat and relax, Mulberry." I proceeded to add sugar and cream to my coffee as I sat silently wondering what I would say to Mulberry. "Can I ask you a question Mulberry?" "Be my guest Lieutenant." I took a few sips of my coffee before posing my question. "Suppose everything goes as planned, and I retire on schedule. Also, let's pretend, God forbid it be true, that I go ahead and leave my position without solving the murder. Okay, so here's the scenario, you're now in full charge of the investigation and you have no more clues or information than I do, so now what would you do?" Mulberry wiped his forehead and inhaled deeply. "First of all, I would re-interview all of the alleged suspects in the matter. Secondly, I would search the weight-pile once more, but this time using high-tech equipment that can detect the slightest object that is foreign to the weight-pile. Thirdly, I would search all of the white and Hispanic inmate cells for weapons. Of course the weapons would have to be analyzed for blood traces that would match the victim's DNA make-up. It is possible that the white and Hispanic inmates could have taken this opportunity to kill Newton Black, knowing that Tuck Williams and other blacks would be the obvious suspects. And last but not least, I would obtain all of the forensic information from the coroner in charge of conducting the autopsy. That's all I can think of right now."

"Not bad Mulberry. Now it's time for your critique." I handed him a small folded piece of paper. "After I say what I have to say, I want you to read this paper." "No problem," said Mulberry. "I'll follow your order of events and provide you with my opinion. Your suggestion to re-interview the suspects is a very good idea. But, I would narrow the suspect list down to the individuals that can be connected to the case by hard facts, if any.

The interview techniques should differ tremendously from the procedures conducted during the initial interviews. My focus would be directed towards those on the suspect list that most often frequent the weight-pile. The murderer would have to be familiar with all angles of the weight-pile for purposes of knowing when and where a fatal blow could be delivered with minimal visibility. Also, the murderer would more than likely have an excellent memory concerning regiment schedules of the black inmates that lift weights in the weight-pile on a regular basis. In reference to searching the weight-pile again, that may not be a bad idea. Who knows what we might have missed during the initial search. I disagree with you concerning searching the white and Hispanic inmates. Time is of the essence and I believe that this type of search would be a waste of valuable time. The circumstances surrounding the murder strongly weigh against the possibility of a white or Hispanic inmate being able to commit the crime. Remember, the murder took place in the extreme end of the black section of the weight-pile. If a white or Hispanic inmate had been present in that area, they would have stood out like a marshmallow in hot chocolate. And to address your last statement in regards to the coroner, you're absolutely right. Matter of fact, I'm going to pay the coroner a visit today. Forensic information could possibly exhibit areas that might help us solve this matter."

"Now read that slip of paper that I handed you," I said with confidence. Mulberry unfolded the small white piece of paper and read it silently to himself. "Looks like you covered the same areas that you wrote on this paper, except for one of course." "We're just about on the same page, you'll get there sooner than you think," I explained to Mulberry.

The hour was almost 2:00 p.m., as I glanced down at my old reliable, black-faced Pulsar wristwatch. I had spoken to the coroner, Dr. Bishop, earlier from my office and he agreed to meet me at his office. To be honest, I had no clear idea why I was going to the coroner's office. I guess it must be attributed to my gut feelings.

The one-way street that I was traveling appeared to be filled with coin meters in each block. As I pulled my vehicle in front of the coroner's office, I found a curbside spot with a posted sign that allowed me an hour to park at no charge.

The exterior of the one-story building appeared to be shabby and was heavily concealed under a multitude of green ivy. I began to walk briskly through two iron gates that were partially open. Approximately ten yards from the gate I could clearly see an open door on my right hand side. As I got closer to the door, I could see a man sitting behind a tan metal desk.

"Can I help you sir?" the man said in a pleasant voice as I entered. "My name is Lieutenant Price, and I am scheduled for a two-fifteen meeting with Doctor Bishop." The medium-sized man was dressed from head to toe in a white surgical gown. I was sure that I appeared visibly uneasy to the man as I peered nervously around the room. The room was fairly small and home to several tall gray file cabinets. The walls were off white and partially covered by large chart boards that were host to several names.

"Doctor Bishop is finishing up some work in the back and says that he will be with you momentarily." I nodded my head in acknowledgment. After all of my years spent investigating prison murders, this was my first time inside a coroner's office. Once I become established with my business, I'm sure I'll have to make several trips to this place. Everyone has to make a living doing something and I guess it's time for me to learn the ropes.

"Can I offer you a glass of water," the man offered kindly. I was really thirsty but for some reason I couldn't fathom the thought of drinking out of a glass that might have been used to house organs from a corpse. My God, what a morbid thought.

"No thank you," I said. "First time visitor, hmm?" the man stated with an unconcealed grin. At this point I longed for a full-length mirror to closely examine my body language. I was in unfamiliar territory and there's no way that I was going to play Mr. Big Shot. "You're right. Now tell me how you know that?" He continued to display a grin before speaking. "Lieutenant, I've been in this game for many years. I don't think that

I would be much of a player if I didn't know when a rookie was entering the playing field." He has a valid point, I said to myself while adjusting my shirt collar. "I can't argue with you there, sir. Of course I've had the occasion to come across a few dead bodies in my line of work, I just never imagined being in the same giant-sized refrigerator as ice-cold stiffs. No pun intended." The man's grin immediately changed to a raised brow. Just as he had begun to respond to my comment, a large white-hinged door flung open. "Howdy Lieutenant," shouted Dr. Bishop. He was covered from head to toe in yellow; a head cap, body suit, and material covered shoes. To be quite frank, he looked like a giant lemon-head.

"I suppose you met my assistant, Ted Simmons," he announced as he extended his hand towards mine. "Oh yes, we did meet." Dr. Bishop is such a jovial guy, to be connected to such a grim occupation. "Can I get you something to drink?" "No thank you doctor, I'm fine." Doctor Bishop walked to a nearby desk and grabbed a clipboard. "Just give me a couple of minutes, Lieutenant, I'll be right with you." I could clearly see that the doctor was jotting down some information that he appeared to be taking from the large chart boards in the room. Instead of standing idle in the middle of the room, and to avoid any further conversation with Ted Simmons, I took the initiative to look about the room. Just as I began to step over a six by three foot metal platform nestled within the floor, Dr. Bishop proceeded to comment. "That's the floor scale we use to weigh the bodies when they're first received here." "Interesting," I said in a less than enthusiastic manner, I continued to explore the room. There was not much to look at, just charts, posters and a dingy sports calendar. The particular chart that I was gazing at listed names with numbers beside them. I had got a strange feeling that these names meant much more than I wanted to know.

"Miller, Roberts, Lewis, Tedley, Gonzalez, Turner and Rodriguez. They're all scheduled for autopsies this week. That's what we do around here, Lieutenant; we cut open bodies and provide answers and causes for death. That board to your left is the homicide board. All those unfortunate folks were murdered in some form or fashion and it's my job to find out how. The board over here is a list of bodies that are scheduled to be picked up by various mortuaries. All these bodies have been drained of all body fluids and prepped for the mortician. We're very organized when it comes to our bodies." I felt like I'd just gotten a crash course in coroner care. This man must really love his job. "What's that board over there used for, Doctor?" He adjusted his prescription glasses and looks up at the board that I was referring to. "Oh, I almost forgot about this board. These folks are John and Jane Does. The dates beside their names list when they first were received at this facility." I took it upon myself to walk a little closer to obtain a better look at the board. "The number four John Doe has been here for over two years, is that date correct?" Doctor Bishop mustered up a smile. "Yup, he's still in the refrigerator." "Thank you for that brief overview of your daily operations, Doctor." "Oh, don't mention it, that's the least I could do. Come on in and let me show you around." We both walked through the large white-hinged doors and down a long dark corridor. On the left side of the corridor was a large opening. We both entered the room. In the center of the room was a large stainless steel platform with many unfamiliar gadgets attached from different angles. The large platform was very similar to a medical surgical bed. "This is where I do the majority of my work. The body is placed flat on the platform for me to begin the procedure. Feel free to sit in on an autopsy one day." Doctor Bishop grabbed a white towel off a stainless steel countertop in the front portion of the room. He began wiping the left side of the stainless steel platform with the towel. "Gotta keep her shined at all times," he bragged. After about a minute of wiping, he threw the towel down on the counter and I followed him as he walked out of the room to the corridor. We continued to walk down the dark corridor until we reached a large metal door that resembled a freezer. Doctor Bishop reached into his pocket and pulled out a white facial mask. "Here Lieutenant, put this on." I followed the instructions given by the doctor by placing the mask over my face. An adrenaline rush raced through my body as I anticipated what I would see behind the large metal door. Doctor Bishop reached out and twisted the handle located on the large metal door. The crackling sound popped in my ear as the door slowly opened. A gush of cold air consumed me. "Try not to touch anything, some of the stuff in here are contaminates." Is he serious? Why would I want to touch dead humans, loose organs, bloody guts and any other weird thing in this cold box.

"Step on in and have a look, Lieutenant." As I stepped into the large refrigerator, I was amazed to see several dead bodies partially covered with blue sheets. They were in front of me, to my left, and to my right. The bodies located near the walls were stacked five high on stainless steel shelves. There were also several bodies lying on gurneys in the middle of the floor. Doctor Bishop strolled slowly around the refrigerated room as he glanced momentarily at a couple of bodies. "We like to keep the frig at about fifty degrees. As you can see, sometimes we do get a little crowded at the Cold Inn," he chuckled a bit.

Once we were back in the front office, Dr. Bishop and I were consumed in the discussion of the Newton Black murder. "He bled to death in a very short period of time. His heart was strategically penetrated. His left ventricle and his pulmonary vein were both severely punctured. Hell, Lieutenant, you saw the pool of blood that was around that young man." I took a moment to consult my notes as I analyzed the information that I had previously jotted down. "Would the killer need some type of medical background to be able to deliver such expert fatal jabs?" I asked pointedly. Doctor Bishop placed a colorful diagram of a human heart in front of me and continued to explain his position. "Look right here below the aorta, you can clearly see the pulmonary vein and just below here, is the larger area of the left ventricle." I took a moment to visually study the diagram. My expertise is by no means in biology but in my opinion, if a person were stabbed in any of these colorful areas, I would think that the person would most likely die. "Tell me something Doctor, did any particular stab wound cause Newton Black's death?" Doctor Bishop grabbed a red marker from the desk and proceeded to place red dots onto the heart diagram. "These are all the areas where the object penetrated the heart. The wounds are so close in proximity; I believe that any one of them could have caused his death. If you have a moment, I can retrieve his autopsy report and give you all the particulars concerning the cause of death." "That won't be necessary, I think I've seen enough today. But I would appreciate you sending me a copy of the report." "Not a problem, I'll have it sent to you before the week is out."

The atmosphere was calm at the prison as I entered the administration building. I trotted slowly down the long corridor headed for Captain Davenport's office. We had agreed on a 4:30 p.m. meeting. As I approached his office, I saw the door was wide open and Captain Davenport was nowhere to be found. I took the liberty to creep into his office and take a seat.

"Good afternoon, Lieutenant," bellowed the Captain as he entered the office while holding two blue cans of soda. "How are you doing Captain?" "Oh, I can't complain, I just thought I'd go get us something to drink since one of us is obviously late," he said with a snicker. My own mentor shooting me down, it must be a bad day. The Captain handed me one of the soft drinks. "Thanks, Captain." "That's the least I can do for a man that's about to reach the pinnacle of his career." I suddenly felt a strong sense of baiting going on, I wondered what the Captain wants to tell me. "I agree with you, Captain, retirement is a good thing, when a man is truly ready to take that leap." "You're absolutely right, Lieutenant. Matter of fact, I'm glad you brought it up." "But you..." "Listen T.P., I want to make this transition of retirement as smooth as possible for you. You should not be bogged down with the worries of a murder investigation. I'll be the first one to admit that we made a mistake in asking you to take on this lengthy and difficult investigation. You have your family and your new business to think about. Believe me T.P., I have no intention of prolonging any of your retirement plans. I'm not going to force you off the case, but I really feel that you should reconsider your position on the matter." "Captain, I'm going to finish this case, even if I have to delay my retirement to complete the task," I said firmly. Captain Davenport sat back in his chair, kicked his feet upon the desk, popped open his can of soda, and took a large gulp.

"Tell me one thing, Lieutenant, what can I do from an administrative standpoint to better assist you in this matter?" A glistening of sincere concern trickled from Captain Davenport's face. If this man only knew that I was doing this for him as well as myself. The sad part about this whole scenario is that the Captain was absolutely correct in his concern about the severity of this investigation. "All I need is your blessing, Captain. Just believe in me as you did when I was a young go-getter. One part of my body is telling me to let the whole thing go and concentrate on my new business. But my inner spirit continues to tell me that I must complete this mission." "And don't tell me, Lieutenant, but my guess is that your spirit is in complete control." "You're absolutely correct, Captain."

I could clearly sense that Captain Davenport finally understood that I was serious about completing the investigation. I swallowed the last drop of my soda, shook his hand and headed for the door.

As luck would have it, or in my case it was a blessing, I saw Ethel Williams heading down the corridor towards her office. "Slow down Ethel!" I yelled without considering my surroundings. She turned around quickly mimicking the body language of a model. She was adorned in a dark-green, silk, skirt suit. Her green pumps appeared to be alligator. Her bright smile lit the entire corridor as I approached her.

"My, my, Lieutenant, to what pleasure do I owe this visit at the closing hour of the day." "I didn't mean to startle you by yelling, but my mouth reacted when I saw you, because my mind knew I needed to speak with you. All I need is one favor from you." "This won't entail any overtime will it, 'cause I left some neck-bones at home cooking in the crock pot?" This sister appeared to be very serious about her neck bones, so I thought

I should speak my peace and let her be on her way. "Hopefully this won't take up too much of your time. All I need from you is those files that we were reviewing last week." "Oh, you mean the files that we had spread all over my desk?" "Exactly," I agreed. "That won't be a problem T.P., I still have the names written down in my notes. I can probably have them ready for you tomorrow by noon." "Thank you Ethel, you are surely a lifesaver. What would I do without you?" She displayed her usual bright smile and I smiled right back at her. "I don't mean to be forward, Lieutenant, but if you're not busy tonight, I could sure use some help eating those neck bones. Let me tell you what else I'm having. Black-eyed peas, string beans, candy-yams, fried corn, mashed potatoes, and sweet corn bread. And I do promise to put my foot in it." Oh my God, she didn't even take a breath as she spouted off a soul food feast fit for a king. The meal sounded delicious, but I wasn't ready to be anyone's king at this stage in my life. Plus, it's hard for me to imagine her foot or any other female's foot in my food. I've seen some women's feet in my day. It's hard for me to imagine an un-manicured, crusty, ashy, chipped-polish foot in my food. I wonder who invented such a crazy way to describe good cookin'? At least people could illustrate a more becoming body part that God created to be associated with food. My mind was really going off on the deep end while this woman awaited my answer. "Tonight is not good for me Ethel, I have tons of work to do on this murder case. I do appreciate the invitation." "Okay Lieutenant, suit yourself. But all of us need rest at some point in time." She gave me her large smile and waved good-bye as she turned into her office.

Nineteen

The sun was slowly dipping over the small hills adjacent to the prison. Being tired was no prerequisite, or excuse for me to go home just because the clock said so. As I sat down in my office staring out of my window, I felt a sudden sense of urgency. I was on a mission and willing to stay there all night to place a small dent in this case if I could.

Answers were a valued treasure at this point. I was beat, whipped, and I honestly didn't know what to do. Just as I lifted up my phone to place a call, I quickly hung up the phone and dropped down to my knees. I began to pray. "Lord, help me. I'm at my wit's end and I don't know what to do. I'm asking you in the most humble way I know, for you to intervene and give me some positive leads concerning this case. And please, forgive me for being so stubborn and not concentrating on my retirement. Amen."

Just as I got up from kneeling on my knees, Officer Mulberry slowly pushed opened my partially closed door.

"Just the man I need to see. We've got a multitude of work to do starting right now. First of all, Ethel Williams, the woman you met from the records department, will be re-pulling the files that we previously reviewed. There's some specific information that I'm looking for that may lead us in the right direction. I took a trip to the coroner's office today and spoke with Dr. Bishop in detail concerning the case. I believe that whoever committed this murder knew exactly how to cause certain death. I'll get more into that theory once Ethel has the files ready for us tomorrow. Next, I need you to go snatch the two jerks out of Ad-seg who were involved in the fight on the basketball court at the time of the murder. I'm definitely interested in hearing what these clowns have to say. Oh yea, and tomorrow at approximately one hour after shift change; I want a full search of the entire weight-pile. I want rakes, shovels, picks, medal detectors and anything else you can think of to conduct a thorough search. As you young fellows say, 'it's on'." Mulberry appeared to be overwhelmed after ingesting all the information I had spouted off. "Anything else T.P.?" he stated with a blank stare. "No, I think that'll keep us rolling for a while." "Okay T.P., I'm on my way to Ad-seg. I'll be back with the first guy in about ten minutes." My intentions were not to tie-up Mulberry's time at the end of the day, but that's how the ball rolls sometime working in a prison. He should be all right, besides he'd be paid overtime.

"Before you go, I just wanted to let you know that you're doing an excellent job in assisting me with this investigation." "Thanks T.P., I'm just doing what I was hired to do." Mulberry tipped his hat.

Twelve frustrating minutes had passed before Mulberry finally arrived back with Chris Collins. Honestly, this guy didn't look as if he could harm a fly drowning in buttermilk. If I didn't know any better, I'd think he wasn't a day over 21. He's about 5 feet, 8 inches tall. He's clean-shaven and walks with a slight limp. I would imagine he sustained the apparent leg injury during his basketball brawl.

"This is Chris Collins, Lieutenant." Mulberry carefully guided Collins to the chair positioned in front of my desk. As Collins squatted to be seated, he kept his bent head towards the floor.

"Mr. Collins, no need to be shy with me, I'm not going to fight with you. I simply need you to answer a few questions." Collins slowly raised his head. "I had a fight on the basketball court. I think that about covers it." Here I go with another high-strung youngster with a smart mouth. "No Mr. Collins, I don't believe your actions were simply a fight. My spirit tells me that there was a bigger game than just the basketball game going on that day. You see, Mr. Collins, we had a vicious murder take place at exactly the same time that you engaged in a fight with a Mr. Ken Dixon…" "…You trippin' man, I don't know nothin' about no damn murder!" "Boy, you better lower your voice in my office, I don't play that mess," I demanded while pointing my right index finger towards Collins' face. "This is how I operate, I ask the questions and you give the answers in a calm manner. Your attitude doesn't faze me one bit. And if you're not careful, you'll spend the majority of your prison time in the hole." Collins was displaying obvious tension in his face but really didn't care. Most of the youngsters in prison think they're tough guys until the going really gets tough, then they melt like little sissy pops. "Now that we have a clear understanding of my rules, I'll continue. How long had you been playing before the fight happened?" "What's this all about, 'cause I don't want to be nobody's snitch," he said in a much lower tone. "I'll make it plain and simple for you, Mr. Collins, if you don't cooperate you don't see the sun shine. Furthermore, without your input and some sufficient answers, I'll more than likely have to consider you as a murder suspect in this matter." "What does playing basketball have to do with this murder?" "Diversion, Mr. Collins. I think that you and your battle partner staged the fight to give the killer ample time to murder Newton Black." "Naw, man…!" "…Watch your voice." Collins is visibly nervous as a few drops of sweat trickled down his forehead.

"Lieutenant, I was on the court just ballin', I don't know nothin' else. I didn't know the dude that got murdered personally, but I do know who he is. I would have to be a fool to murder the man with the top juice card." Collins was singing the blues. It's like taking candy from a baby. This is how one can distinguish the inmates from the convicts. In other words, the boys from the men. "What happened on the court that day, Collins?"

"Me and some of the homies from my housing unit had been playing on the court about twenty minutes before the fight happened. We won our first game, and then another set of dudes wanted to play five on five. Of course we didn't care who we played, 'cause we usually smoke everybody anyway. I remember before the game started, the dude that I had the fight with was telling his partners that he wanted to guard me. But it was more like he had to guard me. Anyway, we were up six to three and I got the ball and hit a twenty-footer for the seventh point. When I turned to run down the court, homeboy cold-cocked me in the back of the head and I just fell out on the black top." "So what you're telling, is that this individual knocked you in the head with his fist and you fell down on the court?" "That was how it started. But I couldn't go out like that, I got up and rushed homeboy and we was straight squabbin'. He got a couple punches in and I damn sho' got in mine." This kid sure was opening up to me now. His story appeared to be raw but yet sincere and he was more than likely telling the truth.

"So tell me Mr. Collins, what did you hear if anything once you and this other individual were engaged in battle?" "There was a lot of cheering from the fellas on the court, I remember. The cheering only lasted a short period of time, once that cop in the tower start yelling that he was going to shoot somebody unless we all hit the ground. I wasn't crazy; I hit the ground real quick. But I did sock homeboy one more time before I hit the ground."

"When did you first notice there was some action at the weight-pile," I said. "I never did. The first time I heard about the murder was two days after being locked down. I overheard some officers talkin' about it." Hmm, this is real interesting I thought to myself. If what Collins was telling me was true, he was possibly used as a pawn in this situation.

"Thanks a bunch Collins, that will be it for now." Mulberry gestured to Collins to stand up and they both exited the room.

Why would Dixon hit Collins for no reason? This was looking more and more like a set-up, which diverted attention from the weight-pile. If I could make the connection between Dixon and any of the black inmates in the area of the weight-pile in question, this would more than likely lead to the murderer. Something told me that I was getting close to solving this case. Murderers can run, but they can't hide. Especially when the fact remains that the murderer was still present with us here on the yard behind bars and barbwire. There had been no escapes lately to my knowledge. The bottom line remained that the individual who inflicted death on another human being was still lurking amongst us.

The fuzzy sound of a two-way radio could be heard clearly from the hallway in front of my office. I could hear Mulberry giving clear instructions on how to enter my office. I was anxious to meet the character that held the key to my many unanswered questions.

Officer Mulberry and Ken Dixon walked slowly into my office. For some reason, I expected to see a tall, rough-looking young man. Much to my surprise, Ken Dixon is approximately 5 feet nine inches and clean cut. His honey colored skin is smooth and his hair is neatly groomed into a short style. As he entered the room he did not exhibit any facial expression.

"I need to know your prison number, Mr. Dixon," I said.

"V-57663," he expressed in a low tone. I could see now that I was going to have to pry any answers out of this guy. My job was supposed to be getting easier in my last few days.

"Mr. Dixon, it's late, Officer Mulberry is working beyond his scheduled hours, and personally I'm tired and I want to go home." Dixon didn't move a muscle and appeared to be less than enthused with my comments. "Listen Dixon, I'm going to cut straight to the chase. Why were you fighting on the basketball court?" Dixon smirked and rolled his large light-brown eyes.

"Things happen when people are involved in a heated game. Dude kept putting his hands on my body. I guess he called his self hand-checking me and I told him I didn't play that mess." "So that's why you hit him?" "He's the one who pushed off after taking a shot at me. I had already warned his young-ass that he was gonna get stole-on if he put his hands on me,"

Dixon said angrily. Maybe if I just put my hands around his throat for about two minutes, maybe he would tell me the truth. Just a thought.

"Basketball can be a pretty rough sport but murder is even tougher," I said sternly. Dixon began to rub his hands together in a rapid manner. This guy just might have a conscience after all.

"Do you realize that someone was conveniently murdered at the time you were having your basketball altercation?"

"No."

"You sure?"

"Yeah man."

"Don't B.S. me, Dixon."

"Like I said, I don't know what you're talkin' about. I was on the court handling my business. It ain't my fault that somebody took advantage of the moment."

"I think you know more than what you're telling me, Dixon. Somebody used you to help murder another human being. If you're a part of this thing, I'm taking you down. The District Attorney's office will hear about you. Accessory to murder is a serious charge which carries substantial time."

"Do whatever you have to do, Lieutenant, I'm not mad at you," he snickered. This idiot was obviously hiding something. But, he wasn't willing to talk about it.

"Mr. Dixon, does the name Newton Black ring a bell?"

"Nope."

"Do you know a Tuck Williams?"

"Can't say I do."

"What about a Craig Battle?"

"Never heard of him."

Dixon undoubtedly felt that he was a smooth operator. He's smooth all right, he was going to be smoothed out of the little freedom that he used to have.

"Mulberry, take this inmate back to the Ad-Seg unit, we wouldn't want to keep him away from his new home. He is to remain in the lock down unit until this murder issue is resolved."

Dixon's smile quickly turned to a frown as Mulberry gestured to him to stand to his feet.

"Let's go Dixon," stated Mulberry. Dixon began to walk sluggishly towards the door. "This ain't right, you know y'all doggin' me!" he yelled. "I'll be glad to sit down and chat with you when you're ready to talk, Mr. Dixon. Have a nice evening."

The day was somewhat productive, but I couldn't wait until tomorrow.

Twenty

The alarm clock startled me as I jumped out of bed to flick it off. Coco was fast asleep at the foot of the bed and didn't seem to be bothered at all by the noisy clock. It was good to know that somebody in this house had some peace of mind.

I reached over and grabbed my wife's picture off the nightstand and pressed my lips against the framed glass, providing her with a morning kiss. Some mornings I miss her more than others. She was my whole world and I wish she were still here. The only reason that I push forward in my endeavors are because that's what she would want me to do for our daughters and myself.

I slipped on my brown suede slippers, grabbed my burgundy robe, which Coco happened to be nestled on, and headed for the bathroom.

As I stood in front of the bathroom mirror, I realized that I hadn't taken a serious look at myself in weeks. Don't get me wrong, I do brush my teeth, wash my face, and shave on a daily basis. But, sometimes people don't take the time to look at the man in the mirror. The mirror told me that I was weary and tired. The mirror also told me that it was time to take care of myself and move on to the next level with my life. I no longer wanted to fight against the mirror. I planned to retire on time as scheduled. If the murder case was not resolved prior to my retirement, then so be it.

For the first time in several days, I finally felt relieved. As I walked into the barbed-wire gates of the prison, I felt no pressure. A large security gate slammed behind me as I headed towards the "D" yard. Several officers greeted me as I continued on towards the plaza gate. The officer that is usually present at the "D" yard plaza gate is Officer Garcia. Once I reached the entrance to the "D" yard, Officer Garcia emerged from the guard shack with keys in hand. "Good morning T.P.," he said in a chipper fashion. "Good morning to you too, Officer Garcia. Would you agree that it's a lovely day?" Garcia nodded his head. "I'm just glad to be at work, sir." Garcia opened the plaza gate and I began my long stroll across the yard.

Much to my surprise, there were several officers present on the weight-pile. The majority of them appeared to be dressed in black jumpsuits. There was digging, spikes swinging, and metal detectors. The sight was impressive, to say the least. Officer Mulberry appeared to have the situation in control. As I approached the weight-pile, Sergeant Little turned around and waved at me. Sometimes I wondered if he was still assisting me with this case. I had not received any updated reports from him in the last few days. He was going to burn the midnight oil on this case whether he liked it or not. Mulberry had been the key individual in assisting me in this matter. Sergeant Little seemed to want to supervise the inmate culinary feeding procedures more than necessary. He should be officially named the head food tasting inspector. "As you can see, T.P., the search is in full swing." I would like it better if you were actually in the weight-pile assisting officers with the search, I thought to myself. "Yeah, looks like Mulberry has them all humping," I said with a bit of sarcasm. "Oh yeah, we got'em going good. I'm telling you Lieutenant if there's something there we'll find it," stated Sergeant Little with a gleam of confidence. "I want something found, Sergeant, and I want it found today. I want every piece of dirt and sand examined. An empty hand is something I don't want to see today." Sergeant Little pulled a king-size Snickers bar from his left front pocket and unwrapped it. "You have my word T.P., we're going to find the murder weapon," he groaned as he bit into the candy bar.

In the confines of my meager office, I flopped myself down in my office chair and removed some documents from my center drawer. These particular forms were past due in accordance with my own time frame. The State of California should waive the six thousand hours required for my private investigators license due to my peace officer status. Today was the day to complete all of the important forms that I was delinquent on. This should take my mind off the specific tasks being conducted on the investigation. I carefully placed all the documents across my desk from left to right in the order of importance and urgency. I removed my pager from my leather belt and set the alarm for twelve noon. Quite frankly, I didn't want to be bothered by anyone until possibly lunchtime. It was about time that I took a break from this madness.

Just as I nestled my backside comfortably into my office chair, Officer Blue appeared at my door. "Come-on in Blue," I instructed. "Pull up that chair over there and have a seat." Blue picked up the metal folding chair and placed it in front of my desk. "I apologize for not calling you, sir, but this is something I think you need to be told in person. With all of the commotion going on the weight-pile, I felt that this would be a good time to sneak over and speak with you."

"What's on your mind, Blue?" Blue reached over and handed me a 1-15. This form is used to document wrongdoings and disciplinary problems committed by inmates. "I wrote this report last night while working overtime. This youngster in the report was busted with a small roach." "Steven Potts, hmm. Was there any evidence that he actually smoked the marijuana and if so, was a urine sample taken?" "No sir." "Was a presumptive test performed to confirm that the material was marijuana and not a warned down cigarette?" "No sir." "Well why are you handing me this report and you haven't even followed through on..." "Sir I think there's something you need to know first," he said mildly. "The floor's yours, Blue, I'm listening." "First of all, while I was conducting a routine pat-down of this kid, I discovered the roach in his right front pocket. He claimed that the denim jeans he had on belonged to someone else but he knew he couldn't prove it. I proceeded to question him further and he was in obvious fear of being written-up. He's a first-termed and he's set to parole in two months."

I was trying to appear attentive to this roundabout situation that Blue was so set on presenting to me. I gestured to him with my hand for him to proceed with the story.

"This guy was visibly shaken-up concerning the situation. Within moments, he slowly whispered something to me." "What did he say, Blue?" "He said that he knew something about the murder. I asked him what murder, and he stated, 'The one that happened out there,' while gesturing with his head in the direction of the prison yard. I moved closer to him and placed my mouth near his left ear. I asked him who committed the murder. He said that he would answer my question if the disciplinary action was squashed and his safety was guaranteed."

This information was interesting to me, in light of the fact that I was desperate for answers. "Is he already in Ad-seg," I asked. "Yup, he's locked down as tight as a tuna can," said Blue. "Good, let's go see him right now."

Normally, I would have an inmate brought down to see me in my office, but when guys are under administrative segregation or in protective custody, I tend to see them in their cell if at all possible. My visit to the lock-down unit shouldn't place the young man in any obvious jeopardy. The inmates were accustomed to seeing my face in the Ad-seg unit.

As the electronic doors opened leading into the administrative segregation unit, the usual volume of noise could be heard throughout the building. An obvious glare from a mirror held by an inmate reflected brightly in my direction. It is not uncommon for inmates to hold mirrors or pieces of mirrored glass sideways from their cells in an attempt to see the officers or medical staff that walk the tier.

Officer Blue and I headed to the unit office where we were greeted by four officers and a sergeant. Each officer was dressed in green fatigues accompanied by a protective vest. "Good morning all," I said in a cheerful manner. Everyone said hello in unison. "How can we help, Lieutenant?" said Sergeant Meeks. Sergeant Meeks is one of our newer sergeants. But according to the seven hash marks down his right arm shirt sleeve, each representing three years, and his head full of gray hair, I know for a fact that he's not new at this prison game. "Congratulations on your recent promotion." "Thank you Lieutenant. It's been a long time coming. I need to be retiring too," he said jokingly.

"I'll just be browsing around the unit, don't mind me," I said. "Our house is your house, Lieutenant, be our guest," offered Sergeant Meeks.

Officer Blue and I walked throughout the unit peering into the small, elongated windows present on the doors of each cell. Just in front of us, an inmate was quickly reeling in a fish line under his cell door. Fish lines are utilized by inmates to pass pencils, paper, toiletries, and even contraband. The fish lines are usually made out of some type of string or from a bed sheet that has been severed. These guys are so creative in their methods of survival within a prison facility. We didn't observe anything illegal attached to the fish line so we ignored it and continued to patrol the unit. We stopped at some of the cells only to chat with inmates whom I've known for a number of years on the yard. As we approached the cell that housed Steven Potts, Officer Blue began to walk briskly ahead of me. Once he reached the cell, he immediately placed his face against the glass window and looked inside. Inmate Potts was fast asleep. I took a quick glance, and immediately signaled to Officer Blue for us to leave the unit.

Neither one of us said anything else, until we were completely out of the unit. "What happened T.P., did you change your mind about this guy?" Blue asked. "Not at all Blue, I just decided to let the guy sleep. Furthermore, if he really knows something about the murder, I want to handle this situation with kid gloves." When I was a kid, my daddy would always say he'd handle important situations with kid gloves.

And as an adult, I tend to refer to a situation as being handled with kid gloves too, when the situation is of delicate importance.

As we crossed paths adjacent to the weight-pile, Sergeant Little and Officer Mulberry waved their hands to get our attention. We stopped walking as they came forward briskly in our direction. It appeared that most of the officers working within the weight-pile were taking a break as the majority of the digging had ceased. Either this was a good sign or it could be that the officers were working much too hard.

I could see that Officer Mulberry was holding something in his hand. I could surely use some good news. "The men recovered some items from the weight-pile, T.P.," said Officer Mulberry as he held up a brown paper bag. "I don't think it's anything that significant," mumbled Sergeant Little. Officer Mulberry uses his gloved hand to remove the items one by one from the bag. I removed a pair of rubber gloves from the small black pouch on my belt. After placing the gloves on my hands, I received the first item from Officer Mulberry. "Hmm, a filed down kitchen fork." All of the prongs had been removed except for one of the middle pieces. This single-sharpened prong could cause some serious injuries. There appeared to be some dried blood around the base of the one remaining prong. This is a typical weapon utilized in many prison-stabbing incidents. The next item he handed me appeared to be a kitchen spoon. Both sides of the rounded portion of the spoon were filed down flat, bringing the tip of the spoon to a sharp point. The object closely resembled the tip of an arrow. This weapon could also cause some serious damage. The next item appeared to be a hard piece of plastic approximately four to five inches in length. There was surgical tape wrapped around one of the ends. The object was pink in color and appeared to be shaved on all sides with one end sharpened to a fine point. It could be a comb, a toothbrush, ink pen or some other unfamiliar item. The last item handed to me by Officer Mulberry appeared to be a long, narrow metal object approximately five to six inches long. It was approximately a quarter-inch in diameter, and sharpened to a fine point. There also appeared to be dried fragments of blood present. "That item was discovered in the immediate vicinity of where Newton Black's body was found. It was buried about five or six inches beneath the sand."

I was pleased that these items had been discovered, but I wouldn't get my hopes too high just yet. There's no telling how long these items had been buried within the weight-pile.

"Should we have the work crew break for lunch or should we call it a day and cease the search?" said Sergeant Little. Breaking for lunch would be the obvious game plan on Sergeant Little's mind. I felt that Officer Mulberry would be the ideal person to answer that question. "What is your assessment of the search at this point, Mulberry?" "The crew has literally combed every inch of the weight-pile. Practically every grain of sand has been picked, tossed, and turned. I feel that the search has been quite thorough. There were some other spoons and forks discovered, but none of them have been altered in any manner such as the items in front of you."

It amazes me that the silverware count clears each day with the amount of forks and spoons hidden in the weight-pile. Normally, the procedures deem that the yard does not open for recreation until the silverware count is accurate. When the silverware count is allowed to clear each day with one or two pieces missing, the results are what had been found today in the weight-pile.

"Good job men," I said with a smile as I handed the items back to Officer Mulberry. "Sergeant, wrap up the search project and prepare the yard for food procedures. Let's try to have the first housing unit reporting for lunch within one hour." Sergeant Little nodded his head in agreement and turned and walked back to the weight-pile. "Thanks a lot Blue, for that information, we'll interview him later." "No problem T.P., I'll go back to my unit and prepare for feeding." "Mulberry, I need you to come with me to my office."

As we entered my office I noticed a pile of C-files on my desk. I presumed that Ethel must have left them there. A yellow post-it note confirmed my suspicions. This day was getting better and better. "Ethel Williams, from the records office left these C-files. I need you to read each of the probation reports and see if you come across the name of Ken Dixon." "Isn't he one of the guys who was involved in that fight on the basketball court?" I handed Officer Mulberry the files. "Yes, he's the one. I've got to know if he had any past relationship with any of the inmates we interviewed last week." Mulberry opened one of the files and began to read. "I'm here at your service, Lieutenant." "While you're doing that, I'll call Dr. Bishop to schedule an appointment to have these shanks (prison knives) analyzed."

"One of these days they'll get some decent phones in this joint. These buttons are always sticking," I said while pushing the buttons. Mulberry nodded his head in agreement as he continued to flip through the various pages of one of the C-files.

"May I speak with Dr. Bishop," I petitioned. The individual on the phone informed me that Dr. Bishop was not in the office, as usual. "I'm Lieutenant Price, with the Department of Corrections. Could you please let him know that I will be sending over some items by courier for him to analyze?" He agreed to deliver the message to Dr. Bishop.

"Any luck so far, Mulberry?" "No T.P., but this material does rate for interesting reading," he said with amusement.

I was pleased that Mulberry had the patience and stamina to deal with the search for information. Most people don't have the skills necessary to conduct a thorough investigation. Unfortunately, a prison setting is not the most exciting place to conduct an investigation. It's a boring, limited, void-of-color, cement-encased city of destruction. Meaning, the possibility of destruction exists daily, both physically and spiritually. People who work in a setting such as this always change in some form or fashion whether they choose to or not. It's definitely a life-changing experience, either for good or bad.

"Is there a reason why you didn't have Ethel pull the Ken Dixon file," he murmured. Quite honestly, I never even thought about pulling the C-file on this character. I was so caught up in finding out if his name appeared in any of these other individual's files. "You know something Mulberry, that's a very good question which I don't have an answer for. It couldn't hurt one bit to see what this guy is all about. Thank you for that suggestion."

I picked up the phone once again and began pressing the sticking buttons. "Hello Ethel, this is Lieutenant Price." I took a brief pause to allow for her to respond. "First of all, I want to thank you for pulling those files and having them sent here right-away." I took a brief pause once again. "You delivered them yourself, well God bless you even more." I could tell from her conversation that she was really happy that I was pleased with her assistance. "I hate to bother you Ethel, but I was wondering if you could do me just one more little favor." She agreed without hesitation. "Would it be possible for you to pull a file on a Ken Dixon, prison number V57663, within the next fifteen minutes?" She agreed once more. "You'll do it in five minutes, great, I'll be right over."

I slammed down the phone and headed for the door. "I'll be back shortly, I'm headed to the administration building as you probably overheard." "No problem T.P., I'll hold down the fort."

Upon entering Ethel's work area, I could clearly hear that she was involved in an ongoing phone conversation. At her desk, I could see that she was taking some notes. She was fashionably dressed in what appeared to be a gold and black pants suit. I was unable to see her entire outfit as she was seated behind her desk. She displayed her familiar signature smile just as she hung up the phone. "I told you five minutes Lieutenant, and it's only been four." "Oh, oh, oh, I'm sorry Ethel." She smiled once again. "Just kidding Lieutenant, I've got your file right here. I'm sure that you're interested in the probation report, so I've already turned to it and placed a paper clip there. I'm not trying to take over your investigation or anything of that nature, Lieutenant, but I saw a name in the report that you might be interested in." I must admit that she had my undivided attention. "And what might that name be?" I said with eagerness. She reached for the file, which was placed on the upper left corner of her desk. She carefully flipped through a couple of pages and moved the file slowly across the desk in my direction. She gently pointed at the contents on the page and moved in closer to get a better look.

"Oh my God," I yelled with sheer disbelief. This is definitely the break I've been looking for. "Craig Battle, the brother that gives attitude a bad name." "So, if my thinking is correct, he's the guy that you went to visit in county jail?" "That's right." "Correct me if I'm wrong, Lieutenant, isn't he good friends with Tuck Williams, your prime suspect?" "Bingo, pay the lady. You're absolutely right Ethel." This woman is sharper than a blade cuttin' butter. "Thank you so much Ethel, I don't know what I would do without you." I hoped that wasn't out of line; she took it exactly the way I meant it.

I dashed out of the administration building and walked briskly all the way to my office.

Things were happening fast and I couldn't stop the rhythm now. I'd decided to interview all the major players again. But first, I had to see exactly what Steven Potts knew about Tuck Williams.

Just as I entered my office, Mulberry abruptly lifted his face up from one of the files. "Did you have any luck T.P.?" "Luck isn't the word for it, Mulberry, we've hit a potential gold-mine. Ken Dixon was involved in a drug transaction with our favorite menace to society, Craig Battle. It seems that they both grew up in the same neighborhood. Of course this means that a Tuck Williams connection is evident." "Good work T.P., so where do we go from here?" Mulberry slammed the file shut and stood at attention. "First, we get Steven Potts in my office. Sleep is not a luxury I care about today. In other words, wake his butt up and get him down here. After I speak with him, I want Corky Price, Todd Henderson, Bobby Nelson, Ronnie Phillips and finally the man himself, Tuck Williams."

"The whole Tuck gang, hmm T.P., I'll have the first client here in ten minutes." "Thank you Mulberry, you've been a priceless assistant."

Before Mulberry returned with Steven Potts, I really felt that I should pray for wisdom and understanding in this matter. So many of my prayers had been answered in this one day, and I really needed to keep everything in the proper perspective. I closed my office door, walked over to my desk and kneeled beside it.

"Precious Lord in heaven, I come before you asking for your guidance and wisdom. Lord, you know the individuals involved in this matter, 'cause you created them, Lord. You know their hearts as well as their minds. Only you know beyond a shadow of a doubt who the killer is, Lord. I'm asking that you would soften the hearts of the parties involved, and allow them to be honest concerning this matter. Give me the insight to gather information and apply it in the manner necessary to capture this killer. The evidence appears to be pointing in one direction, Lord. Please make my investigative path crystal clear. In Jesus' name I pray, Amen."

Just as I got up from my knees, I could clearly hear Officer Mulberry providing Steven Potts with verbal instructions. This kid isn't bigger than a minute. He's about five-five, candy-cane style braided hair. His pants sag and his shirt is creased neatly in several locations. There is not a wisp of hair on his face except for his eyebrows.

"I presume that you are Steven Potts," I said in a stern manner. He appeared to cringe in fear. "Yes sir, that's my name." "I understand that you have some information that we could possibly use to assist us in our investigation of the Newton Black murder." The kid still appeared to be nervous, as he twiddled his fingers. "What guarantees do I have that nobody is gonna kill me for talking with you guys?" My first inclination was to inform the young man that one of the drawbacks of coming to prison is that you face injury and murder on a daily basis. "Let me tell you something, young man, you know as well as I do that we can walk on this yard on any given occasion and possibly be attacked. Personally, I don't believe that you are in any danger. It's procedure for us to question inmates once they are placed in Ad-seg and are under investigation for a serious violation. Now unless you have mentioned to anyone else what you're about to tell us, I don't think you have anything to fear beyond the normal woes of prison." "And what about this bogus dope charge against me, what am I going to do...?" "...listen Potts, I'll see what I can do about the violation, since it doesn't seem to be that serious. Also, the information and evidence contained within the report is somewhat circumstantial." Inmate Potts gave me a smile. "All I want is to be released on time so I can go home. You won't ever have to worry about seeing my butt ever again in this place."

Twenty-One

Precious time was slowly passing, and it was now time to get down to the business at hand. "What exactly did you hear pertaining to the murder of Newton Black?" I opened my notepad and pulled out an ink pen from my inner coat pocket. "It happened about a month ago, while I was in the culinary eating dinner. Tuck Williams was sitting at a table right by mine with his boys." "What boys are you speaking about?" "Everybody knows the brothas that hang out with Tuck, but I just know them by their nicknames. It was Coke, Boo, C-Dog, Ronnie P., and some other guy that I didn't know." "Describe the guy that you didn't know," I beckoned softly. "He was someone that didn't really fit in with them guys. He looked cleaner cut. He didn't really look like a gangster type." Could this guy be describing Ken Dixon?

I immediately looked for the Ken Dixon file. Once I retrieved the file from my stack of files on my desk, I thumbed through the contents in search of a photograph. After a brief period of time, I came across a black and white mug shot. Inmate Dixon looked a bit different from his current appearance. I removed the photo and showed it to Inmate Potts. "Does this appear to be the individual you described in the culinary?" Inmate

Potts pondered over the photograph for a moment before speaking. "Well, it looks a lot like the guy, but his hair was shorter and he didn't have a mustache." Meanwhile, Officer Mulberry was looking through some items that he had removed from his shirt pocket just as I presented the photograph to Potts. "I was just curious, Mr. Potts, if this was the guy you saw." I accepted the photograph from Potts and placed it back into the file. Just as I closed Dixon's file, Mulberry held up a small piece of paper. "I've got something you might want to see, Lieutenant," announced Mulberry. Mulberry walked over and handed me what appeared to be a small colored photograph. "Thank you Officer Mulberry," I said graciously. "Why don't you take a look at this photograph Mr. Potts." Inmate Potts leaned over and took a quick glance at the photograph. "Yeah man, that's him," shouted Potts.

This was real interesting; at least this confirmed that Tuck Williams and Ken Dixon did keep company with one another on a minimal basis. Who knows, they could have been planning the basketball court distraction during that culinary meeting.

"So why don't you tell me what you heard that day in the culinary," I instructed Inmate Potts. "The culinary was very noisy like always. I had been sitting with my cellmate for about twenty minutes before he got up and went out to the yard. I wanted to finish eating my pudding. I remember it was chocolate. We rarely get pudding, not to mention chocolate, so I had to get my grub on. Anyway, while I was eating my pudding, Tuck and his boys were laughing real loud. But, after a few seconds they were real quiet. At this point I heard Tuck say, 'I'm gonna kill that black bastard when I get my chance. Black, black, get it?' Then they all started laughing real loud once again. I got up and took my tray up to be washed. I was pissed-off, cause I didn't get to finish my pudding. But like I said, I don't think that they suspect I heard anything. After I dropped my tray in the kitchen slot to be washed, I looked back over towards their table and none of them were looking at me. I thought that was a good sign, don't you Lieutenant?"

The kid caught me off guard; I wasn't really expecting his question. "Oh yeah, you're right, they probably didn't suspect a thing. One more question Mr. Potts, are you sure that Tuck Williams was the person at the table who made the comment in question?" "I'm positive Lieutenant, because just at the moment when I got up to take up my dirty tray, I took a quick glance at Tuck while he was speaking." "Thank you so much for your cooperation and for your help, Mr. Potts."

Mr. Potts got up from his seat, smiled and walked out of my office with Officer Mulberry.

I sat idle awaiting the Tuck Williams' clan who were about to be interviewed. As I sat quietly in my office, I made a conscious decision to re-interview everyone in the group except for Tuck Williams. My hopes were that all of his boys would run back to him with different reports of how they had been questioned.

The door was pushed fully open and Mulberry escorted Todd Henderson, A.K.A. Boo, into the room. He was smiling, which I didn't understand for a guy who is in prison and also a murder suspect.

"Have a seat Mr. Henderson, I'll be with you in one second." Inmate Henderson continued to display his devilish grin. Officer Mulberry retired to a nearby corner and awaited the start of the interview. I opened my desk drawer and got out a brand new writing pad to begin this portion of the interviews. I was about to interview all of the key players in this situation for the second time and I knew I needed to document every detail.

"Mr. Henderson, I want to be straight forward with you and I'm hoping you'll be the same with me. On the last occasion that I interviewed you, I asked you questions concerning Newton Black. As you know, Mr. Black was murdered almost two weeks ago. I gather from our last conversation that you did not murder Newton Black?" Inmate Henderson appeared to be a tad bit more serious now as he quickly erased his smile. "Naw, naw, Lieutenant, I didn't kill nobody." "That's great Mr. Henderson, but I think you know who did…" "…say what, I don't know nothin'!"

"You do realize that if you're holding back any information pertaining to this case you'll go down just as well. Twenty, thirty, forty years in prison or even life, that's what you would be facing, Mr. Henderson." "Look Lieutenant, I swear to you that I don't know anything." "What if I told you that Tuck Williams is the murderer, would you believe that Mr. Henderson?" "Hmm, hmm…" "Is your memory coming back to you now, Mr. Henderson," I shouted. Henderson appeared visibly shaken, his face was puffy and he cringed. "I'm telling the truth Lieutenant, you've got to believe me." "I don't have to believe anything you say, young man, I'm in charge here. Get him out of here Mulberry, and bring me the next clown."

Inmate Henderson huddled into himself as like a wounded teddy bear and shuffled slowly out of my office.

My motives were genuine but my method with Inmate Henderson was definitely artificial. I didn't mean to be harsh on the guy, but different methods work on different people. I must admit that I did believe that he really didn't know anything about the murder.

Only ten minutes had passed before Officer Mulberry finally arrived with Bobby Nelson. The tactic I just utilized on Inmate Henderson would probably be ineffective on Bobby Nelson. He is a streetwise hoodlum who fears no one in authority.

The guy's muscles appeared to flex with every slight move that his body made. I'm sure he's probably intimidated many people in his day with his muscles.

"So we meet again, Mr. Nelson." He nodded his head in a less than enthusiastic manner. "You refused to speak during our last contact, Mr. Nelson, but I felt the need to provide you with one more opportunity. I think your boy Tuck Williams killed Newton Black. I also think that you know all about it, but you're concealing the truth." Nelson snickered under his breath as he gazed up towards the ceiling. "I realize that prison has never scared you in the least, but I'm going to try my best to make it your permanent home if I can." Nelson guided his eyes in my direction attempting to intimidate me, "mad dog" effect. "Mr. Nelson, let me tell you something, I've dealt with murderers, rapists, child molesters, and major drug dealers for over thirty years. I've been in the middle of several prison riots, and I've been threatened with many weapons. My advice to you today, sir, is to affix your eyes on something or somebody who really worries about intimidation. I'm not saying that you're doing that, but I just thought I should give you a friendly warning." Nelson quickly adjusted his focal point and looked away. "Yeah, whatever you say." "Now that I have your undivided attention, Mr. Nelson, I'm going to give you one last opportunity to tell me what you know about the Newton Black murder or risk living in prison with Tuck Williams until you die." "Look man, I don't know nothing about no murder, and I don't have nothing to say to you."

"You have a nice day, Mr. Nelson, I'm sure we'll be talking again in the future." Inmate Nelson did not display any emotion as he exited my office.

This job doesn't get any easier after twenty-nine years. There was a time when I used to just go with the flow and allow things to happen. I'm too old for those tactics now. I've got to make things happen or they won't happen. Just two more guys to speak with and I'll be finished. Either these guys really didn't know anything, or they were all going out on a limb to protect this clown. I understand prison loyalty with the homeboys, but to risk being an accessory in a matter such as this is crazy.

Just as I gathered my thoughts together, Sergeant Little walked into my office. "The chow is ready T.P., I just wanted to make sure with you that the weight-pile is clear to your satisfaction before we let our hotel guests out of their lovely suites." This man had never delayed feeding on my account unless I had given prior orders to him to change the time. I was shocked. I guess the saying is true that you're never too old to learn something. Maybe by the time I leave Sergeant Little will become a top notch supervisor. "Lieutenant, do you have anymore of that red licorice?" Of course what I just said was wishful thinking. This man must be crazy asking for my private stash. I love licorice. "To address your first concern, Sergeant, you can go ahead and begin sending the housing units to the culinary to eat in about ten minutes. I need to make sure that Mulberry brings me the guys I need to interview before you start feeding. Matter of fact, why don't you sit in on the next interview while Mulberry goes to get the last guy. And as soon as the last guy gets here, you can go ahead and commence with feeding." "Whatever you say T.P., I'm at your service." "Here, you can take the licorice with you," I said while handing him the package.

Inmate Ronnie Phillips strutted into my office as though he were sauntering down a runway as a fashion model. It's no secret that he is known as the pretty boy on the yard.
"I see that you're in a good mood today, Mr. Phillips." "If I complained who would listen, Lieutenant, I'm in prison, remember." "You make a valid point, Mr. Phillips." Inmate Phillips rewarded himself by clapping his hands together lightly and smiling as he sat down in the chair in front of my desk. "Tell me something, Mr. Phillips, how much more time do you have to serve in this joint before you're released?"
"Just two more years and I'm out of this camp." "That's great news. So, I imagine you wouldn't want anything to spoil that happy day, would you?" He folded his arms together while displaying a puzzled expression. "Of course not Lieutenant, nobody wants to stay in a nasty, stinky, hellhole like this a minute longer then their scheduled release date." "Good, good, it appears that we understand each other clearly, Mr. Phillips. Please don't take this as a threat, but if you don't tell me what I need to know about Tuck Williams or if I find out that you are in any way connected to the murder of Newton Black, instead of getting out of here in two years, it will be more like twenty." Inmate Phillips was clearly demonstrating anger. "Why you sweatin' me like this, Lieutenant? You weren't trippin' with me last time you talked to me about this murder crap." "That was

then, and this is now. The stakes are much higher now, Mr. Phillips." I do believe from Inmate Phillips' reaction that I got my point across.

"Have you ever had occasion to hear Tuck Williams threaten to kill or do physical harm to Newton Black in your presence?" "Tuck said a lot of things and it was a lot of people he didn't care for. But, I honestly can't recall any specific moment where he actually threatened to do harm to Newton, whatever his last name is." This guy was slightly difficult to read, but he appeared to be telling the truth. "What is your main purpose for hanging around a character such as Tuck Williams?" "Everybody has homeboys on the yard, Tuck and the rest of the fellas just happen to be the ones I hook up with most of the time. I do know other people of course." "I think that your homeboy Tuck, killed Newton Black. I also think that you and your other homeboys know something about the murder. I want to leave this message with you before you go, Mr. Phillips, somebody is going down for this terrible crime and I won't rest until they do."

"I see that you're getting tough in your pre-retirement days," chuckled Sergeant Little. Undoubtedly, Sergeant Little hasn't conducted too many murder investigations in his career. At first I wanted to ignore his comment, but then I decided that no one is too old to learn what they don't obviously know.

"Sergeant, haven't you ever heard the words interrogation, strategy, psychology? I was just fishing with a scenario, it's his job to make it truthful, not mine. My job is to shake a suspect to the point of breaking. A suspect breaks, and we, for all intents and purposes, refer to that as being busted."

"You know I was just kidding T.P., I like your style." In walked Mulberry with Corky Price, A.K.A. Coke. "If you don't mind T.P., I'm going to head back to the culinary and await clearance for feeding," requested Sergeant Little. "Be my guest Sergeant, I'll radio you when we're prepared to commence with feeding." Sergeant Little exited the office and Officer Mulberry directed Inmate Price to the chair in front of my desk.

The last time that Inmate Price and myself parted company, I was praying to God that we weren't related. I'm sure that it's just a coincidence;

thousands of people in the world have the last name of Price. "This pains me just as much as I'm sure it pains you, Mr. Price, to have you back in my office. I have some unfinished business to take care of and I feel that I cannot complete that business without your assistance." So far, Inmate Price didn't seem to be as vocal as he was during our previous meeting.

"Assistance, what do you mean by that? I'm not into being a flunky for the police." "I'm not asking for you to sell your soul or anyone else's. I am simply wanting some questions answered concerning the Newton Black murder." "I thought I answered all your questions concerning that Newton Black individual." I sensed some hostility coming from Mr. Price. "You're absolutely right, Mr. Price, you did answer my questions concerning Mr. Black. But, today is a new day and new days bring new concerns. Today I need to focus on Mr. Tuck Williams." Inmate Price squirmed in the chair. "What does Tuck have to do with anything?" "That's exactly what I need to know from you, Mr. Price. It's no secret that you and Tuck Williams are part of the same click. I think you're one of his flunky soldiers." "I ain't nobody's flunky," Price said angrily. This was my opportunity to play on his emotions. "That's not what I heard. Matter of fact, I was told that Tuck tells you guys when to eat, sleep, and take a…" "…you trippin' man, ain't nobody told you no bull-shi…" "…watch your mouth in my office, young man. You can do all that cursing on the yard, but don't do it in here." Price was visibly shaken as his jaw ground his teeth.

"Like I said before, I don't know nothin' about no murder."

"So you deny being in the weight-pile with Tuck and the rest of the clan on the day of the murder?" "I didn't say that. All I said is that I don't know who killed homeboy and I couldn't care less."

"You do realize that if you are found to have any connection to Tuck or any of your other homeboys that may have committed the murder, you're going down too. Twenty-five years to life would be my guess." "I'm not concerned with that, because I know I didn't do anything. Furthermore, the threat of time has never scared me, I can do it standing on my head."

"Well, you just might get that opportunity if I happen to connect you to the murder." "Sorry Lieutenant, there's nothing to tell."

A true soldier never tells. It's quite possible that Inmate Price and some of the other guys were covering for Tuck Williams or for each other. After twenty-plus years in this system, it still amazes me that individuals are willing to relinquish their innocence and freedom for one another.

"Well Mr. Price, if you don't have any information for me, you're free to go." Officer Mulberry instructed Inmate Price to stand to his feet and exit the office. "Mulberry, Mr. Price can escort himself back to his unit." Price left the office.

"What was that all about, T.P.?" "I just wanted Mr. Tough Guy to have something to think about as he walks by himself to his unit. Who knows, maybe he knows something, or maybe he doesn't."

The telephone rang just as Officer Mulberry attempted to ask me a question. "Hold that thought while I take this call."

This ancient phone has got to go, I thought to myself as I picked up the receiver. "Hello, Lieutenant Price speaking," I said in a cheerful manner. "This is a pleasant surprise to hear from you, Dr. Bishop." Doctor Bishop has just informed me that he would be in town and wanted to meet with me at the local Sheriff's station. "One-thirty sounds fine with me, Doctor. I'll meet you in the front lobby."

My work schedule was very busy to say the least, so I hoped the doctor had some information worth my while.

"What were you going to ask me before I picked up the telephone?" "I was going to ask you about Tuck Williams. Have you decided if you are going to interview him again?"

"Let's put it off until I get back. Doctor Bishop said that he was going to be in the area on business and wants to meet with me at the Sheriff's station. In the meantime, I need you to go over to the culinary and let Sergeant Little know that he can begin feeding procedures. Keep an eye on Tuck Williams, I'm sure his boys are going to break the news to him that he's on the hot seat."

Twenty-Two

The noontime hour was in full swing as I arrived at the Sheriff's station. I parked my car in front of the beige-bricked, one-story building and walked towards the tinted, double-glass doors. I pushed open one of the doors that was clearly marked "Sheriff" in yellow paint. Doctor Bishop was standing by the reception window that is adjacent to the front door. He turned around and saw me, and began to walk in my direction. His brown wing-tipped shoes clicked loudly against the linoleum floor. He was dressed in a two-piece tan suit that had to be at least thirty years old.

"Glad to see you made it, Lieutenant," stated Dr. Bishop. We both smiled and shook hands. "You're a busy man, so I figured that it must be something important or you wouldn't have called me."

"I'll let you be the judge of that, Lieutenant. Quiet as it's kept, I cherish these rare moments during my workweek when I get to do business with live bodies. You are alive, right, ha, ha, ha?" he pointed his index finger in my direction. "As far as I know, I'm alive." Doctor Bishop is always full of jokes. This man is unbelievably jovial, to be involved in such an occupation. I would imagine that a good sense of humor would be beneficial while working with the dead.

"We can meet right here in the lobby if you don't mind, since I only have a couple minutes to spare," said Dr. Bishop.

"Let's do it Doc, I'm ready to talk." He pointed towards two chairs covered with orange-vinyl material and we both took a seat. "Well Lieutenant, I took the initiative and got those items analyzed that you recovered from the weight-pile. As you know, a couple of the pieces were filed-down silverware. There was no blood at all present on those items. The thin, pink plastic item did have some blood present on it, but I knew that last week."

"Why didn't you tell me this information last week?" Doctor Bishop just sat silent. "I always thought that a metal object caused the murder." "I never once told you that the murder weapon was necessarily metal, and furthermore, you didn't ask."

"Well, tell me this, Doctor, is the plastic item still an assumption or do we have something." Doctor Bishop removed a green paper document from his inner coat pocket. "This document clearly states that the blood and DNA found on the pink item belongs to Newton Black."

The biggest break-through of my career had just unfolded before my eyes. The blood of the victim was confirmed by the DNA analysis. The murder weapon was a pink plastic item, possibly a comb, or toothbrush. From this day forward, the investigation would now take on a different light. I knew my work was now cutout for me, so I thanked Dr. Bishop for his work and information and I rushed back to the prison.

The time was approximately 3 p.m., and the prison yard was full of restless inmates. I rushed across the yard headed for my office. Sergeant Little, Officer Mulberry, and Officer Jones were all standing in front of the entrance of the culinary. I motioned with my right hand for the men to meet me in my office.

Upon entering my office I waited patiently for the men to arrive. Within my mind, I was attempting to formulate a game plan we could utilize to connect clues to the new evidence in question.

"Come on in gentlemen," I said softly. Sergeant Little made himself comfortable as he sat in one of the metal chairs placed in front of my desk. Officer Jones followed suit and sat in the other metal chair. Officer Mulberry stood in a military fashion, positioned in his usual corner. "Due to the time factor and the urgency of the matter, I'll get right to the point. Today I met with Dr. Bishop, and he revealed some very crucial evidence concerning the murder investigation. Traces of Newton Black's blood were discovered on the pink plastic object which was found in the weight-pile."

I took a moment to reflect, as all the gentlemen stared in my direction. I remembered stating on several occasions that we needed to dispose of all of the silverware and metal trays just as many other state prisons have done. There was never any doubt in my mind that a metal object had caused the murder of Newton Black. My embarrassment was apparent; no non-metal object had ever been my focus of attention. In my many years in the department, I've witnessed various items and objects that have been used to injure, maim, and murder. Some of the items were strange to say the least and I was never surprised at the shape or size of the items. But, the damage done to Newton Black's chest cavity revealed injuries associated with a sharp-pointed metal object, in my expert opinion. Not to mention the fact that Dr. Bishop left me hanging for more than a week before informing me of the confirmed murder weapon. I must admit, gentlemen, I am shocked that this pink, plastic item is the weapon we've been looking for." I held up the clear plastic baggie, which the item was placed in, and positioned it toward the ceiling lights.

"Officer Jones, are there any pink, colored instruments utilized for cooking or any other function in the culinary?"

"There's nothing in my kitchen that's pink and looks like that. It sort-of looks like a small comb or a shaved toothbrush to me. But, we're in prison and who would ever think about having a pink brush or toothbrush in the joint." We all chuckled a bit.

"Mulberry, I need you to have all the P.I.A. (Prison Industry Authority) programs checked to see if any of them are involved in using any hard pink plastics." The Prison Industry Authority have a number of trade programs within the prison system. For example; dental technician training, carpentry, wood and metal shop, and other viable programs.

"Sergeant, I need you to go to the canteen and find out if any pink plastic items such as combs, hair brushes or toothbrushes are sold within the store inventory." Sergeant Little's eyes lit up as he shook his head in agreement. He'd be a big kid in a candy store, as soda pop, candy, potato chips, soup and cookies occupy the majority of the small facility. "You can count on me T.P., I'll definitely check it out from top to bottom."

"Please make sure that each of you report back to me by sundown with any information. Officer Jones, feel free to return back to the culinary to finish preparing dinner."

Once the men were out of my office and on their way to their destinations, I decided to follow-up on a hunch. My idea was to check the bed cards of all the men who were alleged as suspects in the investigation. Of course I was hoping to find something pink, if possible. The bed cards are kept in each housing unit and they usually contain the personal items belonging to an inmate.

As I entered the housing unit, Officer Blue immediately greeted me. "What's going on, Lieutenant?" he asked cheerfully.

"I know this may sound crazy, but I need to look at all of the bed cards of all the individuals involved in the murder investigation." Officer Blue expressed a look of curiosity as he reached down to open the gray file cabinet that housed the bed cards. "Sure T.P., I have them right here." Officer Blue pulled out the box of bed cards and placed them on his desk.

"Thanks Blue. Do you mind if I sit at your desk and go through the cards?" "Be my guest T.P., I hope you find what you're looking for."

I carefully went through the bed cards one by one. Nothing seemed to be out of the ordinary. Most of the individuals had deodorant, toothpaste, hair grease, combs, etc. Unfortunately, the bed card did not list the colors of the toothbrushes or combs. My hunch went down in defeat. "Thanks for your help, Blue. And I know this might sound crazy, but keep an eye out on the guys and if you see anyone using any pink personal items, let me know." "No problem T.P., I'll keep an eye out." We both chuckled a bit and I went on my way.

Just as I entered my office, I observed a note on my desk. The note was from Officer Mulberry, with information stating that there were no pink plastics found in the P.I.A. facilities or in the canteen. On this note, I'd retire to my home, I thought to myself. Tomorrow is a new day with new discoveries, I pray.

The sun set with an orange array of light, just as I pulled my vehicle into the driveway of my home. Coco gave me a warm greeting as I entered the front door. There was a pile of mail on the floor just inside the door. After the mailman drops the mail through the door slot, Coco stands guard over the valuable material. I imagine that if anyone touched the mail besides me, little Coco would probably maul the person.

I gathered the mail from the floor and thumbed through it briefly. Much to my surprise, there was a large beige envelope from the California Consumer Affairs Agency. I hoped that it was good news concerning my investigator's license. As I began to open the envelope, I saw the words "CONGRATULATIONS" in bold black letters. The letter stated that my investigator's license would be granted and the required six thousand hours would be waived due to my peace officer status.

I jumped up and down with excitement and Coco followed suit to share in my excitement. We both ran around the house until we were literally out of breath. We both hopped onto my bed and took a well deserved-rest.

The good news concerning my investigator's license had brought me face to face with reality. My official retirement date was less than two weeks away and I had yet to solve the Newton Black murder case. I was determined to pursue my dream as the owner of my own business, but it was tough to move on to the next step in my life without solving this last murder investigation. This situation was a tough period for me but somehow I always manage to push forward. I hoped that I would be able to go on with my life if for some reason I didn't solve the investigation before my scheduled departure.

My daughters and the rest of my family have been in my corner throughout the years and I didn't want to let them down either. All of them have always given me the utmost support and love during difficult periods in my life. My desire is to be the best support system I can be for my girls as they move further into adulthood. When I look at my daughters I see my late wife. They are just as beautiful and caring as she was.

Coco nestled her warm furry body against my lower left leg. I looked over my shoulder and reached for the small portrait of my wife above my headboard.

My God, she was such a beautiful woman both inside and out. If I had just one more opportunity to hug her close to me, God knows I would give everything I own to do so. It's been so tough at times to carry on without the person I loved more than life. Without the love and comfort of the Lord, there's no way I could go on. There is only so much emptiness in my life that can be filled by my daughters and the rest of my family. Lord knows there's nothing that compares with a good wife.

The phone rang and Coco jumped up and runs towards it as if she would answer if she could. After a couple of rings, I got up and answered the phone.

"Officer Blue, what a surprise. Are you calling from work or home?" Surprisingly, Officer Blue was calling me from the prison. He said that he had some important information to share with me. "Go right ahead, you have my undivided attention." Coco took a seat in the center portion of the bed as she looked directly in my eyes. As my head moved from side-to-side, Coco followed suit and moved her head from side-to-side as well.

"I can't believe this, who would have ever imagined that this piece of the puzzle would be practically right in front of our eyes." Officer Blue had an idea to do some research on his own. He contacted the officers in the R & R facility and had them check all the property cards for any pink items that may have been mailed into the prison. A written record is logged for all the items mailed into the prison for each individual inmate. Ironically, Officer Blue had just informed me that there was one pink item mailed into the prison. The item in question was a pink toothbrush. "Who does it belong to," I requested with genuine anticipation. My chin dropped down to my chest and I grabbed my forehead with my right hand.

"For some reason I'm not surprised but yet I never thought of him as being a true prime suspect," I said softly to Officer Blue. Officer Blue sensed that I was a bit puzzled over the situation. "Oh no, I'm not disappointed, I'm just shocked."

As precise as this evidence might appear, I knew that this didn't necessarily mean that this person murdered Newton Black.

"Here's the deal, I'm going to have Officer Mulberry escort this individual to my office in the morning for questioning. Please feel free to stop in for the festivities, I'm sure it'll be a real interesting meeting." Officer Blue said he wouldn't miss this meeting for the world.

Twenty-Three

The night dragged on as I finally got to retire to my bed. I was able to eat, wash dishes, feed Coco and read my bible after speaking with Officer Blue. My hope was that I didn't toss and turn all night in anticipation of confronting the possible assailant. Once I got on my knees and started praying, I petitioned the Lord for a swift end to a complex situation.

The morning arrived with a glimmer of sunshine as the bright rays trickled through my bedroom window. The birds were chirping in the backyard and Coco had probably gone outside through the doggie door to greet them. Breakfast was not a part of my agenda on this particular morning as I quickly showered, got dressed and headed out the door.

My drive to work was unusually quiet as I purposely kept the radio turned off. I must concentrate on the matter at hand as I might now have a new prime suspect. How could it be someone other than Tuck Williams, I thought out loud. Tuck hated Newton Black. He had a motive and an opportunity to commit the murder. Tuck's prison buddies were considered suspects initially but realistically I knew deep down inside that none of them had committed the murder, until now.

Upon my arrival at the prison my first inclination was to pay a visit to my mentor Captain Davenport.

Betty Wilkins greeted me as I entered the administration building. "Long time no see stranger," Betty stated with a large, gingerbread grin. "Please forgive me, Betty, I've really let this case do a number on me. But at the same time I've learned a valuable lesson." "And what might that be?" I extended my hand towards Betty's hand and she reached out to take hold of mine.

"Listen Betty, I know beyond a shadow of a doubt that there is nothing in this world more important than family. This case has taught me a lot. Trust me, I will be retiring as scheduled." "Now that's what I'm talkin' 'bout," Betty announced proudly. We both laughed and embraced momentarily. Betty is a good friend and co-worker whom I would miss. "I'll never forget all your years of assistance, Betty." "You're just retiring, you're not going off to live on a remote island." We both laughed once again.

"I don't mean to change the subject, but have you seen Captain Davenport this morning?" "No I haven't seen him this morning and I've been here since seven-thirty." I removed a small notepad and a pen from my pocket and began to jot down some information. "Betty, can you please do me a favor and give this note to the Captain when he gets here?" Betty nodded her head in agreement and took the note.

"Have a great day Betty, and thanks for your help." "You don't have to thank me for anything, you just go ahead on to your office and take care of your business."

My office was dark and cold but I had a feeling that things were about to heat up. I took a moment to reposition my desk and chair. I reached behind my large gray file cabinet and grabbed four black folding chairs. My office would probably be full of folks as I was expecting more company than usual.

Just as I flopped down to have a seat, Officer Blue entered my office. "You're awfully early this morning, Officer Blue." He walked in and sat in one of the chairs in front of my desk. "I wanted to make sure that I spoke to you before anyone else arrived. Last night I conducted a routine search of your new prime suspect's cell and I found this note in his pocket." I reached forward and accepted the small piece of paper from Officer Blue. The note read as follows: GUESS WHO, I THOUGHT IT WAS ME AND YOU. THAT SITUATION IS WACK, TO HELL WITH THE BLACK. FOOL BETTER LEAVE US ALONE OR GET IN THE MIX AND BE GONE. COME ON NOW, STOP TRIPPIN' IT'S OUR NEW DAY. IT AIN'T NO THANG TO FORM A SIX, CAUSE I DON'T PLAY. DON'T DIS, DON'T RAT, KEEP IT PHAT. IT'S ALL ABOUT 1-8-…GO STRAIGHT TO HEAVEN. Looking at the note, I quickly digested the information.

"So what do you think T.P., does it mean anything significant?" asked Officer Blue. "Oh yes, it definitely means something, and the writer was speaking directly to another person."

Just as I said this, Sergeant Little entered my office along with Captain Davenport. "Hey Captain you must have received the note I left you." "Since you're retiring soon, I thought I'd better give you all the support you might need during these last days," bellowed Captain Davenport.

"Please have a seat, gentlemen. Our guest of honor will be arriving shortly. I'll explain later why I invited all of you here." My purpose in this matter was to intimidate the newly spotlighted suspect, in hopes that he would slip and provide the crucial information I was searching for. I preferred to keep my plans to myself to discourage unwarranted suggestions from my counterparts. I do value other folks' opinions, but concerning this case, the delicate ingredients must be kept in my personal cookbook.

Just as I glanced at my wristwatch, Officer Mulberry and the new prime suspect entered my office. I pointed to the empty chair in front of my desk, and Officer Mulberry carefully escorted the inmate to the chair. "Please have a seat sir," I said with a smile. The inmate sat down without a word, giving away nothing. Officer Mulberry immediately stepped back and stood at attention in his usual spot. Everyone in the room noted the silence, wondering what was about to unfold. "I'm sure you're probably wondering why I had you brought down to my office, but first let me introduce everyone to you. To your left is Officer Blue, on your right side is Sergeant Little, and to the right of Sergeant Little is Captain Davenport. And you're probably familiar with Officer Mulberry, the gentleman who escorted you here from your building. Of course, we've met, and you know me as Lieutenant Price, but I don't mind if you call me T.P. today." "And I don't mind if you call me Sweet Pea today," stated the inmate. None of the files that I reviewed ever mentions him by the name of Sweet Pea. Since the ice appeared to be broken I decided to play right along with Sweet Pea's suggestion. "Okay sir, I'll call you Sweet Pea." He smiled a bit and then gazed around the room, remembering that he was not amongst friends.

"What's all this about, T.P.?" inquired Sweet Pea. I had already made up my mind that I intended to be completely honest with the young man. "I feel that there's something on your mind that you want to tell me." "Something like what?" "Let's be real, Sweet Pea, you have all the answers and all the pieces of the puzzle. What made you hate Newton Black so much?" Sweet Pea sat still without moving a muscle. "Newton Black was doing something that you didn't like. This upset you very much and you felt that you had to eliminate the problem. You knew that no one would suspect you because of your reputation." Sweet Pea did not appear to be moved by my comments. "Mr. Lieutenant, sir, you must by trippin' 'cause I don't know what you're talking about." "So if I told you that you are the only inmate in the entire prison to have a pink toothbrush on his property card, what would you say about that, Mr. Sweet Pea?" Sweet Pea's eyes bulged out.

"Uh, huh." "And what about this note you wrote, sir, 'Guess who, I thought it was me and you.' Were you worried about your relationship with someone? I'll read on. 'That situation is wack, to hell with the Black.' Sounds like you're upset with Newton Black to me. Then you write, 'Fool better leave us alone or get in the mix and be gone.' Sounds like a bit of jealousy to me. Especially if you believe this next line, 'Come on now, stop trippin' it's our new day.' It's getting deep now, wouldn't you say Mr. Sweet Pea?" Sweet Pea shrugged his shoulders as he looked about the room. "It ain't no thang to form a six, 'cause I don't play.' Could you possibly be speaking of a grave? People are buried six feet under the ground. 'Don't dis, don't rat, keep it phat. It's all about 1-8-'. You might as well add the seven, because we know you're talking about murder. Then you conclude by saying, 'Go straight to heaven.' Somebody dies, right, Mr. Sweet Pea? That's how the story ends, a dead body right outside on the weight-pile."

As I glanced around the room at my co-workers, they all appeared to be in shock.

"Must I go on, Mr. Sweet Pea? You know as well as I do that you killed Newton Black. He must have done something that pissed you off, hmm? What was it? Did he steal from you? Did he force you to do things that you didn't want to do? Did you like him but he didn't like you? Or could it be that someone put a hit out and ordered you to kill him?"

Angry wrinkles soured Sweet Pea's face. "Nobody tells me to do a damn thing, Lieutenant, not even you." "Is that right, you don't sound too tough to me. Matter of fact, I wouldn't doubt it if Newton Black was the one that called you Sweet Pea." "That punk didn't give me that name, Boo gave me that name." "Ohhh, the Boo that's better known legally as Todd Henderson," I said with a hint of sarcasm. "Don't nobody mess with Boo," mumbled Sweet Pea. Pretending not to understand Sweet Pea's comment, I decided to ask him to repeat himself. "What did you just say?"

Sweet Pea caught himself, realizing what he had just said. He kept silent for approximately fifteen seconds and then repeated himself with boldness. "I said nobody messes with Boo!" "Did that include Newton Black?" Sweet Pea kept silent.

I decided to add some excitement to the situation with some grilling.

"So it appears that you and Boo had more than just a friendship. Did he help you murder Newton Black or did he just cover for you?" Sweet Pea continued to remain silent. "Maybe Boo held him down while you plunged the weapon in his body. Or maybe you seduced Newton Black and Boo stabbed him." Sweet Pea is becoming very upset by my intimidation. "Don't you think for one minute that I'm going to let Boo get away with this murder, no matter what role he played in helping." "Boo didn't stick nobody in the chest with no weapon," Sweet Pea exclaimed. "You're absolutely right, Boo didn't stick Newton Black in the chest with a weapon, you did. How did you know he was stabbed in his chest, I never told you, nor did anyone else Mr. Ronnie Phillips, or as you call yourself, Sweet Pea. You're nothing but a low-life, lying, mixed up little punk. You murderer, murderer, murderer, murderer, murderer...!" "That's right, I killed that no good bastard. He shouldn't have been messing with Boo, trying to convert him over to his religion and another type of lifestyle. I'd kill his ass again if I had the chance." Ronnie stood up and became even more belligerent. "He needed to be dead trying to brainwash people with his madness. I ain't scared of nobody, I'm Ronnie Phillips, Sweet Pea, I don't take no mess from nobody!" Officer Mulberry and Officer Blue rushed toward Ronnie Phillips and physically retrained him. "I'm warning you, Lieutenant, leave my Boo alone. He didn't do nothin'. I killed that punk by myself!"

This entire scene was way out of hand and someone could be easily hurt. "Get him out of here now!" I shouted.

Officer Blue and Officer Mulberry grabbed Ronnie by his arms and dragged him out of my office.

"Good job Lieutenant," Sergeant Little smiled. "Thank you too, Sergeant, of course I couldn't have done anything without a great set of staff members such as yourself." We shook each other's hand.

"Did you want me to bring the infamous Boo in here for questioning?" "No, that won't be necessary at the moment, Sergeant. We got our man and he admitted to committing the crime and that's good enough for me." Sergeant Little waved and left the office.

"Now do I have your blessing to venture safely into retirement Captain?" Captain Davenport stood up and approached my desk. "I'm not buying it, T.P., retirement is merely a word for you, you'll be up and operating your business and you won't know when to quit. Retirement, huh." Captain Davenport embraced me. "I'll miss you T.P." "I'll miss you too, Captain."

What a day, what a day, I thought to myself. Finally, the Newton Black murder was solved. Thank you Lord for answering my prayers, not in my time but in yours. What a blessing, I'm able to retire in peace.

Officer Mulberry entered the office as I was in the midst of completing documents for the Warden and the District Attorney's office. "That guy never stopped running his mouth from the time we left your office," exclaimed Mulberry. "Hopefully, he's securely locked-up in Ad-Seg." "Oh yes T.P., he's not going anywhere any time soon."

"I want to thank you again for all of your diligence and input regarding this investigation." "Don't mention it, T.P., I'm just glad to be a part of your legacy. You're the best example an officer could have." "Trust me Mulberry, you're going to make a fine investigator one day. You'll go far in this department."

"Tell me something T.P., how did you know that Ronnie Phillips was the actual murderer?" "When the murder weapon was traced back to Phillips' property, that still did not prove that he committed the murder. Anyone could have taken that toothbrush and used it on the victim. To be honest with you, I wasn't convinced that Phillips was the murderer until I read that letter and I saw his eyes admit guilt. I had a slight hunch that he might be addressing Todd Henderson, AKA Boo in his letter. During my interview with Henderson, I remembered that he was the only one who spoke well of Newton Black. It was obvious to Phillips that Newton Black had an influence over Henderson and he probably was on the verge of having Henderson join his organization. Also, I remembered that Officer Parker saw Phillips and Henderson hanging out beside the weight-pile on the day of the murder. He recalled that Phillips was braiding Henderson's hair. During one of my early interviews with Phillips, he stated that he was next to the weight-pile with Henderson during the murder. He further stated that he laid beside Henderson during the ordeal when everyone was ordered to get on the ground. He stated that his clothes got dirty with sand after lying down. My question was this, why would he have sand in his clothes if he were lying beside Henderson outside of the weight-pile? He should have had grass stains if anything, because grass surrounds the weight-pile. Somehow, Phillips slithered his way onto the weight-pile and acted quickly to dispose of Newton Black.

"But when everything is said and done, there's nothing like hearing a suspect verbally admit to a crime."

"Man, T.P., he went through all of that trouble to commit murder?" "Jealousy is a dangerous thing that can even lead to murder."

Mulberry headed for the door. "Should I get Mr. Henderson in here sir?" "No, that won't be necessary, I'll leave that one up to you and Sergeant Little to resolve."

"Hey Mulberry." He turned and faced me. "Yes T.P.?" "Come see me when you retire, I think I'll have a position for you."

"Sure thing T.P., it would be my pleasure to work with you again."

My, my, my, it's been approximately three weeks since Ronnie Phillips, AKA Sweet Pea, admitted to murdering Newton Black. One thing that has since puzzled me is why the nickname Sweet Pea never appeared on any of the gang information sheets.

Anyway, I can't believe that I'm sitting here in the midst of my retirement party daydreaming about the investigation.

I refocused my attention and slowly scanned the room in amazement to see so many of my relatives, friends and co-workers.

The large ballroom is decorated with royal blue and black balloons and party favors. The centerpieces on the tables are filled with beautiful, vibrant flowers.

All twenty of the linen-draped, round tables are completely filled with guests.

I am privileged to be seated next to my beautiful daughters, my brother and sister-in-law, Captain Davenport and his wife, Betty Wilkins and her husband, and my date for the evening, Ethel Williams. By the way, Ethel cooked all of the food.

My youngest daughter points to a small, neatly wrapped gift that is placed in front of me on the table. "Daddy, please open your gift." "Okay pumpkin, I'll open the gift."

I smiled at my daughter and proceeded to open the package. My eyes slowly fill with tears as I gaze at the gift. It is a gold-plated nameplate with the words inscribed, "P.I. Tiger Price." There is also a card attached. It reads, "PLEASE ACCEPT THIS SMALL TOKEN OF OUR LOVE TO YOU FOR OVER TWENTY YEARS OF FAITHFUL SERVICE ON YOUR JOB. NOW, MAY YOU BE SUCCESSFUL IN YOUR OWN PERSONAL ENDEAVOR, IN BUSINESS AS A PRIVATE INVESTIGATOR. MAY GOD BLESS YOU AND KEEP YOU."

The next mystery to be released by Erick Benson is entitled, **Framed Justice.**
Take a wild ride on the crooked side of an American Courtroom, where everyone is suspect of foul play. The court clerk, attorneys, the court reporter, and even the judge is vulnerable to an investigation. Tiger Price, takes on his first investigative case after retiring from the prison system. The doors of his new business had been open less than an hour and he already has his first case.
A friend's son is on trial for murder. Tiger Price will leave no stone unturned in his quest to solve this suspicious murder.

About the Author

Erick G. Benson has been published nationally in Essence magazine and his work has been featured on B.E.T. (Black Entertainment Television). Stay tuned for the release of his next book and future screenplays. Mr. Benson also brings 12 years of experience as a Parole Agent and Correctional Officer.

9 780595 133673